What Readers Are Saying About Will Astrike and the Frank Bass Series

Meet Buffalo Robe Bass, the Crocodile Dundee of Wyoming Territory. But wait...his lady friend, Sally Bloom, is every bit his match. This sleuthing pair brings the Old West back to life, keeps you guessing until the last page, and leaves you hoping that Bass and Bloom and company will soon ride again. –Margaret Coel, New York Times bestselling author of *Winter's Child*.

... As a writer who lives in Wyoming and writes about the West, I can honestly say he nails it: lock, stock, and barrel. Speaking of new heroes, when you think Will Astrike, think early Elmore Leonard. - Gregory Zeigler - Author of The Jake Goddard and Susan Brand Thrillers

I loved the whole book. Characters, plot, and descriptions were all excellent. I especially enjoyed the language—the expressions, idioms, and pace were outstanding. It put you back to the 1880s and how people talked, dressed, and acted. Will read the next book. Thanks, Deputy Marshall Bass, for letting me ride.

... the book was well written, the characters fun, and the story interesting. I have read all of Louis Lamour's books, many two or three times and Will Astrike might be just as good a writer.

This was a great read with outstanding characters and lots of action. Would highly recommend this book to all those that enjoy a great Western story.

Book two of the Frank Bass series by Will Astrike. This story was full of mystery and drama. Enjoyed every page. Thank you.

An excellent read. Keeps you tapping the Kindle. The characters are exciting and believable. I am anxious to read more of Ezra Lacy's adventures. All of you cowboys and cowgirls will enjoy this book. So, "Giddy Up."

... I still think Will Astrike may be the best Western author since Louie L'Amour. I look forward to his next book.

A most wonderful read. Gotta love following Deputy Marshall Bass and Sally around and the messes they get themselves into!

Frank Bass series book Three by Will Astrike. I love the character of Frank Bass. The legendary Marshall of the West. This has been a great series and I've enjoyed reading each book. This story's legacy of the young man who wants to clear his father's name is a good one also.

Another great read. Excellent characters, plot, and description of surroundings. But my favorite thing is the dialog. The idioms and meanings of the day are right online. I had never heard of "consists" used as a noun. Keep 'em coming.

5.0 out of 5 stars[1] **Another winner...**[2]

Reviewed in the United States on May 26, 2023

Verified Purchase[3]

I enjoyed the read... fast-paced...I learned a thing or two about how people lived and survived back then...The descriptions of the city of Austin, the bars, hotels, were great...The characters? AWESOME!!!!...I was never a huge fan of Western novels, but Will Astrike has made me a Frank Bass fan for life...can't wait for Book 6?

Robert F. Thompson[4]

    5.0 out of 5 stars <u>Good read</u>[5]

---

1.   *https://www.amazon.com/gp/customer-reviews/R26H0QCY8Q8LCY/ ref=cm_cr_dp_d_rvw_ttl?ie=UTF8&ASIN=B0C46S7751*

2.   https://www.amazon.com/gp/customer-reviews/R26H0QCY8Q8LCY/ ref=cm_cr_dp_d_rvw_ttl?ie=UTF8&ASIN=B0C46S7751

3.   https://www.amazon.com/gp/help/customer/display.html/ ref=cm_cr_dp_d_rvw_avp?nodeId=G75XTB7MBMBTXP6W

4. https://www.amazon.com/gp/profile/amzn1.account.AGVRXE5V3GWY4MVWOFFG4HQQ3K5A/ ref=cm_cr_dp_d_gw_tr?ie=UTF8

5.   https://www.amazon.com/gp/customer-reviews/R19QYQOSC6A2ZN/ ref=cm_cr_dp_d_rvw_ttl?ie=UTF8&ASIN=B0BYMDXKSD

Reviewed in the United States on October 6, 2023

Verified Purchase[6]

I have read Mr. Astride's Frank Bass series also...This one was really good...the colorful characters...the historical figures of the West came alive...The Texas Rangers...The Indian Nations...The Civil War...Custer...Crook...I will read anything else by Mr. Astrike...

Deborah Sue Lacy[7]

5.0 out of 5 stars <u>Great writing</u>[8]

Reviewed in the United States on December 3, 2023

<u>Verified Purchase</u>[9]

You, sir, are an awesome writer, and the story of Amos Getting was the BEST Western I've read in my 75 years, of which the last 65 have been as an avid reader.

---

6.   https://www.amazon.com/gp/help/customer/display.html/
      ref=cm_cr_dp_d_rvw_avp?nodeId=G75XTB7MBMBTXP6W

7.   https://www.amazon.com/gp/profile/amzn1.account.AF453PUPKMFW2CN3CYEP6ZWGA63Q/
      ref=cm_cr_dp_d_gw_tr?ie=UTF8

8.   https://www.amazon.com/gp/customer-reviews/R394E73STG0YX9/
      ref=cm_cr_dp_d_rvw_ttl?ie=UTF8&ASIN=B09SX1JHZW

9.   https://www.amazon.com/gp/help/customer/display.html/
      ref=cm_cr_dp_d_rvw_avp?nodeId=G75XTB7MBMBTXP6W

ALSO BY
Will Astrike
The Knack
The Skills of Ezra Lacey
Legacy
Stolen
Amos Getting: A Life on the American Frontier
The Regulator
Rustling
Gunslingers

Winner of the 2024 International Impact Award for Historical Fiction

Slaughter

By Will Astrike

Slaughter

Will Astrike

A Note To My Readers

The story that follows is based on an actual serial killer case in Austin, Texas, which began in December 1884 and ran through all of 1885. A total of eight victims were murdered under the cruelest and most tortuous circumstances and were reported in graphic detail in the print media of the day.

Mr. William Sydney Porter, who authored short stories under the nom de plume of O. Henry, was in Austin at the time of the killings and conferred the killer with the name The Servant Girl Annihilator.

Though I have tried to mitigate the gruesome nature of the murders, several descriptions are, by necessity, somewhat graphic. The sensational and grisly nature of the crimes, along with a prolonged period of terror, combine to make this a unique case, one well beyond the capacities of Austin's Finest. Small wonder then, as desperation grips the city, a call goes out for . . . Frank Bass.

Prologue

2:45 a.m., March 1, 1888
  Benoit's Boarding House
  225 Neches Street
  Austin, Texas

He lay on his bed, staring at the ceiling and breathing in short, quick gasps. It was a chilly night, but he had not lit the stove for fear that someone else might know he was awake. It didn't matter anyway. He sweat profusely and had returned to his room in such a heated condition that he undressed and now lay perfectly still, naked in the quiet of the darkness. His hands clenched involuntarily, and the muscles of his legs tightened painfully, but he dared not cry out. He closed his eyes and ran the events of the last few hours back through his mind, smiling into the gloom as he refreshed and viewed each scene, speaking softly and congratulating himself.

She was a lovely little serving girl, Colored, of course, he would never have expected a White one to be so obliging. She had it, though, the power that all of her kind had. She just kept it hidden better. He found her by accident earlier that night as she left the local market, packages, and bags in hand. *The bags were nearly the color of her skin, not the deep brown of the African slave, but more light-skinned from, say, the Caribbean. Yes, that's right, not a black African at all. Ah! But the man, the interferer, he was Black. He'll think twice before mixing in again.* He thought again of her and how they met.

She wore a full blue dress with a narrow bodice and the white cotton day cap that identified her position tilted ever so slightly to the left. *Was that another sign?* Her stained woolen coat was slightly torn here and there, and her hex bag dangled from a sleeve as she toted her parcels.

Best of all, she was kind . . . it was a ruse, of course, the Devil's mistress, feigning politeness for those nearby. *Yes,* she guised herself as a young serving girl, with such dark, deep-set eyes, and her voice, speaking in that low sing-song tone they have, as though she were working her wiles on him, asking him questions about his background and where he lived. He knew what she was about, of course. There was no fooling him, but to conquer the demon in her, he had to play along.

He offered to help carry her bags, and naturally, *she allowed it! My God, this one was such a joy.* And now he knew where she lived. He continued to be coy about himself, and she responded with smiles and quick laughter. But she didn't probe further. That was odd. She should want to know more to continue the hex. She was not playing the part. *She was acting coy. How splendid.* He decided to play along, the innocent victim.

"Would you be available later to earn a few dollars? Say at the Trinity Hotel?" It was close to where she lived. He knew she'd expect the proposition, and he was, after all, playing along.

Her reply was perfect for him, sweet and innocent, curious about the money, and then, "How much?" *As if it made a difference.* The little sorceress was back to playing her game. Her eyes gave her away.

She was interested. She looked him over more carefully now. He knew what she wanted to see, and he obliged. A young Magus for her ego. She swelled visibly and agreed to meet him at midnight in front of the hotel for . . . twenty dollars. The money didn't matter; it was part of the illusion.

He had several hours before she would be his, so he decided to spend them in the company of other men like himself. He supposed there might be others, perhaps in that saloon. Others with the skill, the power to see the Evil One among the others. But no matter. She was his now, and nobody else's.

The bar was packed with men of appetite and spirit, strange for Sunday night. It was the Easter season, after all. Holidays always forgive excesses of food and drink. He decided on a bottle and a small round table at the front window. He sat by himself, casually observing the crowds at the bar and the piano. Never eye contact, though, certainly not. His own power might be recognized. 'Best to stay anonymous, visible but anonymous.

Outside, light snow flurries fell. They blew about during the late afternoon when the west winds came up. Not enough to show footprints. He smiled at that. But it was cold. Cold enough to freeze the troughs overnight. She hated water. They all did. But perhaps it might be cold enough to slow the seepage of blood. It didn't matter, of course, but perhaps it would be inconvenient. He knew she would be dressed seductively, wantonly. They always did. It gave *them* a certain thrill to excite their victims before their ceremony. The quarry would be unable to resist. Little did she know how practiced he was at avoiding her schemes.

Again, he had to play along. It was all part of the game. But, he thought, it might also make the result sweeter. He remembered his father telling him as a boy, "you must work hard for what you truly want," and it was true. Before the night was through, her coven would miss a member. *That would bring others, as it always had.* And he would be ready to save the mortal souls of the possessed.

Time passed so slowly in the saloon. He looked at his bottle and decided he'd drunk enough. Spirit liquor affected him differently than normal men. It made his senses keener, his being more alive. *A walk in the night air. Yes*, he thought. Just the thing to brace him for his task. His walk took him through the streets of the south side and eventually to Pecan Street. His watch read 11:55 p.m., five minutes before the proper time. It was all lining up so perfectly. 'Time to slip into the alley alongside the hotel and wait for his temptress. There, in the shadows along the hotel's wall, he waited for her there. Soon, in the lamplight of the street, her shadowy movement approached. She had stopped.

She appeared to be nervous; of course, she was nervous. She was still in the game. She was playing it well, and it excited him. She looked around quickly, careful to make sure no one from the street was watching. Witnesses were a bane for her, too. Finally, she resumed walking toward the hotel, and he made his move. Quietly, quickly, he was behind her now, close enough to smell her, even feel her warmth in the night air. He raised his cane and brought it down hard on the back of her head. So hard he heard her skull crack. It was too dark in the alley to check, but he knew the time was right.

He caught her as she fell, and he carried her into the alley. She was unconscious due to the blow, no chance to cry out or fight back. As he laid her down, he reached into his pocket for the vital element in disabling her dark powers. As she lay before him, he moved quickly, throwing salt on her body. He worked some into her hair and mouth and all about the skin of her throat and breasts. He lifted her dress and rubbed more salt on her belly and between her legs. When he had finally paralyzed her unholy power, he lifted her head and smoothly, with practiced form, drew the blade of his folding scalpel across her neck from one ear to the other.

Now, he watched her on the gravel of the alleyway and reached into his coat pocket for his heavier tools. The sharpened ax and skinning blade. She was unconscious but not quite dead. Her lifeblood pulsing out of her throat, pumped by her still-beating heart. He watched her carefully for seconds and then minutes. At last, he was satisfied the beast within her was gone.

Her body was truly his now, and he reveled in his conquest. He used the knife again and again on her, releasing her true spirit and killing her ungodly soul. He claimed his reward from her, a memento of his triumph. His hands and face were covered with her, and his clothing smelled of the iron in her blood. The young servant girl was now at rest. *What was that?* Someone calling.

"Mollie? Mollie girl, where you at? That you back in that alley!? Damn your soul, girl! Come out here now!"

He cowered back into the shadows, away from the lamp slowly coming toward him. With no time to finish his work, he took his blade and quickly marked her forehead with a slanted cross, a final statement of his dominance, and then he ran at the light, his hat pulled low and his hands before his face. He bellowed as he passed the light, swinging the steel ax at the man and striking his back, rendering him insensible. His work was not completed, but he was no longer in control. He ran into the blackness, away from flickering lamps that were slowly being lit in the houses nearby.

Chapter 1

10:30 a.m. March 28th, 1888

The Prairie Southeast of El Paso, Texas

Ten Miles from The Rail Head

"Watch it, blanket head. Turn those steers into the north." Frank Bass and his friend and partner Paulo Armendez were working their first herd of sixty-two steers to the rail head in El Paso. They'd been sold for slaughter to AG Meat Products in Fort Worth, and that's where the animals were headed.

"I'm fine, I'm fine. You'd best go to find the Becerra that took off up the arroyo."

"Yeah, yeah, you just keep repeatin' to yourself, 'I'm headin' north, I'm headin' north.' We might actually make some money outta this bunch."

Bass pushed his tall mare, Emma, into the ditch and followed the Angus beef about a quarter mile before turning it back to the herd. He reined up next to Paulo, who was a natural-born cowman, and asked, "How far you figure we've come?"

"Maybe five or six miles. A good speed, considering."

"Considerin' what?"

"Considerin' I must deal with a Novato Deputy Marshal who thinks he's a vaquero."

"Ride rings around you any day of the week."

"Only cause your horse is smarter than you."

"I believe you might be right about that, Chato."

They smiled and switched sides, keeping the cattle headed in a mostly northward direction. They'd left Paulo's twin girls, Isabella and Isidra, in charge of the remainder of their herd, which consisted of six calves and cows and twelve yearlings. The girls were nearly ten years old and had been eager for added responsibility around the ranch. Frank Bass had bought the ranch, then called the Grande

View, some years back, and when the neighboring ranch came up for sale, Bass bought it too. His work as a US Deputy Marshall kept him on the move as often as not, so he brought in a close friend from his Ranger days, Paulo Armendez. Paulo and his wife Chinesta, along with their twin daughters, took over the second ranch, refitted the house, and watched both places while Bass was away.

This was their first trip to the El Paso railhead with salable cattle in any number. It was not a long trail, about fifteen miles, but the process of rounding up steers of the right age and weight, having a vet pronounce them healthy, and then making the slow and arduous journey to the El Paso and Southwestern Railroad stockyard in El Paso was taxing. On top of that, because the price of beef had been changing regularly, a profit on their sale wasn't guaranteed.

The E. P. & S. W. charged six cents per animal per mile to ship by rail. In addition, fees needed to be paid to the stockyard and the veterinarian who graded the animals before shipping. The law stated that cattle mustn't be confined in a car for more than seventy-two hours at a time. That meant that if your buyer were more than seventy-two hours away, you'd have to pay another stockyard fee and vet.

According to the railroad, shipping to Fort Worth, where AG Meat would take ownership of the herd, would bill at thirty-eight hours, including water and coal stops, so the seventy-two-hour limit was satisfied. The published distance by rail was seven hundred and four miles. So sixty-two head at six cents per mile came out to $2618 for the train. Add $75 for the stockyard and $12 for the vet, and the total cost to ship was $2705.

They had sold the herd to AG Meats for $75 a head in good condition as certified by the vet. This left a profit of $1945 to be split sixty/forty between the two men, enough to keep them happy in the cattle business. There were always variables in raising and shipping herds, the cost of beef being the primary concern, but there was also the charge by the railroad and the condition the vet appraised the herd at the time they were shipped.

"Chato, they're pretty well strung out back by a quarter mile. Should we be bringing the stragglers up?" Bass asked.

"Nah. There's water ahead; they'll get the scent and bunch up there. So, what you figure, Vato, how many head we plannin' to buy with our hard-earned dinero from this trip?"

"Hard to say right now. I'd like to check a couple of other Mexican Ranchos 'stead of just ol' man Potrero's. I always feel like we been gouged buyin' from him just cause he's closest. Oughta try a few others out further down the Rio. Hell, there's still plenty a wild Longhorns roaming along the river, too. We might just try a roundup ourselves hire a couple a muchachos to help us out. We could even check with some a' the Apaches around town, like ol' Broken Rock, maybe find out how they gentle them wild ones."

Paulo was distracted by something on a distant hill. "You see him, Frances?"

When something was serious, Paulo always used Bass's first name. "I do."

"What's he's doin over there?"

"Counting."

"Damn, believe you're right. Why would someone risk gettin' hanged for stealing sixty-two head of beef."

"Well, sixty-two cows at seventy-five dollars a head is what?'

"I don't know. Need a pencil for that one."

"Gonna be around forty-five hundred dollars. Fellas rob banks for less."

"'Nother man to my right."

"Probably more behind, too."

"Whatdaya wanna do?"

"You stay at point here. I'm gonna go look for strays. You hear anything loud, them two'll prob'ly come hard at ya. Get to cover and let em have it. But hey, let the herd run; ain't no number a cows worth getting killed for."

"Amen to that, brother."

Bass reined off to his left and kept to an easy pace, walking opposite to the direction of the herd through low brush. He made a show of tending his cattle, talking to them, swinging his quirt, knowing any aggressive movement would likely prod the onlookers to action. Bass needed to know how many there were to deal with and, if possible, determine who they might be. He was watchful as he rode to the rear of the herd and eventually spotted two more riders together, sitting their horses maybe fifty yards out. He approached the pair slowly, no point pretending he didn't see 'em. As he did, he took off the denim jacket he wore and draped it around the pommel of his saddle, hiding the gun belt holding his Walker Colts. Then he dropped his hands to the saddle horn and continued at a leisurely walk toward the two men. As he got closer, he smiled just as big as he could. He thought he recognized one of the two as Lyman Tolliver, a known border tramp and gambler. He couldn't place the other man.

"Well, hey there, Lyman. What are you doin' out here? Ain't no card game nearby."

"Hello Marshal, oh we ain't lookin' for no game, are we, Tom?"

Lyman was a small man with a pock-marked face and stringy black hair that slid over his ears and down his neck. He was dressed too well to be out on the prairie checking out stock. The other man was a bit heavy. He had a round belly and chubby cheeks that supported a three or four-day stubble. Bass saw dark hair under his primrose hat and gaps where teeth should have been that gave him a slight whistle when he spoke. He was a brooding sort, Bass determined, quick-tempered.

"Don't believe I've met your friend here, Lyman."

"Oh, well, just pardon me all to hell, Marshal. This man here is Tom Ketchum, friend of mine from Wyoming way."

"That so? 'Seems I heard 'bout a man named 'Blue Moon' Ketchum. Thought he was hung in New Mexico for bank robbin'? Guess that ain't you, huh? Cause . . . here you are."

"'Ats right, lawman, I'm right here."

"Say, Lyman, you never did answer my question 'bout why you was out here?"

"Well, Marshal, me an' my friend are lookin' for work. Thought you could use a couple hands on this drive."

"And your friends up ahead? They lookin' for work too?"

"Just so, Marshal. All we're after is honest labor."

Bass tired of the chit-chat.

"Lyman, you ain't never done nothin' honest in your life; we both know that. And you, Ketchum? Best point your pony away from El Paso or any place else I might happen to be in the future." He smiled big again and watched as Ketchum seethed. From the corner of his eye, Lyman's hand dropped to his gun, and at the same time, Ketchum went for his.

Up ahead, a quarter mile leading the drive, Paulo heard two loud blasts in rapid succession and had no doubt what they were. Two men spurred their mounts in his direction, so he urged his small pinto to a hill above the herd where there were rocks and some cover. He drew his Winchester saddle gun, shooed his horse away, and, kneeling behind a rock, waited for the two men to be in range.

The cattle had become jumpy at the sound of shots; had it been dark, they would've stampeded. They started bawling and swaying; Paulo knew they'd scatter before this thing was over. The two men rode hard in his direction, firing their rifles with one hand and reining their mounts with the other. Bullets whizzed by and ricocheted off rocks behind him.

At seventy yards, Paulo opened fire, toppling one man over the back of his horse. Seeing his friend get hit slowed the other one down, and he was pulling up to turn his horse when Paulo clipped his right leg. The man jerked the reins, and both horse and rider went down. The animal popped back up and trotted to where the other horse stood, but the man stayed on the ground. The cattle had dispersed in different directions, and Paulo knew it'd take the rest of the day to find 'em.

He trotted to his pinto and spurred the horse down to check on the two men and see who they might be. As he did, Bass rode up from the rear of the strung-out herd, and they met at the spot where the wounded man fell.

"You were right. 'Soon as they heard those cannons a' yours, these two came runnin' at me. I don't know this one. I'll check the other guy in a minute. You know this guy?" Paulo asked.

The wounded man was unconscious but breathing. His right leg bled heavily, so Bass tied his kerchief around the wound and cut a leather thong from his quirt as a tourniquet.

"Yeah, this guy is Little David Quay, and I'll bet the dead one is Cherokee Bob Oldfield. They used to ride together. You know it's Cherokee Bob cause he's missing part of his nose."

Paulo walked over to the dead man several yards away.

"Yup. It's Bob, alright." As Paulo walked back, he asked, "What happened to his nose?"

"A whore cut it off over in Deming when he wouldn't pay. That's where they used to hole up, in Deming."

They tied the dead bodies to their horses and confiscated the men's weapons. The wounded man eventually regained consciousness as Bass and Paulo were tending to the dead.

"*Oh, dear Jesus*, I'm shot! I'm shot. *Ugh*, that hurts. Which one a' you durned heroes shot me in the leg?"

Paulo walked over to the man and knelt at his side. "I did. You hurt like crazy, no?"

"Yeah, buster, I'm hurtin' like crazy! Oh, Jeez, it hurts, *hmm*. Can I have some water?"

"Sure as shootin' partner. Cool agua comin up." Paulo walked to his horse for the bota strapped to his saddle and returned, untying the end. "Here y'are, hombre. Tu pierna, eh . . . your leg hombre. It looks pretty bad."

"Yeah, well, that 'bout makes my day, Pedro."

"Paulo."

"What?"

"My name is Paulo, not Pedro."

"Oh, for cryin' out—a touchy Mexican."

"I am not *Mexicano*, hombre, I am Spanish."

"Alright, got it, Paulo. Thanks for the agua. Oh, man . . . I can't move without it hurts."

Bass had finished tying off Ketchum's legs and walked over to see what the chatter was about.

"S'goin on here, Chato? Little David complaining 'bout bein shot?"

"Yeah, he is . . . says it hurts."

"Well, a course it hurts, David, that's why they call it *gettin' shot*."

"Wha—? Say you're bad as the Mexican. I know you, don't I?"

Both Paulo and Bass answered in unison, "He's Spanish."

Bass continued, "Makes a difference. And the name's Frank Bass."

"*Uh-huh*. Heard a' you. Just can't place it."

"I tracked you and your pard across the panhandle for three days. Maybe two years ago."

"Oh yeah, . . . Bass. That's when I was ridin' with Buck Olbey. Say . . . you shot him as I recall."

"You bet I did, David. Just as quick as I could. Now, I got some morphine in my kit. We can't get you to a doc till tonight, so it might make your travelin' easier."

"Bullet still in there?"

"Believe so. I can try to get it out . . . but from my own experience, I believe it's real close to a major blood vessel. If I cut into that, you're gonna bleed out. I won't be able to stop it."

"Yeah, well . . . *ugh*, let's wait for a doc. *Damn*. How many cows you got?"

"Sixty-two."

"Jesus. All this for sixty-two cows. *Whoo—ha ha* . . . don't hardly seem worth it, does it?"

"Crime don't pay, David. Well, most crimes don't. But you'd need a sight more luck than you seem to have to make stealin' cows to payoff. Lemme get the morphine."

Bass carried a pretty complete medical kit with him. In his line of work, it was necessary. Doc Spalding had prepared six syringes of morphine sulfate in 9mg doses. Bass allowed the six syringes should be enough to get him to Doc's office. "Hold still. This is gonna hurt you worse than me."

Little David Quay calmed down after his shot, and that gave Bass and Paulo a chance to collect the bodies of the three dead men and tie them across the saddles of their horses.

Next, they discussed how to get Little David back to the doc in El Paso. He was hurt too bad to ride, and he'd lost a lot of blood to boot. They decided to rig up a travois. Two long, straight branches were cut, and one end of each was fastened to the horse's side. Then, smaller lengths were used to span the gap between the longer poles. They stretched a blanket between the two poles, and the whole thing dragged behind the horse with the wounded man resting on top.

Usually, it worked fine, but Paulo's blanket had too much give to it, and Little David's butt dragged some as the horse walked. Of course, he complained, and whenever he did, one of the two men would call back to him, "Crime don't pay, David," and he'd be quiet for a while.

As they came to the southern railroad tracks that paralleled old McGoffin Rd. Bass turned to Paulo. "Flip to see who goes back to the herd?"

"No, no. You go on and take the Little David man and the others in. I imagine there's lotsa paperwork to do too. First at Doc's, then at the jail. Huh? I'll go watch the cows. I'm better at it than you are anyway."

"Alright, amigo, if that's how you want it." Bass turned in his saddle to Little David Quay and said, "Davey, boy? We're about ten miles from Doc Spalding's. Can't do nothin' more to make it easy on you. So if it gets bumpy, suffer in silence, will ya."

Bass knew Paulo would be alright with the herd for the night, and by tomorrow mid-morning, he should be back for the last few miles into the El Paso holding pens. He tied the dead men's horses off to D rings on his saddle, pointed Emma west down the old cattle road, and started the long, slow walk to El Paso.

Chapter 2

8:45 a.m., March 29, 1888
City Jail
El Paso, Texas

Bass spent the night in jail. By the time Doc Spalding finished with David Quay and Bass had gotten him settled into a cell, it was late, and he was too tired to ride back to the herd. He took a cot in an empty cell and was asleep before his head hit the pillow. The morning sun rarely made it into the jail cells, but as soon as Eddie Voer, the longtime Jailer, came to work, doors slammed, shutters swung open, the stove was lit, and coffee was put up.

"Hey Marshal, how come you're here? Thought you was bringin' your cows up to the railroad."

"Got waylaid, Eddie. Fella in the last cell is Little David Quay. He and a few of his pards wanted to steal our herd. He's all that's left to face trial."

Eddie walked back to have a look at his new customer.

Bass called after him, "He's shot in the leg! Doc got the slug out and patched him. I'll start the paperwork on him after I get some coffee. Then I'm gonna ride out east of town, help Paulo with the herd. Should have 'em in the pens this afternoon."

A few minutes later, Sheriff Bart Mariany walked in. Bart was older but still quick-witted and more than a capable gunman. He'd been the County Sheriff in El Paso County since the days of Benito Gonzalez and the Salt Siege.

"The hell you doin' here, Frank? Thought you and Paulo was bringin' your herd up today?"

"Good mornin' to you too, Bart. And we are bringing 'em. Paulo's out with 'em now. We had some trouble yesterday. I was just tellin' Eddie here."

"Who's that back yonder?"

"Little David Quay. He was part of the trouble. Oh yeah, you can call in the flyers on Tom Ketchum, Lyman Tolliver, and Cherokee Bob Oldfield. I dropped them off at Doc's last night for the undertaker. I'll pick up their horses and gear before I leave to go back to the herd."

Mariany cast Bass a blank stare. He'd just cleared the books on three known outlaws, wanted from Texas to Arkansas, and arrested a fourth without hardly breaking a sweat or losin' sleep. Mariany muttered beneath his breath as he walked to the privy out back with his newspaper, "Don't know why I'm surprised, just natural as fallin' off a stump. Dispatch three dangerous outlaws and bring in a fourth. All in a day's work, Bart, all in a day's work." He turned and said loudly to the back door, *"If you're a by God Army!"*

Bass collected the weapons and effects of the three dead rustlers and had run all four animals down to Pat Farrister's Del Norte Livery. He returned the three older model Winchester rifles, two Colts, and one Remington revolving pistol to the jail armory, which was only an adobe shelter next to the jail's privy out back. It was 1:00 p.m. before he climbed on his horse and headed east on San Antonio Street to meet up with Paulo.

It took him a while, but he found the herd and not where he expected to. They were still several hours away from the rail yard pens, and Bass took the opportunity to lay into Paulo. "What'd you get lost? All you had to do was point 'em north and whistle at 'em. These cows'll practically pen themselves."

"Don't gimme any a' your guff, Marshal. I spent a good while chasing steers away from the Cathcarte's water tanks. I ain't in no kinda mood . . ."

"Well, don't pay no mind, we'll have 'em penned by suppertime."

In fact, with both of them driving the herd, they were at the railhead by 4:00 p.m. and done counting by 5:30 p.m.

"Only lost two, Chato. Not bad at all. I'm more 'n a little impressed with us right now, Paulo; come on, I'll buy you a drink before headin' home."

"You buyin!? Wait . . . by God . . . I think I just heard hell freeze over."

"Oh, that's real funny . . . you wanna talk about miserly people? I've known you to patch a patch rather 'n buy new. Don't even try to deny it. And I know Nesta's embarrassed to be seen out with you 'cause of it. She's just too kindhearted to speak up."

Paulo just shook his head. "Geez, let's get to Hannigan's before you gets apoplexy thinkin up insults."

Both men knew they were dirty and smelled of tired, wore out cattle, but they also knew that Hannigan wouldn't care. Hannigan's was a favorite haunt of theirs, along with any man who wanted a drink or a game of cards without the interruption of belligerent drunks. Hannigan didn't allow them. If anyone became a little too drunk to listen to reason, Hannigan gave 'em the boot. 'Not allowed back for a whole month. Paddy Hannigan wouldn't miss the business, and his regular customers would appreciate it more. And if a shot of Paddy's Irish whiskey went up in price by a nickel, nobody cared. It was worth it to keep Hannigan's open and prosperous.

The other thing about Hannigan's was all the patrons were generally respected, well-informed citizens. It was just as likely, maybe more so, that you'd hear the latest news sitting at Paddy's bar as at home in the parlor reading *The El Paso Times*.

Bass and Paulo walked through the door to a few *howdys* from the men already playing cards or drinking at the bar. They took seats at a table near the front and waited for Louella, Paddy's wife and the only woman regular to the place, to come take their order.

"Well, don't I feel safe in here today? My two favorite lawmen are sittin' right here."

Paulo reacted quickly. "Oh now, Lou, you know I'm just a fill-in. Callin' me lawman makes me feel like a . . . a jerk. Now the other fella there, he's used to it. Been a jerk much longer 'n me."

At that point, Bass spoke up, "Separate checks, Lou, us jerks can't afford to be buyin' whiskey for mere fill-ins."

Paulo sneered and said, Cheap whiskey for me, Lou . . . . Any ice today?"

"No, hon, sorry. And you, Marshal?"

"Old Overholt, straight up."

"Got it. Be right back, fellas."

Louella walked away, and Bass called after her. "And it's Deputy Marshal, you know."

"I know, just hopin you'd be in a better humor, s'all."

Paulo asked, "So, tell me again about the money we're s'posed to get?"

"Sixteen hundred after transporting and vet fees. Figure we'll put some of it back into some more Angus cows and maybe cross the river and roundin' up some Longhorns. Start fillin' out the herd for later this year and maybe next."

"And who's payin us . . . the slaughterhouse?"

"*Uh-uh*. We're paid by AG Meat Packers. They pay the slaughterers who kill and separate the beeves. Once they're cleared by the vet in Fort Worth, AG owns the cows. They'll sell the meat to butchers, the hides to leather tanneries, and the bones and sinew'll be used for glue. Certain parts are sold separately, like the livers, tongue, and kidneys. Back east, they make sausage out of the blood and offal. The whole cow's used. Not much waste."

"I never gave it much thought till now . . . we're starting to get paid for it an' all. Kinda weird thinkin about it. We drive these living beasts to the railroad, and pretty soon, they're steaks. You're from Chicago; you ever seen how all that's done?"

"Nope. I heard my Pa talk on it once. He said it wasn't very *humane*, so we shouldn't think about that stuff, just enjoy our Sunday ham or chicken. We didn't really have much beef; couldn't afford it. You 'bout ready to go?"

"Yeah, I'll go bring the horses around." Paulo was gone before Bass could protest, and he called to Paulo's backside as he walked out the door, "Hey! I said I'd buy ya one drink, not three . . . yeah, fine, go on . . . no, no, no, don't worry, I'll get the whole tab. Next one's on you."

As they rode up to the turn-off, Paulo headed onto the path to his place. "You be careful getting home now, Chato. Don't fall off that big horse and get hurt . . . you gotta kid now."

Bass just smiled and shook his head as he continued on to the gate at TwainHeart.

When he got home, Sally was sitting in a rocker on the front porch, holding Lillian and rocking back and forth slowly. The evening was a little chilly, but they were both bundled up well.

"Home is the hunter, home from the hill. Good evening, my love. Your daughter and I are just enjoying the spring twilight. She's already nursed and ready to sleep."

"Lemme see her." Bass climbed the stoop, his spurs clinging with each step. He tried to be quiet, but he was a big man in chaps, boots, and spurs, and Lilly opened her eyes. She didn't fuss at all but looked up at her father's whiskered and windburned face and smiled.

She started wiggling her arms about. "Yes, yes . . . she's daddy's girl, all right," Sally said.

Bass kissed Sally on the forehead and sat to take off his spurs and chaps. He went inside then and returned shortly with a dram glass for each of them. The baby had drifted off, and Sally accepted the glass gratefully.

"So, cowboy, how was your cattle drive?"

"The drive wasn't bad at all, and Paulo is a whiz at movin' cows. We did run into a team of rustlers along the way."

"What!? Where?" Sally was always concerned about Bass's job, more so now with the baby.

"'Bout a half day from town, maybe twenty miles out. For sixty cows . . . three of 'em died over sixty cows. All I can figure is they musta been desperate as hell."

"You killed three men, Frederick?"

"Two. Paulo got the other one, and one's in jail, wounded. We got the cows to the pens, though. So as the vet checks em, they're on their way to Fort Worth and the AG Meat Packers."

Sally was silent for a moment. "Frederick? How do they do it? Kill them for butchering, I mean?"

"*Huh*, Paulo was curious too. Well, as I understand it, they stun the animal to unconsciousness and then bleed them out. The heart ultimately stops. I'm told the cow has no pain. I remember my Pa would tell me in Chicago, they used a pole ax on 'em. Boy, I just can't imagine the man who works all day killin' cows. Take a certain type of man for that. Anyway, then they're hoisted on a chain, skinned, and gutted, and the carcass is chilled in an icehouse for shipping. Like I told Paulo, nothin's wasted. Every part of the animal is used."

"I know it's necessary, and I'm certainly not finicky. I enjoy beefsteak as much as anyone. I know everything on the ranch has a function. I just don't want them to have pain or fear."

"That's the whole point in using the stunnin' device, hon. Animals don't feel nothin' . . . so I'm told."

"So, on to the really important news. Your four-month-old daughter is laughing and smiling like a little monkey. She really is the most adorable little thing. And she's speakin' too."

"What?"

"It's gibberish, of course, but she looks so serious about it that she must have thought something through."

"The girl's a genius, that's all. A by God genius. Course, she gets it all from her ma. Her brains and beauty."

"That's a sweet thing to say, dear, but what does she get from you, then?"

"*Hmm.* Don't know . . . but I bet when she's grown, she'll drink rye whiskey, Old Overholt, a' course."

Chapter 3

12:15 a.m., April 1, 1888
Trinity Hotel
Trinity Street at 8th Street
Austin, Texas

Eileen Beretta left her customer at the Trinity Hotel and walked north from the building on Congress Avenue. She walked for several blocks and turned right when she got to Hickory Street. Just as she approached Brazos Street, someone knocked her unconscious from behind and dragged her into an alley between the Farnum Theater and Haskel's Department Store. They cut her throat and stripped her naked. Her chest cavity and abdomen were meticulously and precisely opened, and her internal organs were removed. They carved a crooked cross deeply into her forehead, and finally, they rubbed her over with salt. Her attacker was in no hurry; there was no foot traffic at that time of night, and he wanted to make a thorough job of it.

Austin City Police Officer Hardy Jinx walked his beat at 7:50 a.m. that morning when two garbage workers hailed him, both appearing pale and traumatized. When Officer Hardy came to examine the scene, his stomach rolled, and he wretched onto the brick wall of the department store. Once he'd regained his composure, he ran to the police headquarters only a few blocks away and told the duty Sergeant of his discovery.

"Gutted, you say, boyo?" Sergeant McNamara had been on the job for fourteen years but had never heard a crime scene description like this.

"Mac, she was all opened up. I saw inside a' her. My God, there was blood everywhere." Officer Jinx was as white as a sheet as he reported what he'd seen. His knees shook, and he swallowed hard and often.

"Saints preserve us, another one. I'm gonna have to ask himself on this one."

The chief of police was a man named Grooms Lee, a well-known and well-liked administrator who had a reputation for pulling a cork. He was nearing forty years, had black hair, and a Van Dyke beard to match. He had a little more weight to his middle than most active policemen, which he and others attributed to the large amount of alcohol he consumed. When the Sergeant found him, he was asleep at his desk, an empty bottle of Lone Star Texas Bourbon nearby.

"Chief . . . *ahem*, Chief, sir? Bloody sot, wake up ya drunken . . . ah, there you are, sir. We've had a report of a homicide of a particularly gruesome nature, Chief. Do you want t' handle the case? Or should I ask O'Dell to have a look?"

Cillian O'Dell was a sergeant in the department who'd transferred from New York City. While working in the Brooklyn Burrough, he had become known for his skills in detective work. He transferred to Austin, where he hoped life would be quieter so he could read his Irish novels, a euphemism he used for chasing young women. It had become a hobby for him.

"*Goddamn*. I'll have a look. But see if you can find O'Dell anyway, just in case."

The Chief rose on wobbly legs and straightened his blue jacket. He snatched his hat from the hook behind the door and left with Officer Jinx. The ride to Hickory and Trinity Streets was a short one, and by the time they arrived, a small group of onlookers had formed. The garbage workers tried keeping people on the sidewalk away from viewing the scene.

When Jinx and the Chief arrived in their Gurney Cab, the crowd began dispersing. Jinx held the cab's horse, choosing not to see the woman again. The Chief walked up the alley and found the grisly remains of the young woman who was in a posed posture, sitting up, her back against the theater wall with her eyes open and her arms folded over her opened torso. She was hidden from the street by a large trash receptacle that had been moved into place, presumably by the attacker. Her blood slicked the cobblestones, spreading out around the scene.

It had been near freezing in the city overnight, but the blood serum prevented its freezing. The Chief noticed her organs set out neatly in a row next to her and quickly turned to vomit. His head spun, and the smell of the partially-dried blood had reached his nostrils. When he regained his composure, he walked back to where Jinx stood.

"Jesus . . . This one's worse than the last one. Get O'Dell over here and the doctor. Tell them what happened and to get here quick. You two men there, don't let anybody but a policeman get into that alley."

He turned and vomited again before slowly stumbling to his cab. Jinx helped him mount the steps to the coach, and the two headed away from the scene.

After dropping the Chief at headquarters, Jinx went first to the doctor's office.

Dr. Hiram Flotter had been a physician for thirty years and the Austin Coroner for eight. He was a small, grey-haired man with a neatly trimmed mustache and a salt and pepper goatee. He wore spectacles that slid down his nose, and he had a habit of wearing black clothing. He felt it more suitable for his profession. When he heard Officer Jinx describe the scene, he sat down heavily in his office chair and, looking straight ahead at his office wall, said, "Dear Lord in Heaven . . . another one." Quickly, he picked up his bag and coat and left with Jinx. On his way out of his office, he told his assistant, "Find Harvey and send him with his wagon to the Farnum Theater. One body."

The two men left together, but Jinx rode back to the police station to find Sergeant Cillian O'Dell.

9:00 a.m., April 1, 1888
Benoit's Boarding House
225 Neches Street
Austin, Texas

He'd slept for several hours. He always slept better after. Blissful relief in his sleep. It was a curious thing, but all through the quiet, empty time, he rarely slept. But he had no choice. He had to wait for the right time. Oh yes, the time was vital; only then would the process be effective.

He lay again on his bed, naked, lost in the memories of his night out. *She was beautiful, of course, in the same way that all truly evil things have beauty.* He recalled the episode as if he were watching from a gallery and a Chief surgeon was commenting, *He did it so swiftly, so masterfully.*

Yes, that was the word. *Masterfully,* her total defeat took only a few minutes. Twenty at most. His skills were as keen as ever, his hands as deft.

But my tools, my tools, will need to be better, stronger, so they won't break off in the bone as it did tonight. That was my fault using the wrong instrument. Perhaps the cold air of the night? No matter. It would be easily replaced. And they must be sharper, too. Finely honed is the key to swiftness. A saw. Yes, yes, a bone-saw for the breastbone, at least. Then she will open easily, and the vile beast can be got at.

The plan worked flawlessly: a blow to the back of the head, again, a small fracture in the skull, and she fell into my arms, ready to be freed. And the location, well . . . I couldn't have picked a better location if . . . if I picked it myself . . . ha ha.

Quickly, his mood changed, and his face darkened.

Yes, yes, I hear you damnit . . .

I know it's wrong, but it must be done . . . it must, do you hear? I suppose to the lay public, it's horrible. But they don't know; they can't see how much they suffered from her evil. Now, the beast is gone, and their lives will be brighter again. I've vanquished two of the covens, and they are that much closer to the Garden. They will mourn, of course, the fools, but that's neither here nor there. I will continue my vigilance despite their scorn.

What? What was that? The police? April Fools.

Ha!

I suppose the police will have to involve themselves, but over what? It was one, well, two now, but what were they really? To sacrifice the two for the many? Who would disagree that knew the truth? The police matter not a bit.

What do they have? No witnesses, no weapons. Only the remains—

Oh, all right. Yes, I hear you. You needn't yell. I suppose you're right. I will need to create some kind of diversion to keep them busy.

Stop, yes, I'll think of something. You know, in their eyes, it is very wrong to do. But . . . but . . . still. When the time is right, ha! Dear God, it does please me so.

He closed his eyes again and slept till daylight, when he rose, like every other day. He washed himself and dressed for work, his white clothing somehow reassuring him of his purity. He took time to view his keepsakes in their jars and stored them back in their safe and private place. He smiled quickly at his reflection in the mirror and walked into the work-a-day world, holding his secret deep inside.

9:15 a.m., April 1, 1888
Alley along Farnum Theater
Hickory Street,
Austin, Texas

Doc Flotter arrived on the scene twenty minutes after being notified. There was no one in the livery to prepare his buggy, so he had to wait a few minutes for the owner to be summoned. Even though he was a medical man with many years of experience, he was still taken aback at the scene. To see the human form and its contents so blatantly violated deeply offended him. He began his examination of the body with the matted blood at the back of her head. He took detailed notes as he moved from one aspect of the body to another. Naturally, this took extra time, but Flotter was a methodical man. And his memory lately needed help on occasion.

Simply by feeling the indentation in the skull, he surmised the girl would have certainly been unconscious, possibly even dead, as the result of the blow. *'Left throat is deeply cut beneath the jaw, severing the carotid just before the ear, and What's all this? Salt, for God's sake.*

He spent little time on the girl's facial features except to note, *This is a White female, black hair and eyes—though now opaque—appeared to have been blue.* He estimated her height at five feet two inches and her weight at one hundred and ten pounds.

"She was such a frail thing; I doubt she could have put up much of a fight anyway."

The notes continue: *The incision through the sternum is jagged and hints at brute force on the instrument to cut through the bone. The knife must be serrated, judging by the marks on the sternum.* A saw would have left a different mark. "*Hmm.* What do we have here?"

Embedded in her sternum is a part of a broken knife blade. "Best leave that for O'Dell to see." He continued with his exam. *Likewise, her ribs are parted manually without benefit of any rib-spreading utensil. Four are snapped. The spinal cord is visible from the third cervical vertebrae through the fifth lumbar vertebrae. The chest cavity is neatly cleaned,* and the doctor noted *a mass of connective tissue, muscle, and flesh to the left side of the body. Rigor puts the time of death at around midnight, maybe one a.m., though the cold weather could slow the rigor function.*

The abdominal cavity has been opened neatly with an incision beginning at the pubis and ascending to the sternum. The vital organs are displayed on the pavement directly next to the victim on the right. The intestinal mass has been removed and piled up indiscriminately to the victim's left. And she is covered in salt.

He walked back out to Jinx, who waited in the street.

"Has anyone discovered her identity?"

"Not that I know of."

"Who's taking the pictures for us?"

"Don't have no pictures. Chief never called for 'em."

"Unbelievable. Well, see if you can find someone who'll do it and bring him over. And find other officers to protect the scene. Let these garbage collectors get on with their business." The Doc walked to his buggy, muttering. "Damned drunken son of a bitch. Forget his own shadow if it weren't glued to his ass."

"Well, if you say so, Doc, but Chief gets cross orderin' stuff he didn't do himself."

"That's alright, Jinx, my volition."

The doctor had planned to wait for the photographer, but since one hadn't been ordered and he had no idea how long it would take to get one, he decided to return to his office and start his report. He still had his own practice to think of.

Sergeant Cillian O'Dell was a handsome, thirty-six-year-old, red-haired Irishman who had left the crime-weary police department of Brooklyn, New York, for the quieter realms of central Texas. He had been a detective in New York, rising to the rank from Beat

Officer in just a little over ten years. Now, at thirty-four, he enjoyed the more sedate life of Police Sergeant and was happy to help occasionally with the odd murder case.

He was nearly six feet tall, trim, and athletic, his light auburn hair just rolling over his collar and curling at his ear. His eyes were crystal blue in color, and though his sideburns slid down his jaw, he was clean shaven otherwise.

He arrived a few minutes after the doctor had left and had the same reaction as most at the sight of the grisly crime scene. His face betrayed professional distance, and his revulsion at the sight of the victim soon became one of sadness and sympathy for the poor girl. After a moment, letting his stomach settle, he began his observations, thinking and sometimes talking out loud to himself.

"*Ach*, a pretty thing, I'd guess, maybe twenty or twenty-two: several rings but no band and one or two pieces of gold jewelry left behind. And salt, is it? Why would he do that to ye? Who are you, darlin'? How come you're out walkin late at night? Ach. Yeah, I know. Doin' what ya must. No facial cuts or bruises evident. The bastard snuck up on you, didn't he?"

He made a note to ask the photographer for a photo of just her face. "'Have the Beat Johnnies flash it around hotels and saloons. Oh my, he did for you proper, didn't he? Hello? What have we here?" O'Dell carefully removed the broken knife blade from the sternum and examined it. "About two inches, serrated steel certainly, and the blade curving to a sharp point. A bread knife. Huh." Next, O'Dell examined the organs lying next to the girl. "Liver, spleen, kidneys, bladders. *Hmm*. Same as before, 'must've taken the heart with him. *Uh oh*, what's here then?" He was walking along the outside limit of the blood pattern as it spread from the body. "Footprints, by God, he left us footprints."

O'Dell turned to see a slight commotion at the mouth of the alley. "Who are you then?"

"William Breitwish. Copper named Jinx sent me over to take pictures. Who are you?"

"Name's O'Dell, Personnel Sergeant, recruiter. I'm havin' a look about. I don't know you."

"That's right, and I don't know you either. So?"

"So give it a lash, then." O'Dell was surprised at the audacity of such a young man.

"What?"

"Take your damn photos. And make sure you take one of just her face. I wanna couple of the coppers to show 'em 'round the neighborhood."

"Yeah, alright, might take a while, but alright."

"And make sure you take several of the blood pattern spread over here. Looks like footprints. Get 'close as you can."

"Gotcha. Say, who do I send the bill for all this? Gonna be a pretty penny."

"Just send it to the chief of police; he'll voucher it."

As they were talking, the undertaker's wagon arrived, and two men in white dusters climbed down from the seat.

"We're here to fetch the stiff; where is it?"

O'Dell walked over to them. "Not till I say so, bucko. You and your mate cool your heels at your lorry till I'm through with pokin' about, got it?"

The stripes on O'Dell's uniform must have meant something to the two men, so they went back to their wagon and waited patiently. O'Dell continued viewing the scene from different angles and taking notes. When he finished, he whistled at the undertakers and said, "' Soon as that jackeen's done with his camera, you can take her off."

4:15 p.m., April 1, 1888
Office of the Chief
Police Department
Congress Ave. at Peach Street
Austin, Texas

"So, can we at least assume it's the same guy from last month with the Colored girl?

"Yes, Chief, I think it's a pretty fair wager that it's the same man. And now we have his footprints as well." Cillian O'Dell had the Chief's confidence. The Sergeant came from a big city police force and had seen most every crime known to man. He had closed other cases, killings from the year before. He seemed thorough and knowledgeable.

Doc Flotter was at the meeting, too, and could scarcely contain himself from damning the Chief for his drunkenness. At just four o'clock, and the man was tippled already.

"And you, Doc? What do you think? Same guy or cop—copy . . . 'scuse me, copycat," the Chief asked.

"Oh, it's the same guy, alright, 'same pattern of dismemberment, same souvenir taken away with him. The papers don't have that information; it's only our circle that knows."

O'Dell added, "And we've got a piece of the knife blade. 'Looked like a serrated bread knife to me. There are a few more things I'd like to keep from the chancers at the papers. The knife tip bein' one and the cross dugout on the forehead bein' another. And the salt on her, that has to mean somethin' to our guy, too."

The Doc cut in, "I agree. This is the tip of one knife; the bastard that did this murder used at least three blades, and he knows what he's doing, too. All were clean cuts, not a tear in the skin or a nick in an organ. And he was probably workin' fast. Breaking down a body like that takes time." Doc was quiet for a moment, "You know, it's almost like he performed an autopsy, same basic incisions, organs removed, examined."

"Oy . . . the leecher's right, might be a fine place to start lookin'. Coroners and Mortis might have the cliste." O'Dell said.

Chief Lee looked out through bloodshot eyes, "The hell you just say?"

"I said the doctors right, coroners and morticians have the cliste, the smarts, the ah . . . the know-how. Might be a good place to start looking, Chief."

The Chief, hearing his name again, looked up. "Oh, alright, let's start on that assumption then. When will we have the photos?"

"The lads workin' on 'em now."

"See that he brings 'em to me first. I'm the damn Sheriff of this burg. I need to be kept up to date."

Chapter 4

10:15 a.m. April 30th, 1888
  Sheriff's Office
  City Jail
  El Paso, Texas

Bass had come down from his upstairs office to review new flyers and any flash alerts that may have come in on the morning wire. He checked the communiqué and paid some attention to the information from Austin indicating that a second woman was found mutilated about seven blocks from the location of the last murder. The wire read, "The Austin Police have no leads and are asking for info on doctors or coroner workers who might be in the area."

Bass read the alert twice. "Could just as easily be medical students, too. They'd have knowledge of the human body, or least know where to find out about it."

Bart Mariany asked, "Who's the Chief in Austin, Frank? You know him?"

"Yeah, 'guy named Grooms Lee. I know him. When he was town marshal, he was very good. Honest, hardworking, active lawman. I hear he's drinking now, though." Bass continued reading the wire. "Here's one, a BOTL (Be On The Lookout), for Frank Coe. I remember him from Lincoln County. He musta just got out."

"They say why he's wanted?"

"Nope, just be on the lookout for him."

"You know, his brother George lives up to Las Cruces. Think he'll make for him?"

Bass answered, "Sure do. I remember Frank as the meaner of the two. Real bad temper. Killer."

"He do his time in Huntsville?"

"Nope, Yuma, I believe. There's a good chance he'll come to look up his brother, though. 'Don't know 'he's got anywheres else to go.

I'm headin' to Las Cruces next week. I'll look up George, 'see if he's heard anything.

"Oh say, that reminds me, Francis. I asked Georgy Vale to come in and talk to you 'bout bein' a city deputy. I know you sent him up once, so I thought you'd wanna be involved."

"Alright. When he was younger, I brought him in for robbin' coach passengers around San Antonio. He was just a kid then . . . maybe eighteen. What's he doin now?"

"He's a day worker out to Driscoll's. Odd jobs, cowboyin', I guess."

"*Hmm.* I'll talk to him. Like I said, he was just a kid when I brought him in. Scared, nobody around. Didn't strike me as a bad sort. I'd like to talk to Driscoll's foreman too."

Bass went to the back room for half a cup of cold coffee when Bart asked, "How's that little girl, Frank? She got you twisted round her finger yet?"

Naturally, Bass smiled. "Oh, Bart . . . she's just beautiful. She's smilin' already. Just couldn't be any finer."

"Smilin' huh . . . sure it ain't gas?"

"No, it ain't gas, Bart . . . what do you know 'bout it anyway?"

"Say I raised two boys out on the Llano west a' Lubbock. I know 'bout gas in babies, I guess."

"*Uh-huh*, you sure got plenty yourself, I'll say. You gotta be careful with that, you know . . . a man your advanced age."

"I can still whoop you, junior, with one hand tied behind my back."

"Maybe at a game a' cards you can." Bass smiled to himself. He loved goading the older man.

"Y'damn right, sonny . . . I got skills!"

Bass laughed, and Mariany smiled and chuckled along with him. "Paulo comin in today?" he asked.

"No. I asked him to ride into San Isidro, see 'bout buyin' some cattle down there. Why? Somethin' goin on?"

"Yeah, I planned to bring in Matt Lane today, and I thought I'd like some company."

Bass already knew Bart wanted help with Matt Lane, a younger man, more slippery than most. He also didn't want to admit he needed the help. Bass didn't want to let on, so he said, "You just want someone to talk to; I'll ride out there with you, Bart."

"No, no. This ain't worth your time. I'll take care of it."

"You sure? Got nothin' else to do today . . . it'll get me outta this building."

"Nah. I got it. You stay and get ahead on the paperwork you been puttin' off. And 'seems like I still ain't seen shooting reports from over a month ago."

"Jesus, Bart, I hate doin' them things. I can never remember the details."

"Yeah, well, maybe if you sat down and did 'em right away, you'd remember. Those shootin' reports were your idea anyway. I 'spect you forgot that too."

"No, I ain't forgot . . . I still have you to nag me about it night and day."

Bart smiled. "Wanna go 'cross the street? Get some lunch?"

"You bet." Bass dropped his files on the desk and grabbed his hat.

11:45 p.m., April 30, 1888
Mesquite Street and River Drive
Austin. Texas

Beatrix Lowe was a waitress at the Winslow Hotel dining room, and she would occasionally take work as a housekeeper when the Hotel was short-staffed. She was an unwed mother who lived with her parents in an apartment downtown on Congress Ave. She paid all she earned from the hotel to her parents for room and board for herself and her two-year-old son.

She was desperate to get away from her parents, who were devout people and unrelenting in their disappointment and anger at their daughter's decision to keep the child. That they allowed her and her son to live under their roof was constantly thrown in her face, and her parent's embarrassment over her pregnancy had forced them to leave their church.

Because she gave everything she made to her parents, the only way to make any kind of money to keep for her "moving away fund" was to take side jobs now and again. She discovered that an attractive, attentive young woman could make a sizable sum quickly by entertaining visiting businessmen at the local hotels. She would never consider working her secret job at the Winslow, though. Too many people there knew her name and situation. But further downtown, there were hotels that catered to that sort of trade, a place where out-of-towners' could drink, play cards, and enjoy the company of young women . . . for a price.

She told her parents she was going to work that Thursday evening and might take an extra shift as well. She walked as usual to the Winslow, but rather than go into the employee entrance, she took a trolley to the Pierce Hotel on Live Oak Avenue across from the Union Pacific Depot. She went immediately inside, avoiding the lamp lights in the lobby walked up the stairs to the mezzanine. She dressed provocatively in a frilled skirt with a low-cut bodice that displayed her femininity to its fullest potential. She caught the eye of several men as they came and went from the gaming room, but nothing seemed to gel until a youngish man she had seen before stopped at her chair, sat in the one next to it, and began a conversation. She had seen the man a week before in the hotel dressed as a Dandy and assumed he'd pay well. But that night, she was already committed to a peddler from Baton Rouge.

As she listened to his patter, she decided he was not handsome but not unattractive either. He was tall, dressed quite well, again, in an expensive-looking dark suit, and carried a beaver hat and ebony cane. They chatted for some time, during which she made it quite clear that she would expect to be paid for her time and even offered the amount. The man smiled and, after checking his watch, suggested that she accompany him to his room to sample a special liqueur he'd bought. She smiled coyly and agreed, so he walked her to the stairs. His room was on the third floor, he explained, and they climbed the rear staircase two flights to the third floor.

By necessity, her waist and torso stayed cinched tightly, and she was breathing heavily when they reached his room. He mumbled something as he fumbled for his keys, and as she walked into the room, her back to him, he brought the heavy metal crown of his ebony cane brutally down on the back of her head. He felt her skull cave as he struck and held her around the waist as she fell forward. With practiced haste, he closed the room door and dragged Beatrix Lowe onto the bed.

9:30 a.m. May 1st, 1888
Pierce Hotel
Live Oak Avenue
Austin, Texas

Dorita Remosa was one of the housekeepers at the Pierce Hotel. There were only two maids working regularly at the Pierce. It was a smaller hotel with modest rates that appealed to traveling salesmen and overnight visitors from the train on a budget. It was also popular with women in the professional escort service who often shared their fees with the hotel staff in exchange for their discretion. Of course, the police department knew exactly what happened there. Still, as long as no serious disturbance was made and no formal complaints were filed, the department concerned itself with more serious crimes against persons and property.

However, what Dorita Remosa found this morning changed all that forever. At first, she thought it could not be real; a human being could never be made to look that way. But then the sickly-sweet odor struck, and the sound of the flies buzzing about through the open window caused her to realize what she was seeing. She ran screaming from the room in hysterics that carried out to the street and caused passers-by to stop and wonder at the cause.

The beat officer this time was Allen Wallsetter, a young man new to the force, who heard Dorita's wailing and ran inside. The rest of the hotel buzzed, wondering at the cause of the disturbance when Officer Wallsetter climbed to the third floor and found poor Dorita siting on the floor sobbing and babbling incoherently. Wallsetter tried questioning the woman, but all she could do was point to Room 31, which was still open, the door ajar from her rapid exit.

As he walked toward the room, an eerie feeling fell over him, one that foretold he was about to view another victim of the city's first serial killer. As if to protect his own soul, he peered cautiously around the door jamb and beheld the ghastliest scene anyone could imagine. It was too horrible for his mind to process, and yet he stayed transfixed in his position until his throat closed, and he backed away, gagging and retching.

10:00 a.m., May 1, 1888
City Police station
Congress and Peach Street
Austin, Texas

"What? Another one you're sayin?" Sergeant McNamara knew what he was supposed to do. They'd been over it often enough over the last month. But his head still buzzed at the thought of such a devil at large in his beautiful, important city.

"Oh dear God, Sarge," Wallsetter was still pale and glassy-eyed as he spoke, "who could possibly do that to another human?"

The Sergeant was at a loss as well. "I don't 'ave an answer for ye me lad. But I know we'll catch the demon sooner or later, and when we do . . . won't be needin' no trial, now mark me."

"Well, what do I do now? I'm sure I have to write a report on it, but I'm not sure I can, Sarge."

"Don't worry 'bout it now, lad . . . run fetch the doctor, will ye? And see if you can find the picture taker, too." The Sergeant called after Wallsetter as he left on his chores, "Don't let anybody into that room, now!"

5:30 p.m. May 1, 1888
Office of Mayor Joseph Nalle
City Courthouse
Congress Ave.
Austin, Texas

Joe Nalle was a successful businessman who had a career with the railroad before getting into the lumber and cotton trade. He had a checkered past in that he'd shot a city councilman over a political issue. He was found not guilty, a result of politics again, and after failing in the election once, he took the Mayoral office in a landslide election in '87. His stance was always tough on crime. Physically, he was a short, round man with a broad mustache who wore spectacles and celluloid collars with bowties.

Police Chief Grooms Lee knocked on the Mayor's office door. It was after hours, and the Mayor answered himself.

"Come in, Chief, come in, sit down, will you? I'd offer you a drink, but I see you beat me to it."

The Chief had had enough to drink that he chose not to suffer another slur from the panty-waste bureaucrat who was elected Mayor last year. He added a sneer to his tone when he responded. "At's right, your honor. You wanted to see me . . . sir?"

"I've asked you before, Chief, and you've chosen not to answer. Have you made any progress on this 'Annihilator' case yet? I'm catching all kinds a heat for it from the Chamber of Commerce over it. The colored girl worked in Judge Brady's house, for Pete's sake."

"The *what* case?"

"Annihilator. That's what the papers are calling it. O. Henry came up with the name. He told a friend the 'town is fearfully dull except for the Annihilator.' Can you believe that? And people say he has wit."

"Joseph, what is it you want of me?"

The Mayor looked at him sternly. "Damnit, Grooms, I want you to quit drinking and find the bastard! This business is giving Austin a black eye. Folks'll stop coming here before long for fear of being axed to death. Now listen to me. I've called in the Pinkertons on this."

Grooms Lee leaped from his chair, nearly stumbling on an end table. "You've what? Called in the . . . why you simpering little weasel. Was a day not long ago I'd have you fer breakfast . . . calling in the Pinks. How dare you?"

"You sit down and listen to me, or I'll have you replaced. Now, you and your department don't seem to be making any progress, so as Mayor, I have to take action. They're sending an investigator down. And if you know of anyone around here who can help you find this butcher, I'd advise you beg him to try. Now get out of my office."

Chapter 5

Noon, May 13th, 1888

> *Las Cruces*

> *New Mexico Territory*

"Hey Eddie, how's tricks?"

"Used to be pretty good till I got so old. How you doin' Frank?"

"Fine, Eddie, just fine."

Eddie Del Gato was in his mid-forties and starting to feel the effects of twenty years in law enforcement. He'd been shot three times, once almost fatally, and twice in the same leg, though several years separated the shootings. As a consequence, though, Eddie walked with a noticeable limp, not necessarily because of being shot but because of the arthritis that settled in his knee fifteen years later. Eddie was an affable sort, the kind of man you met, enjoyed chatting with, and then forgot three days later. But as pleasant as he could be, he could also summon up the devil when need be. He was as cold-blooded a killer as walked on legs, and Bass was glad he chose the right side of the law. As the Sheriff of Las Cruces in the New Mexico Territory, that kind of personality served him well.

"I heard somethin from Bart last time I was in El Paso. Said that you and Sally had a little girl . . . 'at so?"

"It is true Eddie named her Lillian for Sal's Grandma. And I do believe the sun rises and sets on that little baby."

"Daddy's girl, no doubt. I hope she has Sally's looks . . . and her brains. Come to think of it, 'don't know what good she'd get from you. Prob'ly be a good pistol shot, I guess."

"Sal and I were talking 'bout that the other day. I said Lilly'd probably grow up with a taste for rye whiskey."

"*Ha*! She might at that. So, what brings you up our way?"

"Got a BOTL on Mad-dog Frank Coe 'bout a week ago. Guess he got outta stir recently, and I figured since his brother has a place here . . ."

"You figured Frank'd come by. Right? See his brother? You remember what he said he'd do to you, don't you?"

"Eddie, if I heard it once, I heard it a hundred times: *I'm gonna fix you, Bass. 'Soon as I'm out, I'm gonna fix your wagon good.*"

"So you ain't takin it serious then?'

"Oh no . . . I take it plenty serious. Specially from someone as mean as Mad-dog Frank Coe. Figured I'd rather meet him straight up than wait for a bullet at his convenience."

"And you allowed he'd come to see his brother first, huh?"

"That's it. Have you seen George recently? Like around town or the rail yard."

"Yeah, I have, in fact. I saw him two days ago, 'come into town to do a few things. 'Saw him come outta the Territorial Savings Bank the other day. Didn't think much of it till now. 'You saying Frank's out? 'You know when they sprung him?"

"Didn't mention a date, but the wire came in on the thirtieth. The wire's usually pretty prompt."

"You know there's an East bound due in today, 'couple hours from now. You wanna hang around . . . see if Frank Coe's on it?. . maybe say howdy?"

"You know I think I will, Eddie. In the meantime, I'd like to see ol' George and catch up with him on old times. You tell me where his place is?"

"You bet. It's two miles west of town across Rio. Take Amadore Avenue over the bridge and turn left when you see his sign."

"Thanks, Eddie. Don't plan to be long." Bass lifted his hat off the hat rack at the door and walked back down to the railroad freight yard where he'd left his tall mare, Emma. She'd done quite a bit of train traveling in the last three years, but she still needed time to get her land legs back.

It was a beautiful Wednesday afternoon, not too hot with just enough breeze to be cooling and not strong enough to kick up the dust. He crossed the Rio on the Amadore bridge and couldn't help but notice how slowly the water moved. The Rio always had the smell of mineral silt to it, but when the stream slowed down, it became more disagreeable.

George Coe's place was south of the road, just as Eddie had said, and from the road, it looked like a strong wind might topple the whole shebang, barn and all. There was nobody outside working, so Bass assumed George was inside. It was possible, Bass allowed, that George had taken himself a wife since the last time the two met, so Bass tried to be polite when he knocked on the door. After the second knock, he heard a woman's voice call down from the second floor.

"Who is it, damn your eyes, Go 'way. We ain't cookin' no whiskey no more. Go 'way I say, or I'll sic the dogs on ye."

"Whoever you are, I don't care if you're making whiskey or not. I'm just out to pay a social call."

"We ain't sociable people, so hit the road, mister."

"Well, alright. Tell George that Marshal Frank Bass was by to see him."

Bass heard someone stumble coming downstairs. "Damned dog, get outta the way."

Finally, the door opened, and a large woman in a gray smock with frizzy hair greeted him. "Say I'm awful sorry 'bout all that talk. I sure wasn't expectin' no law man out here today. I'd have you come in, but I ain't spruced the place up lately. I cook my own corn whiskey out back, and locals is always poking 'round for a taste. Would you care to try a swalla? George ain't here, I'm afraid. Has he gone and done somethin he shouldn't a'?"

"No, no, nothin like that, Miss . . . ah Miss—?"

"Oh! I ain't no Miss. I'm *Mrs.* Mrs. George Cole. Call me Freida, won't you?"

"Freida? Ah. I think I'll stick with Mrs. Cole. Seems more proper."

"Well, suite yourself, Here try this . . . fresh yesterday." Mrs. Cole handed Bass a tin cup with a clear liquid in it. He sniffed it, and the fumes of pure grain alcohol watered his eyes. He was thankful he hadn't been lighting a cigar at the time.

"Oh, go ahead and try it. You're a grown man, for Pete's sake."

Against his better judgment, Bass took a sip and let the fluid slide into his stomach. At first, he was pleased at how smoothly it went down, and he took another longer swallow.

"There now, ain't that just like nectar? It gets better as you go."

Bass took one last swallow and suddenly began feeling the heavy effects of the first sip. Beads of sweat popped from his forehead and down the center of his back. His tongue swelled, and his eyes crossed.

"*Well, thack you vemmy muth, Mithes Coe. I beleee I come back at a lather thime.*"

Bass tipped his hat at the woman, who was all smiles at this point and began weaving a path back to Emma. He had difficulty lifting his foot to the stirrup because both his legs were numb, but eventually, he made it to the saddle and urged Emma from the yard.

Bass wasn't quite sure which way Las Cruces was from the gate, so he let Emma decide. It took nearly thirty minutes for Emma to carry Bass back to the Sheriff's Office and another twenty minutes after that for Bass to be able to speak a clear sentence. Eddie Del Gato had a good laugh at Bass's expense.

"I should a warned you 'bout Freida Coe's home squeeze. 'Takes a certain kinda fortitude to withstand that brew. She sold me a bottle of the stuff last year, and after two swallows, I was blinded. 'Saved the rest to burn in the lamps at home. Don't worry, though. You'll be alright in a half hour or so."

"Thank God a' that."

"I saw George down at the livery while you were gone. He was rentin' a saddle horse. I asked Kurt, the liveryman, about what George wanted the horse for, and he said that George didn't say. Only that he'd have the horse back in a week or so."

"Think they're plannin' somethin?"

"Yes . . . I do. Maybe here, maybe down your way. Maybe the coach between here and El Paso. Or maybe they're just goin out for a picnic . . . who knows."

"Well, I'll tell you what, let's both meet Mad-dog Coe at the train station . . . maybe plant the notion that we know he's here and we're watchin him. Might dampen whatever they're plannin' a bit."

"Sounds good to me, Frank. Drink some a that cold coffee over there, might help the double vision." Bass smiled, though Eddie Del Gato wasn't too far from right.

The east bound El Paso and southwestern train was fifteen minutes late pulling in to the Las Cruces terminal. Passengers slowly climbed down the steps of the cars, helped by the porters, and made their way into the freight building to collect their bags. Bass and Eddie Del Gato waited along the tracks near the cattle pens until they saw Maddog Frank Coe step off one of the Pullman coaches.

They began walking his way, watching his movements; he seemed to be searching for someone, probably his brother, but neither Bass nor Eddie saw George anywhere. Suddenly, from behind them, several pistol shots rang out, one striking Eddie painfully in the lower back. At the same time, Mad-dog Coe, true to his name, sprinted at the two lawmen, firing his pistol. At the first shot, passengers and rail workers scrambled for cover, confusing the scene and making it difficult for Bass to see his assailants.

Bass caught a glimpse of George as he pulled Eddie to the relative cover of a freight pallet. With Eddie at cover, Bass turned to mark George's position. Frank Coe still ran directly at him, shooting at each opportunity and keeping Bass from taking any kind of action.

Finally, out of desperation and to draw fire away from Eddie, Bass made a dash for an open-wheel cart loaded with duffels and bags. On his way, he took two shots at George's horse; he screamed in pain and toppled over, pinning George on his left side. Bass couldn't see if George, who was the further of the two, had retained his gun in the fall, but he was no longer shooting.

Bass could no longer see Frank Coe's position, so he rolled quickly to his right, his pistol extended. When his target was in view, Bass fired three shots into Mad-dog Coe's middle, dropping him on the spot. Bass could still hear George cursing his horse and walked cautiously in his direction. When he saw that George lay immobilized under his animal, Bass checked on Eddie Del Gato.

As he went to Eddie, he called back, "George, you stay put under that horse. I don't wanna shoot you too, but if you run, I won't miss."

When he was in earshot, Eddie called out, "I'm alright, Frank. Bastard George hit me just above my belt. 'Caught my side and went through. I'm bleedin pretty good, though. Spare your kerchief?"

Bass smiled at Eddie's matter-of-fact attitude and was thankful George wasn't a better shot. Then he jammed his kerchief into the small hole in Eddie's side and told him to keep pressure on it.

Bass called to several of the onlookers, "One you fellas go fetch the doc, will ya."

"What happened, Frank? I was turned away from the action . . . didn't see anything."

"Well, I shot George's horse, and he fell on top of him. I guess he lost his handgun 'cause he didn't shoot anymore. Mad-dog kept comin down the middle of the walk shootin' at me when he could, so I shot him . . . he's dead over yonder there. I'm gonna go check on George real quick. I'll be right back."

Frank approached the man beneath the dead horse. "Well, hello, George. 'Guess you woke up with wild hair today. Lucky you ain't dead as your horse here."

"You no-good . . . dirty . . . *damn you*! Get me outta here. Will ya? Damn horse has broken my leg."

"Do I look that stupid to you, George? You just cool your heels in the dirt there for a few more minutes till I get Eddie Del Gato taken care of. Then I'll see about extricatin' you."

Bass picked up George's pistol and tossed it across the tracks. Then he went back to Eddie. The Doc had a few men carry Eddie over to his office to get stitched up. He told Bass that Eddie would be alright once the stitches healed. Two to three weeks, he figured. Bass had the town mortician pick up Frank Coe and watched as he was carted off. He wondered why a man would do five years in the penitentiary only to return home to get shot. He planned on asking George about that. He and two others finally pulled George out from under the horse and carried him over to Doc's as well. Doc said his leg was broken in two places and would take a long time to heal. Bass said that would work out fine 'cause where George was goin; he'd have plenty of time to heal up. Bass asked George what his brother's plan was when he got to town.

"Pretty sure he wasn't expectin' to see me."

"No, by God, he weren't. Now he's gone, guess it don't matter none. We was plannin' on hittin' the bank over to town. My brother figured as to how you'd probably be the one to come after us. He'd set a trap and gun you down. You and Del Gato beat us to it, I guess."

"You guess? Your brother's laid out in a hurry-up wagon somewhere, and you're headed to the penitentiary all lamed up. You guess? Shameful is what it is. George. 'Stead a startin' over fresh;

your brother's finished. And by my hand, too. 'Had to kill a man. I ain't never alright with that."

"Well damn, Marshal, you put it that way . . . still, it's a might harder on brother Frank, though."

Bass chuckled as he left the room. George was right; it was a lot harder on Frank. He decided to spend the night and look in on George in the morning. He also figured he'd hang around until Eddie could call in a deputy to watch the town when he'd gone home.

Chapter 6

10:00 a.m., May 12, 1888
City Jail
El Paso, Texas

Bart Mariany and Frank Bass were still finishing the morning pot of coffee when a messenger arrived. It was normal for morning wires to be delivered rather than called for. Like the Army's Flash system, the wire provided information from the previous day or the very early morning hours of the day it arrived. The wires contained information pertinent to individual marshaling districts and held brief statements regarding new crimes, wanted individuals, and, until fifteen years ago, Indian movements and warnings about the area.

"You got a private wire here from that Chief named Grooms in Austin. What kinda name is Grooms, anyway?"

"Irish, let's see."

This wire, however, was a private message from Sheriff Grooms Lee to Marshal Frank Bass. It read:

Frank—

'Need help with serial killings. 'Don't know where to start—got to stop this butcher.

—Grooms

"Somethin up, Frank?"

"Yeah, the Sheriff of Austin wants me to help him with their serial killer." Bass began thinking of the ramifications if he decided to go.

"You know the guy, Frank? Well enough for him to ask?"

"We Rangered together. He saved my life once in Los Trios. He's a capable guy, but I heard he's been drinkin for a while. 'Imagine he's getting heat from the town council, Austin bein' state capitol an' all. Dick Reagan's the US Deputy Marshal there, but I heard he's bein' replaced. *Hell*, I'll talk to Sally about it. Let him know tomorrow. I'll be upstairs if you need me."

Bass walked to his office upstairs from the jail. The stairs had recently been replaced but still creaked like they'd crumble any second with each step. His office hadn't changed in the almost four years he'd been there. The same worn sofa-settee next to a broken-down steel filing box against the same faded yellow paint he'd been looking at for over four years. A small parlor stove stood in the near corner to the door. Eddie Voer used to start a pot of coffee in his office but slacked off when Bass started coming downstairs. There were pictures of Rutherford Hays, James Garfield, and Chester Arthur spaced just so above the sofa. A framed picture of Grover Cleveland had been installed behind the desk, and on his left side hung an American flag. To Cleveland's right, the Texas Lone Star banner took its place. On the wall next to the door was a picture of George Washington, the President who established the US Marshals Service with the First Judiciary Act.

Bass sat in his chair and leaned back, considering the wire he'd just received from his old friend. In the Rangers, they'd pretty well partnered up, went everywhere together, and also watched each other's back. They were much younger then, of course. Grooms left the service to get married, and he and his wife bought a house in Waco where he'd taken a job as Sheriff. He rarely heard from Grooms Lee after that. Bass had his own life to think of, too. He continued with the Rangers until his company rescued captives from a Comanche stronghold, and one of them, a Blackfoot maid named Moon in the Winter Sky, stole his heart. "Everybody makes their own way, I guess." Bass read whatever he could find on the killings in Austin to give himself a better idea of what he was up against. He'd pretty much decided to go and help out his old friend.

He went to the local newspaper office of *The El Paso Times* and asked the editor there, Tim Archuleta, if he'd find any articles he could on the Austin Killings and send them over to the jail. Tim was busy with the daily press run, but Buffalo Frank Bass was a newsmaker, and it paid to stay on his good side. Forty-five minutes later, Bass was upstairs reading about the Annihilator.

"*Holy*—my God," Bass muttered various phrases as he read. "How the hell is this guy even walking the streets? There's gotta be a record somewhere about a guy that's this dangerous. This kind of depravity doesn't just spring up. Somebody knows this guy. Somewhere, somebody knows him."

Bass finished his reading and checked his gold Elgin watch for the time. It was nearly five, time to go home. He wanted to make a quick stop at Doc Ira Spalding's office on his way. He talked with the doctor for about twenty minutes and was surprised at some of the answers he heard. He felt better now about a starting point for Sheriff Grooms Lee.

It took forty minutes to ride out to TwainHeart, his and Sally's place along the Rio. He rode straight to the barn, as was his habit, and saw to putting up his horse for the evening. Fresh water, a pale of oats and alfalfa hay to keep her busy, and he was off to the back porch and the kitchen door. Sally was in the kitchen cleaning Lilly's pacifiers. She had two when Bass walked into the mudroom and took off his spurs and boots.

"You're home a bit early. Is something wrong?"

"Nope, not a thing, just can't stay away from my girls." Bass kissed Sally's neck as she stood at the sink.

"Thought it time to clean these properly. She drops them so regularly, and rinsing doesn't get them quite clean enough."

"What'd she do today? She reading yet?"

"Yes, yes. She's finished the paper, and now she's scanning the dictionary."

"Say, I'd almost believe it. She takes after you so well."

"Nonsense, she's her daddy's girl and will probably be all her life. Marianna's coming over tonight while Theo's away. She hasn't seen the baby for over a week, 'says she feels empty. She's so sweet. We're lucky she's so close. Her English has improved since taking that class, don't you think?"

"Oh, I ain't no judge; she always spoke better 'n me anyway. She does just fine. I wonder how long they're gonna wait before startin' a family. Feed store's doin' good, real good, actually. I know that's what Theo was worried over."

Sally nodded. "Well, I hope it's sooner than later, for Marianna's sake. She nearly swoons with yearning every time she's around Lilly."

"*Hmm*. Smells good. What's on the stove?"

"Just what was left from the last two nights. Nothing keeps in warm weather, even with the icebox. We need more ice. Oh, we got a letter from your sister today. I think it's your sister, Grace Whitworth?"

"Yeah, that's her, let's see . . . what'd she say."

Bass grabbed a biscuit from a bowl on the table and walked into the front room to the bar. He poured them each a whiskey and went back into the kitchen. He set Sally's glass on the counter next to her and sat at the table, nibbling on the biscuit. Her back was to him as he spoke.

"Says here she and Levi bought a place, hey whatdaya know. It's up outside Livermore near the Wyoming border. Say's they got three hundred sixty acres of grass and forest land . . . good water, she says. Hell, this was dated the end of March. Wonder why it took so long to get here?"

Sally was still at the sink. "You know I've never met your sister . . . I'd certainly like to. Can we plan a visit?"

"Why sure, I reckon. It's a long ways . . . well, you know that. How will Lil do on the trip like that?"

Sally dried her hands and sipped her whiskey, "Oh, I think later in summertime, she'll be alright for train travel. We'll have to make accommodations, of course, but it should be alright. Gracie doesn't know about the baby, does she, Frederick?"

Bass sipped his drink. "Guess not. I don't write like I should."

"Well, I'm sure she forgives you. You've told me I know, but how many children does she have?"

"Four boys . . . two oughts to be grown by now. Their own place, well, good for them. I'll have to find out where this Livermore, Colorado is . . . and speakin' a' getting word from friends, don't believe I ever mentioned a friend of mine from the Ranger company named Grooms Lee."

"No, I should certainly remember a name like that."

"Well, he's the sheriff in Austin. I guess now he's chief of police; anyway, he asked me to come help on an investigation he's havin trouble with."

"Austin? Oh God . . . it's not that terrible Butcher case, is it?"

"Yup. He's at a standstill and needs some help, hon."

Sally paused and then turned back to the sink, swallowing the rest of her drink. "Frederick, I'm worried about this. Oh, not because I'm afraid you'll get hurt, though that always worries me. I'm afraid of what this kinda crime, its victims, seeing them and all . . . I'm worried what it'll do to you . . . inside."

"I've thought about that too, Sal. When I was with General Crook, I saw some awful things too. Things that make you wonder about a man's sensibilities . . . his *ah,* his humanity." But if I can speed up findin' and stoppin' this animal from doin' more harm to folks, I believe I should."

"I know. And you're right to put others first." Her shoulders sagged, and she asked,

"When will you go?"

"' Wanted to talk to you first, so I really hadn't figured. I suppose tomorrow afternoon . . . on the six o'clock eastbound."

Sally turned around and walked to him, hugging him tightly when he stood. "Go wash up. Suppers ready."

Bass went into the lavatory that Silas Pratt had built under the stairs to the second floor. It had its own basin, tub, and a flush toilet as well. Silas called it a 'crapper' for the Englishman who invented it. A knock at the door came just as Bass finished up, and he went to open it. Marianna stood on the porch holding a bag of things that looked like baby things to Bass.

"Good evening, Mister Frank Bass. You're looking well tonight."

"Why, thanks, Marianna, that sounded right-proper, but please don't feel like you have to call me anything but Frank, agreed?"

"Yes, I know it, but my English needs practicing. Where is the *nina*—ah . . . the baby, please?"

"Well, I believe Lilly's asleep, but Sally's in the kitchen."

Marianna left for the kitchen, and Bass sat at the table, still sipping his whiskey. The two women appeared with plates and sat across from each other, chatting between themselves. Bass thought about his trip to Austin, what he should pack, and whether he should take Emma or hire a mount. He thought again about the list Doc had given him of the state-run asylums for the insane and incompetent. One, in particular, piqued his curiosity. The State Lunatic Asylum that was located in Austin.

11:15 a.m., May 14, 1888
E. P. & S. W. Terminal
El Paso, Texas

Bass had just arrived at the passenger terminal after first stopping at the jail to leave instructions for Paulo. He was still tryin to figure why Frank and George Coe were so hell-bent on killing him as soon as Frank Coe got off the train. Part of his instructions to Paulo were to check with the local doctor to see if George had been talkative at all during his time in Doc's office. He also told Paulo about a trial coming up in Marfa and, if he had time, to sit in for him. He'd left a note for Bart to ask Georgy Vale to come in once Bass was back from Austin. He did not know how long that would be.

The E. P. & S. W. train left Tucson at 8:15 a.m. and arrived in El Paso at 5:00 p.m. the same day. It was a daily train as it carried California mail westbound to Louisiana and from there to stops heading north. The train left El Paso at 6:00 p.m. and stopped twice, once in Odessa and then again in San Angelo. Travel time to Austin was about eighteen hours, getting Bass into the Capitol a little past noon the next day. He decided on not putting Emma through such a long trip, even though she handled the train ride generally well. Most horses her age took a full day to recover from that much time in the freight car, and Bass decided he'd just find a livery if the need arose.

He'd already spent quite a few days in train travel this year. It started back when he was asked to investigate the kidnapping of two little girls from their home in the northern part of Texas and ended in Las Vegas, New Mexico, a few weeks later with the death of one of the most nefarious villains Bass had ever encountered. In between, Bass spent much of his time riding trains between El Paso and Albuquerque and several other stops almost every day.

Once onboard the eastbound, Bass noted right away that the seats hadn't gotten any softer. He'd hoped the railroad might spend some money on more comfortable seating in the interim since his last trip, but sadly, they hadn't. He finally got his cushion adjusted properly and settled in for the trip to Odessa.

The view from the car always made him feel like he was riding a tireless horse at full gallop for hours on end. He liked that. Unfortunately, most of this trip would be spent in darkness, and Bass occasionally had difficulty sleeping while moving. This train had a dining car, however, and a club car where drinking alcohol and smoking were permitted. He planned on taking maximum advantage of the latter on this trip. They'd stop in Odessa at midnight and then San Angelo near 4:00 a.m. He planned to be dozing at both those times.

Once underway, Bass walked forward to the Lounge Car, which was not much than a saloon on rails, but the seating was better. He sat in one of the comfortable chairs, lit a small cigar, and ordered a rye whiskey with ice. Having ice was a bonus for train travel. He sat next to a large, shaggy-haired man in a baggy brown suit with a stained vest and wrinkled trousers. Bass assumed the man had been traveling for some time, which would explain his appearance. The fellow spotted Bass's US Deputy Marshal badge and introduced himself.

"Marshal, my name's Howard Fine. I sell linens and cotton goods all over the tri-state area, Mississippi, Louisiana, and Texas. I always say, 'my bolt goods are good, but I'm mighty fine.' Get it? A play on words there so they remember my name next time. Headin' to Austin to pitch several hotels there. You goin' on business or pleasure?"

"Business, Mr. Fine. I've been asked to come by a friend."

"Say, I'll bet it has to do with them Annihilator murders, don't it? I don't mind sayin' I'm a bit nervous travelin' alone as I am."

"Oh, I think you'll be safe enough. All the victims to date have been women working in the *gentlemen's comfort trade*. I don't believe, even at night, you'd be mistaken for one of those."

"But that's just me point, my point indeed. There is always a likelihood that I might find a woman like that necessary if you take my meaning, sir. I'm unmarried, footloose, and fancy-free, as they say. A strange hotel, a strange city . . . female companionship at times is a Godsend."

"Yes, I can see how it might be in your situation. I believe my best advice, then, is to avoid the chance of a terrible visit to Austin, is abstinence. Yes, I think so. *Abstinence.* With lunatics such as this at large, venturing out of your room at night might be too risky, Howard. I've seen it happen all too often. An innocent uh . . . business associate is in the wrong place at the wrong time, and *pffftt.* The lunatic gets two for one."

Howard Fine's eyes widened as big as saucers, and small beads of sweat formed on his upper lip and forehead. Suddenly, he jumped to his feet. "I believe I'll review my sales calls for Austin. Good evening, Marshal." Howard Fine dropped his paper and turned to head for the door.

Before closing the door, Bass called after him, "Oh, and it's Deputy Marshal, actually."

2:15 p.m., May 15, 1888
Police Headquarters
Congress Ave. at Peach Street
Austin, Texas

Bass walked through the double doors of the police department and found himself standing in a tiled antechamber with wooden benches on each side and an elevated sergeant's desk at the end. On the benches sat a rough assortment of the people of Austin, all here to make their complaints, observations, fears, and hatreds known. Most were there to report petty crimes against property, like minor theft and shoplifting. There was an older man who approached Bass with a particularly forlorn expression and spoke to him with some kind of European accent Bass couldn't quite place,

"Please, *Signori*, oh please, you are a *polizi*, a police. Cana you find her? She's all I have."

Bass immediately turned to the man and asked, "She's missing? Who is missing? Tell me, tell me who"? Bass moved the smaller man to the side, away from some of the noise and loud talking common in police station waiting rooms.

"Tell me again. Slowly. Who is missing? You said she . . . who is she?"

"She is my Greta, my little Greta; she does not know her way. She would not stay away. You can help me?"

"I'll try. Can you describe her? How tall? How old? What color hair and eyes?" Bass gestured along with his questions, hoping the man would understand what he needed to know.

"Yah, yah . . . she isa four years and has long ears, yes? Flap, Flap. She isa so small." The man indicated only a foot or so off the ground. "My Greta, she woulda no stay away."

It dawned on Bass now that the old man had lost his dog or that she hadn't come home last night. On the one hand, he was relieved that it wasn't another possible victim, but then again . . . well, he felt sorry for the old guy but didn't know where to send him. He signaled for the man to stay put and made his way through the throng of concerned citizens to the sergeant's desk.

"'Scuse me, Sarge, Frank Bass, Deputy US Marshal, can you tell me where the dog catcher or city pound is?"

"What? You're who? The pound? Yeah, the pound is through that door and down the hall. Animal Control. Beat it, will ya, pal?"

Bass nodded and went back to tell the old man where he could go for help, but he'd already left. Bass shook his head and went back to the desk sergeant.

"Hey. Back again." Bass flashed his Federal ID card the Sergeant suddenly was all ears.

"Here to see Chief Lee. Can you tell me where he is?"

"This time a' day? He's at the Nightstick bar around the corner. Turn left out the door."

Bass nodded a thank you and gently removed himself from the crowd. Outside, he turned left and walked a half block but saw no tavern or saloon called the Nightstick. He walked a bit further and, looking down a side street, noticed a sign sticking out from a brick wall. All it had on it was a drawing of a police baton. No name, just the baton. *Gotta be it*, he thought and opened the door.

Chapter 7

The Nightstick was strictly a bar, no card tables, no menus for a café, and no dart boards. Only a polished wooden bar that ran the length of the room down the right-hand side. Behind the bar, three barmen in aprons poured whiskey or drew beer taps. There were no waitresses, no cigarette girls, and no women that Bass saw though the place was so crowded it's possible he missed one. He did see plenty of men in the uniform of the Austin Police Department, and at the far end, he spotted their Chief, Grooms Lee. Chief Lee's eyes were half closed as he leaned against the bar at a precarious angle so that a bump or jostle might spill the man onto the floor . . . badge and all.

"Grooms, what are you doin' here, man? My God looks like half your department's bellied up."

"Who's at? Who're you? Bass? Frank Bass? Oh Lord . . . thanks fer coming. I'm in a real fix, brother."

"Yeah, I can see that. C'mon, we're getting outta here. Through the back . . . is there an alley? Must be. C'mon . . . here we go." Bass pulled Lee's left arm over his own shoulder, and with his arm around the other man's waist, he carried the chief to the alley behind the Nightstick.

Grooms Lee spent the first ten minutes of their visit being sick in the cobblestone alleyway. Bass let the man finish emptying out the whiskey that hadn't made it into his system yet and then walked him further down the alley where there was more sunlight. Lee had his back against the opposing brick wall and slid slowly down to a sitting position. He sat for some minutes, his eyes closed against the light and his breathing so shallow it was barely audible.

At last, he said without opening his eyes, "You know what's going on? Here in my city, Frank?"

"Yeah, Grooms, I do. I read the papers. Sounds real bad, Grooms."

"Yeah, Mayor called in the Pinks. Told me so . . . was it yesterday. He knows. Yup, he knows the Chief can't handle it. He's a drunk, Frank. Chief's a drunk."

"It sure looks that way, Grooms. You wanna do anything 'bout that? If you do, I'm here for ya."

A Sergeant poked his head out the door and looked their way, "You need any help with him?"

"Nah . . . I got him. Thanks anyway."

The Sergeant nodded and closed the door. Chief Lee was lying on the cobblestones now, his eyes open, staring, trying to see into the torment that hid behind his eyes.

"You still there, Frank?"

"Still here, Grooms."

"Take me home, will ya?"

"You bet, where d' you live."

"112 . . . damn, ha. 112 Brazos, take the trolley out front." Chief Lee tried standing, and with Bass's help, they both made it to the trolley stop across from the police department. Lee spent the twenty-minute trip sitting up, holding his hat in his lap with his eyes closed.

The trolley stopped at his corner, and Bass helped Lee up the front stoop and into the brick apartment building's lobby. Lee fumbled for his key, and when he finally found it, he pointed at one of the ground-floor doors, and they went in. The place looked to be good sized, though it was hard to tell with all the clothes, newspapers, broken furniture, and glassware strewn about. As they stood in the doorway, Lee, slightly weaving, turned to Bass and said, "Maid's day off."

They both went inside, and Grooms Lee collapsed on the divan, shoving books and newspapers out of the way. Bass covered him with a small blanket he found in the bedroom and got a towel and basin to wipe off the man's face. As he started, Grooms said with his eyes still closed, "She's gone, Frank, Mary. Mary's gone, gone, gone away. With another man. Frank, Mary's gone away with another man."

After that, he was quiet, and his breathing became regular and rhythmic. Bass let himself out. He had to go back to the Nightstick for his bag, and then he needed to find a hotel. He decided on the C Hotel because it was reasonably clean and comfortable, had an inexpensive dining room with good food and service, and a quiet saloon.

7:45 p.m., May 15, 1888
Winslow Hotel
Congress Ave at Ash Street
Austin, Texas

The Winslow occupied a square city block three blocks south of the State Government House. It was a nicely appointed hotel with a large lobby and meeting rooms nearly a hundred guest rooms on three floors. The lamps were carefully polished brass, and the carpets were well-maintained woven rugs from the Middle East and the American southwest. The dining room occupied nearly half of the first floor and, when not partitioned off, could seat one hundred and fifty guests. Still, by Eastern standards, the Winslow was not a grand hotel.

The Winslow catered to businessmen and, because of its location, politicians from all over the state. Bass stepped up to the front desk, set his large carpet bag on the floor, and touched the plunger on the bell. It being nearly eight o' clock in the evening, the desk clerk was in the office arranging the housekeeping schedule for the coming day. When she heard the bell, she walked quickly to the front desk.

"Yes sir, welcome to the Winslow. What can I do for you?"

"A room, please. It's just for myself. I'll be here for a few days, so let's say my stay is open-ended."

"Alright, sir, the rate for a single is two dollars a day in advance. Since your stay is indefinite let's say ten dollars to book the room for the first five days and a settlement to be made when you leave. If that is satisfactory, sign here, please."

Bass smiled at the young woman, and she smiled back. "Are you here on business or pleasure?" Bass signed the registry and spun the book around so the girl could read. "US Deputy Marshal Frank Bass, I suppose then it's business."

Bass nodded. "That's right, Miss."

The clerk quickly added, "My name is Beth Wahlton. I'm off at midnight . . . in case you have trouble sleeping."

She smiled again at Bass, and he said, "Actually, I'm married, Miss Wahlton. Have a baby girl back in El Paso."

The clerk nodded and said, "I suppose you're here to assist in the investigation of the serial killer, then."

"Yes, but mostly to see an old friend."

"Of course. We are all terribly saddened by the most recent murder. She was one of our staff, you see. Dreadful business this. He must be deucedly clever to avoid capture for so long."

"She worked here, you say?"

"Yes. In housekeeping. I'm just now redoing the schedule."

"Gonna wanna talk with her direct supervisor . . . perhaps tomorrow?"

"Of course, her name is Tilly Masters. Her shift starts at 6:00 a.m."

Bass nodded and said, "My key, please."

"Oh yes. Room 225. Turn left at the top of those stairs. At the end of the hall." The clerk smiled in the same practiced way that all hotel clerks smile, and Bass picked up his bag and went upstairs.

His room was larger than most of the hotels Bass frequented but essentially the same. A double bed, an armoire, two armchairs with tables against the windows, and a chest of drawers with a basin and pitcher on top next to the mirror. Bass hung his clothing in the armoire. He'd brought three shirts, two vests and matching jackets, and two pairs of light gray worsted trousers. He brought his nickel-plated .38 caliber Colt Lightning with him; it was lighter and a bit smaller. He intended to use a shoulder holster when in Austin. Side arms were frowned upon as they were reminders of a more lawless time. Bass also suspected that side arms made politicians nervous.

In his boot, he carried his favorite Remington-Smoot five-shot .20 caliber revolver. He'd carried this gun since giving his Remington Rider .32 caliber to Sally when she learned to shoot. She saved his life with that particular pistol, and he'd never think of taking it back. Once he finished his unpacking he decided to go to the dining room for something to eat. He hadn't had anything to eat since the train this morning, and his appetite was sharp-set.

It was 8:30 p.m. when he entered the dining room. It was about half full of nicely dressed men and women talking over their meals in candlelight. Bass sat at a table by a window and watched the evening traffic barely visible in the lamp light. The waitress looked to be in her thirties, attractive and slim, in her hotel uniform of a deep maroon skirt and white high-necked blouse and apron.

"Sir? A drink before dinner? She smiled as she handed Bass a menu and brought her notepad up to the light.

"Please, I'll have a double rye whiskey, Overholt if you have it, on ice."

"Very good, sir. Have a look at our menu, and I'll be right back."

Bass looked at the single-page menu and decided on pork chops and greens with a side of fried potatoes. When the girl returned, he thanked her for his drink and gave her his order and asked quickly, before she left, if she'd known the girl who was killed at the end of last month.

The waitress's face clouded over immediately, and she stood with her hands crossed in front of her. "Yes, I did, sir. We were very good friends. Bea and I had known each other a long time."

"I'm very sorry to bring it up. I can see it's painful for you."

"Yes, it is, sir . . . and our worthless police department can't seem to get a handle on who it is. I apologize for that, sir. I'm quite angry about it. Three girls treated in the most horrible, devilish way."

"I understand completely. Can I have your name, please? I'm a US Deputy Marshal asked to help out on this investigation."

"Well, sir, if you don't mind, can I see your badge, please? Since all of this started, I've become much more cautious."

"Of course, here." Bass showed her both his badge and Government-stamped ID card.

The girl looked at both carefully and smiled. "Hope you understand, Marshal, can't be too careful. My name's Megan Day, sir, like 'the break of.'"

They chuckled. "Megan, stay cautious and tell your friends to be careful too. Now, can we talk sometime tomorrow? Maybe in here or the lobby?"

"I don't think Herb would want us to be seen sittin' around talkin in the lobby."

"Who's Herb?"

"The manager. He's at the front desk just now."

"Alright, don't worry about Herb, I'll fix it with him. I'll meet you in the lobby tomorrow . . . what time?"

"I'm off breakfast at 9:00 a.m."

"Good. I'll see you then."

Megan went back to the kitchen and brought Bass his order. The food was just passable, but the service was good, so he left Megan a healthy tip and grabbed a paper in the lobby on his way to his room.

He poured another whiskey for himself and sat in his drawers reading *The Austin Statesman* until his eyes told him it was time to sleep. Two articles were written about the Annihilator in the paper. He read them both and hoped he'd sleep through the night.

The next morning, Bass was awakened by the sounds of city life. Horses and wagons on the cobblestoned streets, garbage collectors cursing as they hoisted bins onto their wagons. And the normal, noisy beginning of a typical Wednesday in the Capitol City.

He rolled out of bed feeling better than he thought he would. Yesterday had been a long one, starting with short sleep and no food on the train, retrieving and caring for a drunken friend in the late afternoon, and an evening dinner at the hotel, chatting with a possible witness to the horrible crimes that had plagued the city for months. He remembered his 9:00 a.m. appointment in the lobby with Megan and wanted to get there first for a conversation with Herb.

He did a quick brush-up at the basin, cleaning his teeth and brushing his hair into place. He made a mental note to find a barber; his hair was starting to curl over his collar, and a hot shave wouldn't hurt either. He made it to the lobby by 8:40 and helped himself to a biscuit and coffee that was set out on a table under the front windows. As he ate, Herb distributed mail and walked to the front desk. Though Herb saw him, he continued his chore until finished and only then walked to the counter window where Bass waited.

"Good morning, sir. How can I help?"

"Your name's Herb, right?"

"That's right." Herb wrinkled his brow at the question.

"Do you remember me from yesterday . . . checking in?"

"I do indeed, sir."

"Good, now, in a few minutes, I'm gonna conduct an interview with one a' your employees right over there in them two chairs. Her name is Megan Day. She works in the dining room."

"Sir, I'm afraid that's against hotel regulations. No fraternization between guests and employees is ever allowed. We're quite strict about enforcing that rule, and she should know about it, as well."

"*Uh-huh*. Herb, what's your last name?"

"It's Petrie." Bass assumed his most intimidating Deputy Marshal persona and said,

"Mr. Petrie I plan to conduct an official interview with Miss Day this morning, as I believe she may have information useful in solving the Annihilator slayings. She seems to feel comfortable here in the hotel. Now, if necessary, I'll close the hotel for the duration of my talk with Miss Day. No one will be permitted to enter or leave until

I'm finished. She'll be here in a few minutes. You tell me if I need to chain the doors."

Petrie flustered and had to compose himself before speaking. "Well, under the circumstances, I ah . . . it seems . . ."

Bass smiled as warmly as he could muster. "Good. I'm glad that's settled, aren't you?"

Bass walked to the two chairs that were isolated from the main traffic through the lobby and sat in one that faced the front door. A few minutes later, Megan appeared and walked tentatively past Herb at the front desk and sat opposite Bass.

"Morning, Megan. How was your shift?"

"It was about normal. Three hours, and now I'm off till four when we prep for dinner."

"Do they pay you well here? Are you happy with your job?"

"The pay is poor, but we do get tips that we share with the rest of the staff, and thank you very much for yours last night. Wish all my customers were as generous."

"Well, that's alright, you earned it. You say you share tips with the staff. Does that include ol' Herb there?"

"Oh, yeah, and the bellhops, too." Bass nodded and continued,

"You said that you and Beatrix were friends, right?"

"Yes, sir."

"How well did you know her? Um, did you know her family, for instance?"

At this, Megan rolled her eyes and gently shook her head. "I knew her folks; they're real religious, real proper folk. They wouldn't let her go out with us or have any fun. She was tryin' to save money so she could move out."

"Megan, I'm sure you've read that the victims so far have been prostitutes. Is that how Beatrix earned extra money?"

Megan folded her hands in her lap and then began to worry the seams of her apron. "Yes. She didn't do it often . . . only two or three times." Megan's eyes filled with tears, and her voice cracked. "It's all just so very sad."

Bass handed the girl a napkin from the table and waited for her to continue. She cleared her throat and looked up, nodding that she felt better.

"Megan, how did she explain her being out so late to her parents?"

"Well, she would usually say she was working a double shift or wait till they were asleep, though once they went to a midnight prayer vigil and were gone most the night."

"Do you know if she visited the Pierce Hotel before?"

"Yeah . . . she said that there were lots of single salesman types that stayed there between trains."

"Do you know if she had any regular customers? I'm sorry. I know this is hard, but I have to ask."

"Not really. She didn't talk about 'em much. She said once she saw a real rich lookin' fella all dressed up like for a ball or something. Top hat, gold cane, a cape, even white gloves . . . everything fancy. But she never went with him. She never saw him with anyone else, though. When she told me about him, I thought it was funny; I mean, such a fancy dresser at the Pierce."

Bass had thought the same thing; how a man dressed like that would certainly stand out among salesmen.

"Did she happen to say what he looked like?"

"Nah, she never saw his face, and it was only the one-time she said."

"Alright, Megan, That's enough for now. Thank you for answerin' these questions. I know they're tough on ya."

"Oh, that's ok. I really want the devil found, Marshal. If you need me again, I'll be happy to oblige."

"Thanks again, Megan. Go get some rest before you have to come back to work."

Megan stood, and Bass was finishing his coffee when he heard her say, "Tall . . . she said he was tall. Just remembered."

Bass nodded her way and said thanks as she walked back to the dining room. *Hmm. He was tall. Maybe I'll take a run over to the Pierce Hotel this afternoon.*

Chapter 8

10:30 a.m., May 16, 1888
Police Department
Office of the Chief
Congress Ave at Peach St.
Austin, Texas

The State Capitol Building had burned some seven years earlier, and today, after an almost complete reconstruction, was the celebration of the official reopening of the grand building of Austin, bigger, they said, than the capitol in Washington DC. There were festivities around the building, but in the city of Austin, chaos reigned as usual.

Bass walked through the double doors and up to the Sergeant's desk. "Here to see the Chief. Can you point me to his desk?"

The Sergeant leered at Bass for a moment and said, "Below the clock on the wall, the man's office door."

Bass nodded as he walked by and knocked lightly on the door jamb. When no one answered, Bass opened the door and found Grooms Lee, his head on his arms folded on the desk, sound asleep. Bass closed the door quickly, hoping no one else would see the Chief as he was, but then, after yesterday afternoon at the Nightstick, he realized the office probably knew about this and much more related to Chief Lee's behavior.

"Wake up, Lee . . . wake up for God's sake. It's near eleven, man. Wake up."

Chief Lee lifted his head from the desk and seeing Bass, remembered where he was and tried pulling himself together.

"Hey Frank, mornin' to ya. How'd you sleep? . . . Where'd ya sleep, for that matter?"

"I got a room at the Winslow. C'mon man, snap to will ya. I need to know a few things 'bout this case. This is your town, Grooms."

"*Ahem*, yes, yes, absolutely true." Lee stood and walked over to a pegboard with dates, victims, photos, and locales. Brief notes accompanied each victim, and next to the pegboard, a street map of Austin with red dots indicating the radius of the murder scenes. At first glance, Bass saw no pattern on the map, just random dots, but as he looked closer, he noticed the dots were all located in proximity to a hotel.

"Say, look here. All these locations are near or within walking distance of a hotel. By itself, that don't mean much, but we're lookin' for patterns here, and on three killings, that's one. And over on your timeline you got all three killings happening on the first day of the month. That's gotta mean something, and it's another pattern."

"Yeah, I see that. Now the hotels . . . that lines up with hookers as his victims."

"Yeah, except for the first one, says here she was a servant girl at . . . can't read that . . ."

"' Says Brady house . . . yeah Brady, he's a local judge. 'No arrest record on him, clean as a whistle. But there was a guy, a Colored guy tried stopping him and got an ax in his back for his trouble."

Bass listened and said, "Alright. Maybe she wasn't a hooker but happened to be in the wrong place at the wrong time. Now, what about the other man? How is he, where is he?"

"Jesus Frank, I don't know. I turned the case over to our Sergeant O'Dell. He used to do detective work up in New York City. Cillian O'Dell. He's handlin' the murders now."

"*Uh-huh*. Well, from now on, you're handlin' the case, and you're gonna make sure the papers know it."

Grooms Lee looked forlorn. The reporters all knew him for what he was. It was bad enough the whole police force knew; now the whole damn town would know.

"Frank, listen. I can't do this kinda thing anymore. The truth is, I ain't been worth much since Annie left. Hell, I figured just to finish out my term and leave town. I'm in way over my head here."

"Way over . . . say you listen here, ol' chum. A good part of the police work I know was learned from you. 'You remember Abilene? The hours you spent with me watchin' that ol barn? Sittin' outside in them rocks? And damned if you wasn't right too. Bob Vogel did come back that night, and we nailed him dead to rights. That's one of the things you taught me, Grooms, was patience. You used to say, 'if you wait long enough' . . . what was it?"

"If you wait long enough, an outlaw'll trip himself up, and all ya hafta do is put the cuffs on him."

Bass smiled, watching his old friend. "Damn right. And that's what we're gonna do with this son of a bitch, Grooms. We're gonna let him trip himself up."

Grooms Lee took a deep breath, looked at Bass, and said, "Alright, let's catch this sucker."

"Tha's the lawman I know. Now, the Colored guy. Let's talk to him."

"Right, I'll get Cillian in on this with us. He's pretty sharp, Frank. Seen a lot." The Chief left his office and returned a few minutes later with a uniformed sergeant. Cillian O'Dell was nearly as tall as Bass, but his full beard and long, curly red hair made him seem larger than he was. He was barrel-chested and had large, meaty hands, which looked like powerful weapons in themselves.

"So. Who's this hearty lad, then?" His blue eyes examined Bass, taking his measure, Bass supposed.

"This is an old friend, Cill, Federal Marshal from El Paso. Name's Frank Bass. He's here to help with the Annihilator killings."

"Is he then?" O'Dell advanced toward Bass with his hand out. "Seems I've read about a Federal Copper named Bass . . . s'posed to be some kinda super sleuth. Is 'at so, Mr. Bass?"

Bass had taken the Sergeant's hand, and the two began a squeezing game to see who'd quit first. "I've had some success, Sergeant. I hear y'all from up north. Get tired a' the big city, did ya?"

O'Dell released first and offered a genuine smile, "Laddy, I nabbed all the really rotten ones, thought I'd come down here for a wee rest."

Bass and Lee both chuckled. "Chief says you been lookin' into the killin's this fella been doin. What can you tell us about 'em?"

"Boys, this is a sick one. First, all three killin's occurred after midnight accordin' to the doc, on the first o' the month. Second, his MO is the same for all three. He hits 'em over the head, drags 'em inta the alleyway, and cuts their troats. Then, and I havena figured this one out yet, the munter sprinkles 'em with salt. Salt, I say."

Bass shook his head, "Why would . . ."

"Dear God. He doesn't . . . he doesn't eat . . .?"

"No nuttin' like 'at. It's in their hair and down at their feet, too. Then he carves a cross right in the middle a their bean."

"A cross? A cross like the church cross, right?"

"A' course ya slacker, right here." He pointed to the spot between his brows and above the nose. "And the last thing is . . . he takes her heart. Doc says no heart organs 'been found. Naturally, we assumes how he took it with 'im."

Both Bass and Lee looked at each other with eyes wide and full of the natural apprehension at facing down something like this.

"' Wanted to talk to the man that was wounded during was it the first assault?" Bass asked Cillian next.

"At's roight. He's a hard man too. They both work for Judge Wendel Brady. He butlers fer him, and she worked in the kitchen. I tried to ask a few what-fors, but he weren't havin it. S'been a while now, though. He mighta remembered something. Worth a go, Gaffer."

Bass looked at Cillian O'Dell as though he'd come from another world.

Finally, Grooms offered, "Frank, he said the man is the Judge's butler, and he tried interviewing him once before, but the guy wouldn't talk. But since time has passed, it might be a good idea to try again. Gaffer."

"Alright, I know I'm just a dumb Texas hick, but what're you two callin' me with that?"

Cillian said, "Gaffer? Means Bossman."

Bass smiled but still had his doubts about this new language.

The three men signaled for a Gurney cab to take them to the Trinity Hotel at the corner of Sixth Street and Trinity. The hotel was in a commercial part of town and close to the county courthouse and civic center. Normally, the area is bustling with trade and commercial vehicles, but at night, when everything's closed down, there's very little street activity. The man who had been injured by the assailant worked in the home of Judge Wendel Brady. It was a three-story Victorian house on Trinity, close to the corner with Sixth Street. The murder had occurred in the alley that ran between Trinity Street and San Jacinto.

The three men climbed out of the small cab and walked up the steps to the front porch. The house was in a fashionable area near to the courthouse and the Theater District.

Cillian twisted the ornamented doorbell key, and after a few moments, a stiff-looking Black man answered. He looked to be in his fifties, clean shaven, his hair was nearly white, and he had age wrinkles around his eyes and across his forehead. He dressed formally in a starched collar, cutaway coat, and white linen shirt. His trousers were neatly pressed twill with a satin stripe running down the outside of each leg.

"How can I help you, gentlemen?" His voice was deep but controlled to sound welcoming, even though it was obvious that he recognized Cillian and the Chief from prior experience. He would certainly be aware of the nature of their call. Bass answered first, thinking his Federal position might be more impressive.

"I'm Federal Deputy Marshal Frank Bass, and we'd like to ask you a few questions regarding the murder of Mollie Simms. She was employed here, wasn't she?"

From somewhere in the house, Bass heard a woman's voice call, "Who is it, Geoffrey? Who's at the door?"

"It's the police again, ma'am, wantin' to speak with me some more."

"Well, my heavens. Have them wait, please."

Geoffrey turned back to the three men smiling and pointed to chairs on the porch. After a few moments, an older lady appeared. She was a large woman dressed in the style of the day and her gray hair piled on top of her head. Her face was pinched as though she had smelled something awful, and her face was made up with powder and rouge in equal proportions.

"I am Amelia Brady; this is my house. You people have already interviewed Geoffrey once. Why have you come again?"

Again, Bass took the lead. "Ma'am, as I explained to your Butler, I'm a Federal Deputy Marshal, and while it's true these men talked with your man once, I wasn't there to hear any of it. And it's been my experience that, after a time, details can sometimes be recalled. Or perhaps a new question might be asked. In any event, ma'am, we'd like to talk with your Geoffrey once again. Oh, and I'm sorry for the loss of your worker."

"What's that? Geoffrey, what does he mean by that? Has one of those flighty Colored girls run off again?"

"No, ma'am. It was Mollie, ma'am, young Mollie Simms, a kitchen worker who was killed."

"What!? From my house? You can't be serious . . . my God, the scandal this will cause. Oh, and the Judge! Surely, this will land in his lap." The woman had become quite agitated over Mollie's inconsiderate demise. Bass, at first, was incredulous that this woman was so callous about her employee, but then he realized that she, like many other older women of her station, had no real contact with the world they lived in. It was part of the shield their husbands provided and the kind of courtesy they expected.

"Well, if she's gone, have we replaced her?"

"Yes, ma'am. It happened some months ago. You may remember I was injured?"

"You were inj—oh! Was that the reason for the day you missed?"

"Yes, ma'am."

"I see. Well, you look fine now. Was the Judge informed at the time?"

"Yes, ma'am."

"Oh. Well, in that case, do whatever you must with these people and return to your duties post haste."

"Of course, ma'am."

The old lady turned on her heel and walked back into the house, closing the entry door just loudly enough that it could not be taken for a slam. Geoffrey turned to the three men, who all had difficulty believing what they'd witnessed.

"Alright then"—Geoffrey sat in a chair opposite the three—"ask away."

The three men were still seated, and Bass began questioning. "Geoffrey, how long had Mollie Simms worked in the house?"

"Nearly a year."

"And was she in the habit of going out late at night?"

"Gentlemen, let's get it straight. Mollie was a young, pretty gal. She didn't like being cooped up in this ol' museum of a house day in and day out, no sir. She enjoyed the company of men too, Lordy, how she did that." Geoffrey smiled at his memories of the girl.

"I must ask this: did she ever receive money from these men?"

Geoffrey's face clouded over. "Truly fellas I don't know . . . I suspect so, though. She never wanted for new hats or dresses. The Mrs. provides the girls' uniforms and a little cash, walkin 'round money. But never enough for what Mollie had."

"How many servants work here, Geoffrey?" Grooms asked.

"There's four of us. One girl does laundry, one does cleaning, and one does cooking. I'm kinda like the overseer. Oh, I do the servin' at table, and I drive 'em in their fancy buggy too."

Cillian O'Dell listened to every answer and heard every word spoken by Amelia Brady. His 'olde sod' upbringing had fostered a healthy distrust for the Gentry, and as far as he was concerned, this household was due for a comeuppance.

"Tell me then, Geoffrey, since you been knowin' so much about the Grand House and all, do you think maybe the old Judge maya been sniffin' about down in the laundry at all? Maybe when the old woman was out to her tea?"

Though Geoffrey was older he still took offense and stood toe to toe with the younger Irishman. "You cracker trash, you'll take that back bout the Judge, or I'll thump you good."

Bass and the Chief were both up and working their way between the two men. Grooms faced Cillian and quietly said, "Outta line, ya dodgy Mick. You'd best apologize and step back so we can finish. Aye, boyo?"

Cillian backed down from his Chief and apologized to Geoffrey. "Sorry, there Geoffrey . . . 'preciate ya bein a sport. Won't say no more."

Cillian walked down the steps to the pavement and waited as Bass and Lee continued.

Bass started again. "Geoffrey, so far, you're the only witness to the man at the scene. If you don't mind, can I ask you to close your eyes and reimagine that night?"

"You boys is persistent . . . I already answered that one, but alright." Geoffrey closed his eyes and was silent for a moment.

Bass asked, "Where were you when you first thought something was wrong?"

"I was come down to the kitchen, I heard the door open and saw Mollie wrap her old brown coat 'round her." Geoffrey kept his eyes closed.

"Did you follow her?"

"No, 'least not right away. I went to my room and started thinkin 'bout it, and I got my jacket."

"Did you go looking for her then?"

"Yessir, I thought about it some more, and I knowed it was late, and she oughtn't be out that time a night. I put my jacket on over my nightshirt and went on out behind her."

"What was it like, the night, I mean, at that hour?"

"Well, it was cold, I'll say. Still some little bit of snow around. And quiet too, you know, like a church is quiet when it's empty."

"Do you remember which lamps on the street were lit?"

"*Hmm*, why yes, I believe the light at the theater was lit, and one a the streetlamps on Trinity was still burning. I remember a moon that night, too, sir. It musta been clear."

"You followed her, Mollie, right?"

"Tha's right."

"How far behind were you? How many minutes do you think?"

"Oh my, I don't know. Maybe twenty minutes or maybe more. Oh Lord, I shouldn'ta waited so long."

"Why did you stop at the alley, Geoffrey? What made you stop?"

Geoffrey's eyes were still closed tightly now, and his face was twisted into a sad kind of grimace. "I see a flash of something, didn't know what, so I called for her, *Mollie*, I said. '*Mollie girl, where you at? That you back in that alley!? Damn your soul, girl! Come out here now!'* Tha's what I said, mister, I cursed her soul, I did. Oh Lord, forgive me, and she was so mangled and dead not a few feet away."

"You mustn't blame yourself, Geoffrey. You had no way of knowing what had happened. Your only concern was for the girl."

Geoffrey shook his head from side to side and small tears had puddled beneath his eyes and perched without sliding down his cheek.

"Now think again, Geoffrey, what happened next?"

"So I was standin' on the walk by the street starin' into that dark alley next to the theater, and quick as a slap, this fella came running at me. He was waving some kinda heavy knife at me. And I turned to run. That's when he stabbed me square in my middle back. He hit me so hard I fell down in the street, too scared even to move."

"Tell me about him, Geoffrey. How tall was he?"

"*Hmm.* He woulda been maybe my size or a tad bigger."

"Was he a White man?"

"Oh yessir, I glimpsed at his arm when he raised it, and he were White."

"Did you see what he was wearing?"

Geoffrey paused to think. "Yessir, he wore like a black shawl a' some kind, but I did see a bit of his white shirt, too."

"Could you see his face?"

"No. He had his other hand in front of his face, and his hat was down low."

"Which hand did he use to cover his face?"

"The uh, uh . . . the right one. Yes, the right one. I can see him coming at me with his right hand up by his face."

"So then you turned away to run, as any man would do, and then what happened, Geoffrey?"

"He struck me a heavy blow that knocked me to the pavement. Truly, boys, I didn't even know I'd been cut till a neighbor came down and helped me."

"You're doing fine Geoffrey, real fine. Just one more question."

"Alright." Geoffrey closed his eyes again as Bass spoke.

"Geoffrey, you're down, lying in the street because a man knocked you down and struck you in the back. When you looked up from the cobblestones, what did you see?"

Again, Geoffrey paused. "I saw him running, but he ran funny like he'd been shot. Limpin' along, goin' as fast as he could, but he was still limping. He had a black wood cane I saw that had a gold knob on top, and he was limping away. Between two houses across the street."

"And which leg did he favor, which one limped?"

"By God . . . his left one, sir." Geoffrey opened his eyes. "Damn. Had no idea I remembered all that." He stood up and said, "Prob'ly gimme night terrors for it."

Both Bass and Lee apologized. "I'm sorry for putting you through all that again. But you know, some of what you told us might help us to find the murderer before he strikes again."

"I hope so, Mr. Marshal, I truly do." Geoffrey went inside, and the three men talked on the street.

"Frank, that was brilliant questioning. And asking him to close his eyes? Extraordinary."

"I'll say so meself, Mr. Federal Man. 'Got way more this time than I did the first. Where'd you learn that, mate?"

"Huh, an old Crow Medicine Woman taught me."

Cillian and Grooms looked at each other and shrugged. Bass watched them and shrugged right back.

"Alright then, who's for lunch?" The other two agreed, and Grooms told them of a place he used to frequent nearby.

"Essie's Diner. Over on San Jacinto. Quiet, good food. Comfortable . . . and no newspaper people.

Chapter 9

12:30 p.m., May 16, 1888
  Essie's Diner
  San Jacinto Street
  Austin Texas

The weather had warmed, and there was no longer a need for outer coats and jackets. All three men carried their coats on their arms to the diner and hung them on the coat rack at the door. Cillian removed his hat and hung it up, too. Chief Lee kept his tweed bowler hat on, and Bass removed his gray slouch hat and set it on the fourth chair at the table.

Bass looked back at Cillian's headpiece and asked, "What kind a topper is that you just hung up, don't believe I've ever seen one afore?"

"*Hmm*? Oh, me bonnet. It's called a scally cap. Got it in Boston 'fore headin' to Gotham."

"Gotham?"

"New York, man. Gotham City. Brooklyn specifically."

"Ah. Got it. What's it made outta?"

Cillian shrugged, "Some kinda wool; never asked." He looked at Bass. "What manner of hat is that one, then?"

"We call it a *slouch* 'cause it droops in front and in the back. 'Keeps the sun off your neck and face, though. What about yours, Chief? Whatdaya call that one you're wearing?"

"Call it my hat . . . you wanna eat or what?"

The waitress was a young girl with dark curly hair, blue eyes, and a fascination for O'Day's hair.

She took the order and finally asked him about it. "In my country, darlin, if ya don't have red hair and a churlish nature, you're English, by God, and you'd best go home."

O'Dell winked at her, and she smiled and left the table.

"Too young, boyo. Much too young."

Bass and O'Dell had each ordered whiskey—Cillian made it Bushmill's, of course—while Grooms Lee ordered coffee. The girl returned with her tray of drinks and went back to the kitchen. Bass began with his thoughts so far.

"Alright, let's review what we got. We all know the nature of the killin's and where they happened. The patterns are there for us. One, Doc says all three were killed after midnight, so the killer may be saying something by striking early on the first of the month. Two, each of the victims were covered in salt. That's got to mean something to the killer, and all we have to do is figure out what.

"Three, so far, the victims are all females and selling for sex. Mollie Simms may a' worked as maid in the Judge's house, but according to Geoffrey, she was in the habit of sellin' herself to make extra money.

"Four, the women were all hit on the head from behind, had their throats cut, and were likely dead before our boy began his work. And five, this is the one that just gets my goat; he takes her heart and carves a cross on her forehead. So there it is. What'd I miss?"

"The hotels, the crime scenes were all in proximity to hotels. One was inside a room. That pretty much bolsters the notion they were whores," Grooms added.

"And now we have a pretty fair description of the tosser, and we can near well assume he uses his cane as a club, a crusher," Cillian O'Dell said.

Bass added, "I talked with a friend of Beatrix this morning, named Megan Day, at the Winslow Hotel. They worked there together. She told me of a man Beatrix once described to her that she met at the Pierce Hotel. She said he dressed to the nines: cape, top hat, gloves, the whole thing. She said he also had a gold cane. Now, I'm sure she was referring to the headpiece, and it may not mean anything at all, but she said nothing about a limp."

Cillian spoke up, "Which reminds me, we have photographs of footprints found at the scene of her killing. Could you tell by looking if the mugger has a limp?"

The dark-haired waitress returned with their order and set plates in front of each man. She stooped extra low when she set Cillian's plate down. Cillian smiled and winked again as she left the table.

As they ate, their conversation continued.

"Let's keep that information under wraps, Sergeant. 'No point telling the killer what we're looking for. 'Seems counter-productive to me. Now, Doc seems to feel that whoever it is he has a knowledge of the human body, maybe even worked a medical practice or hospital at one time," Chief said.

Bass finished his whiskey, " You know we're talking all around it here, boys. Whoever this fiend is, he's obviously insane. Has anyone gone to the asylum yet?"

Cillian raised his hand slightly. "Aye, I rode out there after the first one, talked to the doctor" —Cillian pulled a small notebook from his pocket—"a doc named Marion Gilmore. He's a likely one he is, 'name like Marion. Anyway, he's the chief looney there. I asked a question if any of his patients had talents along those lines. He dinna wanna say. He was tight as a mugger's grip that one. I also asked were any of his lunatics missing. And he got all huffy 'bout it, didn't he, like them buggers, enjoy bein' locked away. I tink another visit might be in order. Specially wit what we got from ol' Geoffrey today. Mr. Marshal, do ya tink ye might work yer interrogation skills on that one?"

"Boyo, be happy ta. This afternoon, though, I'd like to go to the Pierce Hotel. Now that we have both Megan's description and Geoffrey's firsthand look, I'd like to talk with some of the staff who mighta 'seen this maniac. Sarge? How about checkin' into the medical schools and mortuaries? Your doc seemed to think highly of the man's knowledge about the human body . . . so maybe?"

"Will do, Marshal. I'll ask a couple of hoofers who might wanna log some extra time."

Bass looked at him and asked, "Hoofers?"

"Aye, beat coppers, the men walkin or riding. Patrollin' the neighborhoods."

"Ah. I get it. And Grooms? Whatdaya think of goin through your office's list of known felons in the area? Recent parolees who went up the river on a sex-related crime conviction: rape, attacks on women, that sorta thing. The villain lives in town here . . . all we have to do is find him."

The three left the diner in different directions. Grooms headed back to the police headquarters while Sergeant O'Dell took a trolley to Congress Ave a newly new campus of St. Edwards University across from the post office.

2:45 p.m., May 16, 1888
Texas State Lunatic Asylum
Guadalupe Ave.
Austin, Texas

Bass knew his way around Austin from the several State Jurisdictional Meetings he'd attended over the last few years. He'd also had the opportunity to visit professionally on two occasions to arrest and transport outlaws wanted in his District. Still, he'd never visited the lunatic asylum before. He expected its location to be distanced from the general population but not so remote that Gurney cabs wouldn't go that far. He decided since it looked like he'd be here for a few days, he'd go to the nearest livery and rent a mount for his stay.

The Gurney cabs were plentiful around the hotels, the train depot, and the state capitol. He walked several blocks to find one that wasn't engaged and asked the driver to take him to the nearest reputable livery.

"'Tain't real pretty, but the one where I keep my rig and ol' Louie, my bay gelding, is near the rail yard on Live Oak Avenue. Ya want I should take ya?"

"Yeah, sounds like my kinda place." Bass preferred the less fancy places as a general rule. More likely to run into honest, hardworking folks who knew the value of a dollar. It was true he'd been taken a few times but never by enough to change his mind.

He stepped out of the two-wheel buggy in front of a building that looked more like a warehouse than a livery. The sign on the door read Slap and Tickle Livery, Herm Fields Prop. Bass rapped on the door, and a lady's voice answered, "Come on in; don't stand in the weather like a fool."

Bass opened the door and met Lolamike. She looked to be about five feet tall and maybe that wide. She wore her gray-black hair in a ponytail, and her round face lit up at the sight of Frank Bass. She stood up from her table and shuffled her way to the counter near Bass.

"What can I do ya for there, handsome?"

Bass smiled 'tipped his hat. "I need a horse for a few days. A tall mare, not too young?"

"Ha! How would you feel 'bout a short fat one with a ponytail that ain't too young?"

Bass played along. "Sure! As long as she carries me out to the lunatic asylum and back, that'd be fine."

Lolamike jumped back a step from the counter. "*Jiminy*! Why you wanna go out there for? 'S nothin' but crazies from all over at that place."

"I'm a US Deputy Marshal investigatin' the serial killin's. Seems like a natural to head out there."

"Alright then, I got some fine animals out to the coral. Follow me, huh?"

"Yes, ma'am."

Bass followed Lolamike out of the office and through a side door that opened into a long series of stalls on either side of a central walkway. "This your barn?"

"Indeed, used to be a tobacco drying operation till the owner T. W. Smith and his son decided the ground was better in Willis, east a' here. My brother organized us usin' the space, and here we are. Grand, ain't it? My name's Lolamike Fields. I run the day-to-day. Herm runs the business side."

"Very impressive, Lolamike. Who came up with the name? Very original."

"Oh, that was Herm. He said horses sometimes were like women: every now and then ya have to slap their rump and tickle their chin to get 'em to work."

Bass looked at Lolamike for a moment, and a slow smile spread over his face.

"*I know, I know* . . . but he's my brother. And most a' the fellas think it's funny."

"I can see that."

"Well, out here in the coral are the saddle ponies. And you won't find a sweeter bunch a' critters anywhere. Have a look and take your pick."

Bass walked among the horses; there were twenty or so milling about the coral. He decided on a tall buckskin mare with good confirmation and a strong rear end. Her teeth told him she might be eight or nine years old, and her legs were cool and strong. She was recently shod. "Who's your farrier? Did a good job."

"Thanks, that'd be me."

Bass grinned back at her. "This one'll do. Let's see bout a saddle."

When it was all said and done, Bass rode out of the barn on Dotty, two bits a day for the horse, blanket, saddle, and bridle.

Bass road north on Guadalupe Street, perhaps a mile and a quarter, and jogged to the west on Magnolia Street. Then, following his instructions from Cillian O'Dell, he turned north on San Marcos and followed it about a half mile until a magnificent-looking Gothic structure rose up perhaps a quarter mile long with spires and belfries along its outer wall. He rode up the circular drive and dismounted in front of the large white sign that said Welcome to Texas State Lunatic Asylum.

The grounds in front were nicely manicured, and the trees and hedges 'pruned and trimmed to garden quality. He tied off Dotty at the buggy stop and climbed a broad marble staircase to the front doors. Upon entering, a large oval desk in the center of a round lobby lighted by skylights three stories above waited for him. A sign on the desk read Information, and Bass approached a young man dressed in white with an Attendant badge and said, "My name is Frank Bass. I'm a US Deputy Marshal, and I'd like to see Mr. Marion Gilmore."

The young man looked up from the book he read. "Dr. Gilmore is very busy today. Do you have an appointment?"

"No, I don't. See, I'm investigatin' these Annihilator killings, and I need Dr. Gilmore's professional advice.

"Well, I wish you success, of course, with your investigation, but Dr. Gilmore is still busy. You'll have to make an appointment and come back then."

Bass shook his head. It was a long ride out there; it was late in the day, and his patience wore thin. "Son, police officers, includin' me, are never made to wait and get an appointment. I see Doctor Gilmore's office yonder, and I believe I'll just knock on his door." Bass began walking toward the office, but the attendant jumped up and blocked his way. He was taller than Bass imagined, and his white uniform shirt stretched to bursting along the young man's chest and shoulders.

"I said *no*," and with that, he swung at Bass's left jaw.

Bass sidestepped the punch, *thankfully*, he thought, and countered with two quick lefts to the front of the man's face. His nose broke with the first jab, blood spurting like a fountain from the middle of his face. The second jab disoriented him, and he witnessed a display of bright lights as he fell.

Bass proceeded on his way, but just as he was about to knock, the young man's shoes scuffled behind him. The Attendant, now a bloody mess, reached out to grab Bass's right shoulder when he turned from his left and cracked the young man's left jaw with a right fist that drove through and put the young man into unconsciousness.

The commotion drew a small crowd of similarly dressed, large men, as well as Doctor Marion Gilmore, who opened his office door, screaming at the unconscious man on the floor and anyone else in earshot. "*What the hell* . . . Lawrence, for God's sake, you're supposed to be an Orderly . . . and look at you. Dear God, some of the rest of you get him to the infirmary and clean up this mess."

He turned his attention to Bass, "And who the devil are you presuming on my good nature and disturbing my peace?"

"Deputy US Marshal Frank Bass. Doctor, I'd like to ask you a few questions."

Gilmore was a moderately sized fellow with a large belly and short legs. His head was bald on top, and whisps of dark gray and white hair decorated the sides. He wore spectacles perched on his nose, which he kept crinkled up to keep them there.

"Well, well, I've already spoken to the police, you know, that damned Irishman, don't recall his name. Who are you again?"

"Deputy US Marshal Frank Bass. I got some questions for you . . . 'bout the Annihilator killins."

"Damn, well, if you must . . . but wait here a moment."

Bass waited at the door until a thin girl emerged, Bass thought she looked in her teens. She had short blond hair and would've looked very pretty if it weren't for the tears and redness around her eyes. She buttoned her hospital gown as she hurried past. Bass turned to Gilmore, glaring, and the Doctor explained.

"A . . . uh, therapy session . . . you know . . . they become quite emotional."

Then the doctor smiled strangely, and Bass prepared his right fist again. Gilmore opened the door wider and asked Bass to take a chair across from his desk.

When they were both seated, Gilmore asked, "Now, what exactly is it this time that you people want?"

"Same as last time, Doctor. Honesty and cooperation. I'm sure you've been reading the papers about this lunatic?"

"Of course, of course, and we prefer not to use that term. I know it's on the charter and the sign out front, but we prefer to use *insane* or *mentally ill. Lunatic* has such a dreadful connotation, almost comical."

"Alright, then you agree, based on the reports in the paper, the murderer is insane."

"Yes, certainly, but the term is relative. Any taking of human life is, by definition, insane."

"Look, buster, I'm tired of talkin' terminology here. The guy doin' this needs to be hanged or locked away forever, so what I want from you is straight responses to my questions. If you can't do that, I'm happy to run your ass down to police headquarters for a real police grilling. Now, based on your knowledge of the insane, what can you tell me about this guy?"

Doctor Gilmore wasn't used to being addressed this way in his own office. He bristled at the notion of going to the police headquarters and decided to get this business over with.

"Based only on information from the papers, I can say he is an obsessed man, probably in his thirties, with a complete knowledge of human physiology. He has medical training of some kind. From experience, I can tell you he believes, in some bizarre way, that he is helping these women or society in general. Timing seems crucial as the women have all been assaulted around the same time on the first of the month."

"What about his looks? Can you give us an indication of what he looks like?"

"He will look like anyone else you would see on the street. But he will be meticulous in his dress and appearance due to his obsessive nature. He will also have small peccadilloes that are uncommon to the general populace."

"Peccadilloes?"

"Yes, small habits or rituals, slight faults if you will, that may seem harmless to the casual observer. It's all a function of his obsessive nature."

"Doctor, we've found traces of salt on the victims. Have you ever heard of this kind of doings in your experiences?"

"Salt? No, never. I'm sure it is significant to the culprit, but I've never heard of such a thing myself."

"Do you think he's married . . . a family man?"

"Highly unlikely, no. This man probably lives alone and shuns social interactions."

"That helps us some, Doc, thank you. Let me ask you this: if you wanted to apprehend this character, how would you go about it?"

"*Hmm*. I suppose I'd wait till the last day of the month and keep a vigil around the hotels."

Bass nodded. That was an obvious option, but it indicated the Doc's thinking. "Fine then. Oh, one last thing, how many of your patients have you released in the last, say, six months."

The Doctor sat thinking for a moment and said, "In six months? I recall only three, and they were all female. Any discharge must have my approval of course, state law. So I can state with some surety it is only those three. And the police get those reports as well."

"Thanks for your time, Doctor Gilmore. I won't keep you from any more of your 'therapy sessions.'"

Bass rose and made eye contact with Gilmore as he did. He turned to leave, and when he was just at the door, Gilmore called after him, "He'll be wicked clever, you know."

Bass paused and then closed the door. It was late in the day, and he wanted to get back to his hotel. He was tired, and he needed a bath.

Chapter 10

5:45 p.m., May 16, 1888

    Riding on Guadalupe Rd.

    Austin, Texas

Bass was still getting the feel of his rented mount and thinking through the facts of the case, wondering if Doctor Gilmore had helped them at all. *The man being obsessed 'ats pretty easy to figure. Meticulous in appearance, many folks are. Peccadilloes, 'still not sure a' that one, but I'll ask the other guys. Nothin' at all on the salt question, and then as I leave, he tells me the guy's clever. Huh, maybe I shoulda asked 'bout the cross, but 'no point in makin' that public just to get his lip service.*

Bass arrived at his hotel a little after six o'clock and found a stall in the barn behind the hotel for Dotty. He stopped at the bar and ordered a whiskey. As he sat alone at the bar, he began wondering again what the salt meant and how it figured into this maniac's obsession. He decided to try a library tomorrow to see if he could find some kind of explanation.

He finished his drink and walked out to the lobby to organize a hot bath. He was due, he figured, and spending that kinda time with a—what was it they called child molesters in the pen? *Chomo,* that's it—chomo like Gilmore without arresting him was enough to require soap.

Thirty minutes later, as Bass sat in the hot water of his tub, he thought about his daughter and how different he wanted her world to be. He knew he'd be able to protect her for the near term, but twelve years fifteen years out, he knew he wouldn't be able to. He made a pledge to himself that he'd teach her how to defend herself, how to shoot, how to fight and also how to avoid the dangers that life presented. He knew Sally would approve as well.

Back in his room, Bass dressed in a clean shirt and drawers and decided whether he was hungry enough to eat. His Elgin told him it was 7:30 p.m., well into the dinner hour, but for some reason, he just wasn't feeling hungry. He decided to walk out into the late spring night and enjoy the mild temperatures and easy breezes of the city as it quieted. He knew there was a city park not far away with a lawn and benches among the trees. It was west on Ash a couple blocks and then north by one or two. There was a fine-looking church across from the lawn, he recalled. He decided to walk over there to kind of quiet himself. It had been an active few days dealing with Grooms and whatnot.

He remembered him saying in his stupor that Mary had left, Mary had gone. He had only a vague recollection of the woman. He'd met her once but really didn't know her. Obviously, her leaving affected Grooms deeply. Bass knew Grooms Lee as an honest lawman, elected by a wide margin. He had a habit of surrounding himself with good lawmen, like Cillian O'Dell, and his department had never garnered a whiff of scandal in any regard. The Grooms he saw when he first arrived was nothing at all like the man he once knew.

The lamps of the park were all lit, and the sky still reflected the last deep red and pink rays of the sunset. Bass picked a bench and sat down. He leaned back and closed his eyes, listening to the sounds as twilight surrendered to evening.

"Say there, bub . . . you're sitting on my bench."

Bass opened his eyes and saw an older man in ragged clothes, a short stogie in his mouth, and maybe a week's worth of stubble on his face. He wore a collapsed beaver hat and spoke through missing teeth that whistled whenever he tried to pronounce an *S*. Bass was startled out of his serenity.

"Oh, well, I'm sorry I had . . . wait a minute, your bench? What makes this your bench? It's a city park."

"It's my bench, sonny, 'cause I 'been sleepin' on her for the last six nights. Makes her mine, savvy?"

Bass started smiling, and soon, the old man did, too. "Heeltap, you son of bitch. How are you?"

"*Shhh*, not so loud . . . I'm tryin to stay low out here. An' this time, I'm 'Gandy Dave Lomax.' And remember, you don't know me."

"*Ha*. I'll try, but it won't be easy. You in Austin to look into the murders?"

"Yeah, 'Mayor asked us to come, and since I have some experience around the state, they sent me. 'Saw you get off the train. Where 'you staying?"

"The Winslow Hotel on Congress at Ash. 'The hell happened to your teeth, Heeltap?"

"*Damnit*, I ain't Heeltap no more. An' I lost 'em in a boxing match with an old man on De Levan Street in Chicago."

"Oh, an old man, huh? How'd you do?"

"I don't wanna talk about it. How's Miss Sally? 'She found anyone better yet? Wouldn't take much."

"No, Gandy, she's still with me. We have a little girl now named Lillian."

"Really? A little girl? Say, that's awful nice, a little girl. Well, I hope she got her mama's brains cause her Pa's one to stumble on his own feet . . . sleep on another man's bench."

"' Sorry 'bout that Heeltap—Gandy—damn! 'You notice anything yet? About the case?"

"Nah, not much. Police Chief's a lush, ya know."

"Yeah, I know. He's a friend from years back 'asked me to come and help out. He's sobered now . . . I'll try to see that he stays that way."

"Okay . . . he better . . . Mayor wants to fire him for some fella in Waco. Listen up. If I need to see you, I'll leave a note in your hotel mailbox. If you wanna talk to me, I stop by this bench once or twice a day. Leave a note under the leg. I'm gonna go down to the Pierce Hotel now, spend some time lookin' around. You . . . *aw hell*, keep yourself safe." With those words, Gandy Dave Lomax was off down the street.

Bass smiled as he watched him go and thought, "Sally'd get a kick outta seein' him again."

Bass walked back to the hotel and asked the night clerk about the libraries in town.

"Well there's a Texas History Center in the Capitol building and a' course the Austin Public. But the best research library in town is out at Texas State University. I used to use it all the time when I was enrolled."

"Oh? You're no longer a student?"

"Well, not there, it's pretty expensive I plan to go to St. Edwards to study Seminary."

"Oh yes? What's Seminary?"

"The study of religions and faiths, both ancient and modern. I plan to enter the Priesthood."

"Well, good luck to ya. 'Believe I'll take a run out to the state school tomorrow. Say, maybe you can tell me, bein' a religious scholar and all, what does it mean, I mean, in religion when someone puts a cross on yer forehead?"

"Like on Ash Wednesday? It means you've done penance for your sins before God and are ready to meet him. It's kinda a reminder that we're all gonna die, you know 'ashes to ashes.'"

"*Hmm*, okay, thanks, that's a start."

"A start?"

"Yeah, to my readin'...a good place to start. G'night now."

"Sleep well, sir."

Bass picked up a newspaper and went upstairs to his room. He thought there might be continuing articles about the Annihilator in the paper, but he found none. Leafing through the small daily, his eyes grew heavy. He made a mental note to send a wire to Sally in the morning, and he was asleep by 9:30 p.m.

7:15 a.m., May 17, 1888
Winslow Hotel
Dining Room
Austin, Texas

The dining room buzzed that morning. With meetings and a few hearings at the Capitol, Mondays were busy days anyway. Bass ordered his usual breakfast: a pot of coffee, eggs, ham, and fried potatoes. He'd purchased an *Austin Statesman* paper and a street map of the city from the front desk.

Now that he had a horse, he wouldn't be able just to tell a cabby or trolleyman where he wanted to go. And he was pretty sure Dotty wouldn't know the addresses of the places he wanted to get to. He saw that the state university was way out on Elm Street, nearly as far away as the lunatic asylum he visited yesterday. He wondered why it might be so far out and could only assume it was because the school would need room to grow.

After breakfast, he went out to the barn and spent a few minutes getting more familiar with Dotty. He spent time brushing down her back and currying the knots from her mane and tail. Most people said that horses don't feel them, but Bass wasn't so sure. At any rate, it couldn't hurt to keep her groomed. After saddling he led her out of the barn and hopped aboard, and turned her head north on Congress Ave.

The state university was another impressive looking building, but saw no other structures around. He expected to see other classroom buildings, dormitories, and so forth, like the campuses he was familiar with in Waco and Fort Worth. He reined Dotty in at a buggy stop on the west side of the building just off Mathilda Street. There was a small flight of steps to the side entrance, and through the doors, he found himself in a lobby three stories tall with stairways on each side of the building.

Like the asylum, there was an information desk where an attractive young woman dressed in a high-necked white blouse and skirt combination sat ready to offer assistance. Her blond hair piled up and pinned on her head. Bass assumed it was an effort to look older, and she wore very little makeup, perhaps some lip rouge. Bass had tried a semester at Northwestern University, but a classroom education just wasn't right for him. Besides, he didn't have enough money to continue.

Bass removed his hat and approached. "Excuse me, I'm lookin' for the library?"

The girl looked up from the book she was reading and smiled warmly. "Of course, the library is on the second floor, sir; take the east staircase right over there."

Bass thanked her and began walking to the stairs when she called after him, "Is that a firearm, sir? I'm afraid they aren't allowed anywhere on campus."

"I understand, my name is Frank Bass," he displayed his badge and ID card, "I'm a US Deputy Marshal and we're ah, supposed to be armed at all times, miss."

"No! Buffalo Robe Bass?" The girl pulled one of Edward Ellis's dime novels from her handbag. "Why, I'm just one of your most ardent admirers, Marshal. Would you mind signin' my book?"

Bass was startled and a little flattered as well. He hadn't thought any of the books were still in circulation.

"Why sure 'nuff, I will. Let's see, which one you got here? *Buffalo Robe . . . and the Rimrock Riders. Hmm.* I'm afraid I don't remember that one. What'd I do in it?"

"Why, you foiled a bank robbery in Laredo and shot down two murderin' thieves as they made their getaway along the Rimrock hideout, then later you got into a fight with Rattlesnake Willy, and when he tried to knife you, you turned the blade back on him. Don't you remember?"

"Oh yes, yes, of course, I do. It's just that there were so many outlaws that needed to face justice I sometimes get 'em confused. Well, thanks for the directions, miss."

Bass walked away, eyes wide in amazement that folks were still reading those stories. He vaguely remembered a bank robbery in Laredo several years ago but couldn't recall shooting anyone.

The library was two stories tall, with bookshelves lining each wall and several free-standing rows on either side of a central desk. He approached another lady, somewhat older and more proper-looking, behind the checkout desk and asked,

"Excuse me, I'm looking for information about salt." The woman's expression did not change, and neither did she blink. She just continued to look at Bass for several seconds and said, "Salt. In regard to what, sir?"

Now, Bass was in a quandary. He daren't explain that he wanted to know why a lunatic would sprinkle salt all over a disemboweled body. That was to remain private knowledge. And he really didn't know where to go from there.

"Uh, how about its uses in general?"

"You want to know about the use of salt . . . well, let me take you to our encyclopedias. We have the latest Britannica, and I'm sure you'll find therein just scads of information on the uses of salt."

Her sarcasm was not lost on Bass, but he had come this far, so he followed her into the maze of eight-foot-tall shelves to the section labeled Encyclopedia. "Here you are, sir. Do take your time and let me know if you need help with any of the big words." She walked away, and Bass smiled, thinking how silly he must've sounded.

He started with the index, hoping to find a reference to connect salt to a dead body. He found nothing. He found several references to salt and saline as a preservative, but that led nowhere. He tried several other books looking for a connection to the Cross or Ash

Wednesday or the notion of death in "ashes to ashes," as the night clerk mentioned. But nothing that linked salt in any way.

He found pages regarding the various industrial uses of salt and salts' effect on freezing and frozen water. He read that article thinking that the killer may have used the salt to melt ice at the scene, but he knew that would be stretching it. That wouldn't explain why salt was sprinkled all over the bodies and in the women's hair. He spent most of the morning reading so that by noon, he had a slight headache, and his eyes were starting to cross. He decided to head back to the hotel first to send a wire to Sally and then to get some chlorodyne from his medical kit.

Bass parked Dotty alongside the hotel and walked into the lobby to the mail desk.

"I'd like to send a wire today, please." The clerk turned from the mail slots and sat down with pencil and pad.

He wrote, "to Sally Bass, address is TwainHeart Ranch, El Paso Texas." The message read:

My Love,

> *All's well. Staying at Winslow Hotel. Working with Chief Grooms Lee. Not much to report so far. Austin is a fine city. Will keep you appraised of developments. Kisses to Lil.*

Frederick

He didn't want to be too specific or mention that he'd seen Heeltap, though he knew she'd want to know. "Send that today, please. How much for a special delivery?"

"A dollar extra. Go out today 'soon as the runner gets back, yes, sir. Total is two dollars fifty. Yes, sir."

Bass paid the clerk and began walking to the stairs when another voice at the desk called out. "Marshal? Marshal Bass? A note, sir, in your mailbox."

Bass opened the note as he walked, thinking it would likely be from Grooms. But as he read, he noticed the signature "Gandy Dave."

The note read, "Found a dead dog this morning . . . throat cut . . . Now, who does that to a dog?"

Bass put the note in his pocket and continued to his room.

Chapter 11

1:45 p.m., May 17, 1888
    A Bench on the Park Lawn
    Near the Governor's Mansion
    Austin, Texas

Bass hadn't noticed it in the dark last night, but the park bench where he met Gandy Dave Lomax was near the Governor's Mansion. Bass checked around the bench first thing before sitting down in case there was some other message that Gandy had left. Once he was seated, he took a long look at the house that the people of Texas provided for their Governor. *Stately, that's what, stately, I guess it should be.*

Bass was impressed with its size and the detail work around the eaves and chimneys. The second-floor windows facing his position were long, possibly floor to ceiling and Bass conceived that perhaps a ballroom or maybe a banquet hall was behind the walls. He couldn't see the front facade but was able to see one of the white columns on the end closest to him. He'd only been to the Capitol Building once before and it was at night. He'd never seen the Governor's house.

"Mighty impressive. S'pose it outta be with a state as grand as Texas."

While Bass stared at the mansion, Gandy Dave arrived and sat on the bench next to him.

"*Whew* . . . Lord, I caught your scent 'fore you sat down, Heeltap. Don't they let you wash at all?"

"Damnit, it ain't Heeltap, and no, I don't wash. It ain't seemly for the people I'm with or the places I go. Now, you got my note, I guess?"

"Yes, I did. Where'd you find this dog with the cut throat?"

"Down near the river in the bushes on Willow Street, close by to Gardiner's Lumber Yard."

"Well damn, you know there was an old man at police headquarters the other day sayin' his dog was missing. Didn't speak English well. Sent him off to the dog catcher's office down the hall."

Gandy Dave nodded, "Might be the same. There's immigrants livin' in that neighborhood. 'Area has boarding houses, run-down shanties, folks livin' on the fish they catch from the river. But the thing that got me 'bout the dog was its throat was slit. Now, who does that? Stray dogs pesterin' folks, children, barkin' all hours, ya shoot it, right? Maybe throw stuff at it . . . but to walk up and cut the animal's throat? I'm thinkin it's our man, Frank. 'At's his MO."

"You're right 'bout that, and it very well coulda been our guy, you know? Maybe practicing, he lives nearby, and the dog's barkin' disturbed him, wanted it shut up quick."

"Or maybe the dog was barkin' as he returned late at night, an' he had to be quiet about it. Wouldn't do to have a shot ring out, police'd be there in an instant."

"Heel—sorry, Gandy Dave, why don't you spend some time in that area, watchin folks come an' go? The doc I talked to yesterday said we'd be lookin' for a young man maybe twenties, and real neat in his appearance. The one witness we have said he limped to the left leg and carried a cane. 'Tain't much to go on, I know, but it's worth a try. I'm gonna see Grooms Lee, the chief of police, this afternoon, and I'll bring him up to date."

"Well, don't say nothin' about me. Police have a habit of interferin' with my kinda work, so don't even mention you seen me."

"Got it."

Gandy Dave Lomax stood up and walked lazily away from the bench, lighting his cigar stump as he walked. Bass watched the ragged old bum saunter away and couldn't help but smile.

He remembered meeting James McParland, a.k.a. Heeltap, a.k.a. Gandy Dave Lomax, in Fort Stockton, Texas, where he was sent to investigate an illegal oil drilling scheme. Bass was there looking into the murder of a young rancher, and the two investigations merged.

Heeltap, as Bass knew him then, surprised both Bass and Sally when he appeared at a railroad station after both cases were closed. He was dressed in his city best, and Bass hadn't any idea who it was until he recognized Heeltap's voice. That was about a year ago and in another part of the state. Yet, here he was again, a ragged-looking homeless bum working once more on the same case.

Bass checked his gold Elgin watch, gifted to him with gratitude by General George Crook for his work as a scout in the pursuit of Geronimo a number of years earlier. Bass saw it was 2:15 p.m. and time for a quick lunch before heading to the police headquarters. He decided to try the Capitol Club, a brass and leather-looking eatery, the kind Sally hated, a block north of his hotel on Congress Ave. The reason she hated that kind of diner was because it catered primarily to men. The generally smoke-filled dining area and boisterous talk of men in their afternoon whiskey was something she preferred to avoid. Bass, on the other hand, loved them. There was one in El Paso called Hannigan's that he and the rest of the men in law enforcement visited . . . regularly. The food was good, the liquor cheap, and the camaraderie was free.

Bass walked into the Capitol Club and found just what he expected: a room full of smoke being issued by men at a bar. He had already seen the Bill of Fare posted on the front door, so when he sat at the bar and the barman asked his pleasure, he was ready to reply.

"Ham and cheese on rye bread and a dram glass of Overholt rye."

The response was pleasant, and the whiskey appeared almost immediately. He peeled the paper wrapper of one of his small cigars and struck a match on his holster to light it.

As he puffed, an older man next to him said, "Rye whiskey . . . Ranger drink."

Bass looked him over as he puffed. The man was older, heavier, perhaps in his fifties. He had a full head of white hair combed straight back to his collar and wore a fitted gray pinstriped suit. He'd set a black-felt Edwardian Homberg on the bar in front of him.

Bass nodded at the man and said, "It is that. Will you join me?"

"Certainly."

Bass raised his hand for the barman's attention and signaled for another drink. "I take it then sir, since you obviously know the whiskey, that you are or perhaps were one of our noble Rangers."

"I was as a younger man, sir. Rode with Captain Leander McNelly."

"And were you fortunate enough to see action with Captain McNelly?

"I was with Captain in DeWitt County for the Taylor-Sutton feuds. Shortly after leavin' that battle-weary area, Captain was laid low by consumption, and I eventually left the service."

"I see. To Leander McNelly."

The man raised his glass in a toast, and Bass followed in form. Then he asked, "May I know your name?"

"I am John S. Ford, a former Ranger, now a state representative. And you are?"

"Frank Bass, Federal Deputy Marshal from El Paso. I'm on . . . well, I guess you'd say detached service here. The chief of police is an old friend."

"I surmise you're assisting him with these horrendous killings then."

"I am. He needs all the help he can get."

"Yes, I'm sure. I met the Chief two years ago, just after his election. Quite a personable young man. I thought certain he'd run for higher office one day."

"Well, sir, Grooms had a difficult time of it lately in his personal life, but I agree with you; he's a likable cuss all right."

The older man excused himself then, and Bass's sandwich arrived. He asked for another whiskey as the plate was set before him. When the bartender returned, he leaned across the bar. "You know who that ol' guy is?"

"Yeah, John S. something."

"Fella, that was the most famous Ranger that ever lived. RIP Ford, John RIP Ford. The RIP is because he wrote letters to the families of men killed in his command and always signed 'em RIP."

"Well, I'll be. I never woulda known. Sure, RIP Ford. I heard a' him years ago. He's a bona fide hero, a bit before my time, but . . . my word. And I bought him a drink, didn't I? My, my."

Bass finished eating and went back to the hotel to fetch Dotty for his ride to the police station. Forty minutes later, he knocked on Chief Grooms Lee's door.

"Hey Frank, come on in . . . what do ya know."

"Hey Grooms, well lessee . . . a couple things to add from talkin to that Doc at the asylum. You gotta minute?"

"Ah, not right now, Frank. 'Had a shooting on the west side last night. Two dead. We're all kinda busy on that. I sent Cillian out early to get the particulars, and I gotta another named meeting with the mayor in a few minutes . . . hey, you wanna come?"

"No."

"*Aw*, come on, Frank, I need a little support with Mayor Joe, and you're a noted Federal. He'll be impressed as hell. Come on, will ya?"

"Shoot. Where's his office?"

"He's comin here. Thanks, Frank, this'll help."

"Alright, alright, just remember it when I need a favor from you."

"A' course, buy ya a drink at lunch?"

"' At ain't nearly enough." Bass sat down in a chair by the front window and started drumming his fingers on the armrests. A minute or two later, there was a knock on the door, and Grooms opened it to reveal not only Mayor Nalle but also two reporters, one with a photographer.

"Dammit, Joe didn't say anything 'bout newspapers." Grooms said under his breath.

The Mayor only smiled at the reporters and showed the photographer where to set up his tripod. When he returned to Grooms's desk, he said, "Nonsense, a little public exposure is good for everyone."

The Mayor walked around Grooms's desk and put his arm on the Chief's shoulder while shaking his hand, "How's this boys? Can you get us both in the frame?"

The photographer used magnesium powder mixed with potassium chlorate. He touched it off using a flint, and the resulting explosion filled the room with white smoke and the acrid odor of a chemical fire. Bass's eyes were blinded as he happened to be looking at the photographer just as the flash went off. He blinked several times, but the bright ball remained, burning in the center of his vision.

Once the photographer had left, the Mayor went back to his office, and the reporters started their questions.

"Chief? Why is it taking so long to catch this maniac Annihilator, as O. Henry has dubbed him?"

"Because, like many madmen, he's devilishly clever, leaving very few clues as to his identity."

"Then you do have some clues, is that what you're sayin Chief?"

"There are always signs left behind at every crime. The trick is in knowing what they mean and how to use them."

"Can you give us a 'fer-instance' Chief?"

"No. I'm sorry but we're not at liberty to discuss the specifics of the case. I hope you understand, as it may tip off any suspect we might be watching."

The third reporter, a skinny man with sharp features and a straw skimmer, asked, "So who is this fella then, Chief? He a cowboy friend a' yours, a deputy, or what?"

"No, boys, this is US Deputy Marshal Frank Bass. You may a' heard of him. He's a friend from way back when, and I asked him to help with our investigation."

There was some jostling and cursing then among the reporters who each tried to ask the first question of Bass. The straw skimmer won out. "So we have a celebrity workin' on this one. How's about it, Marshal? Can't you give us a little more information?"

"*Ha*! If you heard a' me, then you prob'ly know I don't really care for the press. No. I can't give you anything for the same reasons the Chief named. Man, you should be askin' is the Chief's lead investigator, Sergeant Cillian O'Dell. And here's somethin else fer y'all to chew on. Austin's a big city. With big-city crime. Chief's got enough to look after without you boys nippin' his heels."

The reporters took it that the interview was over and started putting away their notebooks and grousing a bit about not getting enough for their papers.

One of them, a heavyset balding man who wore an old, sweat-stained derby hat, said through a smirk as he left, "We get a sight more outta you when you're drunk, Chief. How long you think you'll be on the wag—" the reporter didn't finish his insult, there was too much of Bass's right fist in his face. The man staggered out to the hall, cursing and holding the left side of his face.

"Thank you, Frank, but you really don't have to do that. I'm pretty used to it now. It's just somethin' I'll have to work through."

"Hell, I know that, but any chance I get to stub one a them fellas . . . 'few months ago, I had 'em all over me. In Albuquerque, El Paso. I'd been shot, stabbed, and damn near froze, findin' two little girls was stolen from their home on Christmas morning. Christmas, by God . . . *ah*, I'm sorry if it comes back at you. Just refer 'em to my office in El Paso, or better yet, to District Judge Clarence Hobart. He hates 'em worse 'n me. Now, what about the shooting last night?"

"Well, Frank, it's the darndest thing. A husband and wife argue, and the wife shoots him, that I can see happening. Two men get into it in a bar over cards and shoot each other, that I can see. But by all accounts, the two guys found dead across from each other didn't know each other at all. 'Didn't live near each other, didn't work together. Nothing. Out there on the west side. O'Dell was out there mosta the mornin. He should be around here someplace now. We'll find out more when he checks in. You got anything new?"

"Well, yeah. 'Went out to the lunatic asylum yesterday and had a congenial chat with Doc Gilmore. Sit back down and pour me a whiskey. I'll tell you all about it."

Grooms sat back in his chair and handed Bass the whiskey bottle and a glass from his desk drawer.

"Alright, shoot."

"First off, I rented a horse for the trip out to that place, 'seems the trolly line doesn't run out there, and the Gurney cabs won't take you neither. 'Probably know they won't get a return customer out there. Anyway, I can tell they're quite sincere about their security. I had a light tussle with one of 'em just to get to Gilmore's office. Oh. I plan to arrest him for molestin' underage patients before this is over. I saw one come outta his office, still buttoning her hospital gown and obviously upset."

"You know, I only met that fella once, and I right away didn't like him. Go on."

"Well, he told me the killer was obsessed and probably thought he was doing his victims a favor. He had no idea 'bout the salt. I didn't tell him 'bout the cross in the forehead, but I got somethin there too. Gilmore said he'd probably be in his thirties and 'meticulous' in his dress. Also, he'd have pickledillos—"

"Have what?"

"Sounded like *pickledilloes*, strange little rituals or habits, he said."

"*Peccadilloes.*"

"Huh?"

"*Peccadilloes*, the word he used."

"Yeah, well, he also said he'd be 'wicked clever.'"

"Well, none a that's new, he told mostly the same thing to Cillian. Though not the age part. Wonder how he figured that?"

"Don't know, but then later I asked a 'serminology' student about what the cross might mean, just generally, didn't tie it into the case. He said the cross that a priest put on your forehead is supposed to remind you that you're gonna die . . . you know 'ashes to ashes'? Like on Ash Wednesday? He said it's to make you humble."

"Okay, that's interesting. Why don't you run it by O'Dell and see what he says."

"Right, will do."

The Chief leaned back in his chair and sighed deeply. He said, "Anyway, it don't leave us with much to go on. Salt is a common purchase. Canvassing markets lookin' for anyone who uses salt in a month is pointless."

Bass thought for a moment and said, "Maybe not. The Doc said the killer's obsessive . . . 'think he mighta bought a whole bunch a salt all at one time? Maybe to make sure he always had some?"

"Damn . . . that's right. Anyway, it can't hurt. We can have the beat patrolmen check the markets, maybe on the sly, 'find out if any large purchases of salt were made recently. It's something. A place to start. Well done, Deputy Marshal."

"Thanks . . . and it's Dep—oh, never mind."

Chapter 12

6:45 a.m., May 18, 1888
200 block Nueces Ave.
Austin, Texas

The sun was high enough now to properly illuminate the scene. Down the street from the Railroad Saloon and kitty-corner from Millet's Lumber yard, two men in their twenties had simultaneously decided the other needed to die. The result of the early morning shoot-out—witnesses said they heard the shots around 1:00 a.m.—was that two men lay dead in the street. One was shot through his head, the other shot in the back. The first man lay on the side of the road, and the second one, the one back-shot, lay on the opposite side along a footpath that led from the Colorado River to a small lea between buildings on Nueces. Cillian O'Dell arrived at just after 6:00 a.m. and now stood with the beat patrol officer, Martin Feeley, at the body of the man shot through the head.

"'Ave any of the blighters in the neighborhood come forward, Marty?"

"No, Sarge, this is just how I found 'em. That house yonder by the path? It's the closest. I asked the old lady there if she knew anything and all she'd say is she heard several shots. She's sure it was nearly 1:00 a.m., 'says she has a wall clock near her bed. She peeked out her window but didn't see nothing, not even the bodies, in the dark. She said the dogs stopped barkin', and she went back to sleep."

"Do we know who they was?"

"This one's name is Mike somethin. He hangs around the lumber yard lookin' for work. I seen him a couple times. The other one? I don't know him. Never seen him before."

"Right then. This one's pistol is on the ground by his left hand." O'Dell knelt to get a better look at the man's face. "And he smells a' whiskey. 'Looks to be mid-thirties. The pistol is a . . . popper. A

Flobert a' some kind. 'Can't read the maker. Single shot, rimfire .22. Aye, the hole in his head's a good deal bigga than that. Let's check his mate."

The two men walked to the other body. It, too, lay face down with a bullet hole squarely in the middle of his back. "An' we don't know this fella yet, but oy, do me a favor, boyo. Go back and see did the man, ah . . . Mike, shoot his gun?"

While he waited for Martin to return, he bent to look at the man's face. "So who are ye then? I don't smell no whiskey on ya, 'doubt ya'd been drinking. I don't see yer gun boy, so I'm gonna roll ye over 'n case ya fell on it."

O'Dell rolled the deceased over but still found no weapon. Marty returned as O'Dell was feeling for a wallet or pocketbook that might have an ID. "No gun on ye. So what did you use to kill ol' Mike o'er there? So? What is it then? Did he use his gun or no?"

"Yeah, Sarge, he shot the pistol. It's been fired."

"*Hmm*. Marty, this is a strange one. Mike o'er there was shot in the head. But this one here ain't got a gun. This one here's been shot but not by number .22 popper like Mike's. The hole in his back was made by a bigger gun, a .40 caliber at least. Marty, me lad, all this adds up to one of two things: this guy shot Mike in the head and tossed his gun somewhere when he turned to run. Mike, with a slug in his bloody head, shot a .40 caliber gun at this fella, hitting him in the back, and then hid the flippin' gun, or . . . there's a third arsehole shooter with a big damn gun still walkin' about. My money's on the latter." As soon as Sergeant O'Dell said these words, both he and beat Officer Feely heard a low, piteous wail and looked up to see a woman in night clothes sobbing as she looked at the body of the unknown man not twenty feet away.

Cillian O'Dell went to her first and stood in front of her, blocking her view while hugging her tightly as she sobbed. He stroked her hair and whispered quietly to her, and after several minutes, she had calmed enough to say that the man's name was Eric Smitson, and he was her husband.

"Martin, ride back into town and fetch the picture taker and the doctor, please. I'll stay here with Mrs. Smitson. Go on, now. There's a good lad."

Cillian O'Dell didn't get back to his desk until well after noon and spent a solid two hours writing out reports and starting the murder log. He wouldn't have the photos for a couple of days, but he wrote up what he remembered about the Doc—Flotter's preliminary examinations.

Victim number one, Mike Saddicks' age approx. Thirty-five deceased of bullet wound through and through to head, estimate .40 caliber: victim number two, Eric Smitson, age approx. Thirty-five deceased of bullet wound to the back, severing the spinal cord at approx. T 18 -19 and penetrating the heart in the left Atrium. Time of death estimated to be between 1:00 a.m. and 3:00 a.m. on May 14, 1888. Following extraction of the bullet found in Eric Smitson's chest cavity, the projectile is a .40 caliber Winchester round, forty to sixty-five of that brand. (WCF)

The only firearm retrieved at the scene was a .22 caliber (6mm) Flobert Cadet 'Saloon gun.' It had been recently fired, but the spent bullet was not found, and its trajectory is unknown.

My conclusion here is that there was a third shooter involved, but no trace of him or his weapon was found—photos to follow along with Doctor Flotter's completed report.

—Sgt. Cillian O'Dell

It was after 5:00 p. m. when Sergeant O'Dell put his pencil aside and closed his new murder log. He knew he should report to the Chief, but his baser instincts convinced him of his need for a pint, so he left the station house and walked to the Nightstick. He sat at the bar with several beat officers, chatting about the events of the day and the relative merits of the players on the Austin Senators Baseball

Club. At 6:30, he decided to visit the Chief's office secretly, hoping to find he'd gone home for the day. As luck would have it, Chief Lee was still in and visiting with Marshal Frank Bass.

"Come in, Cill, come in. Sit down. We were just talking about the press, what Frank learned at the asylum yesterday, and the two killings you worked on today. How'd that go down? Where are you on it?"

"Aye, welp 'ere's what I tink happened. Sometime in the wee hours a' this mornin, Michael Saddicks, a young man lookin' for work, walks outta the West Avenue Alehouse headin' for Millets Lumber Yard. He's bee hawkin' 'em for work, and they let him sleep in one of the drying barns. Anyway, and dis is all me own conjecture mind, Michael encounters another man on his way, and they get into it over somethin. Maybe the other bloke's drunk too, I don't know, but it ends with Michael takin' a .40 to the bean, but not before he gets off a shot from his 6mm popper gun. Maybe he hit the fella, maybe not, 'can't find the slug, and it's a cap and ball piece, so no casing left behind.

"Now, down the road, a piece is the home of Eric Smitson. He hears the shots and comes out to see what's what. He's unarmed, and my guess is he sees Mr. Forty-Caliber and turns to run home. Only Forty-Caliber can't leave a witness now, so he plugs Mr. Smitson in the middle o' his back, and the poor beggar dies almost immediately. Mr. Forty-Caliber dashes away and Officer Feeley comes along on his beat about 6:00 a.m. and sends a kid from the millets to come fetch me. That's how I seen it, anyway. Don't make no sense otherwise."

Bass and Lee have been listening, and Bass asks, "Anything at all to indicate that this may have been related to the Annihilator?"

"Nuttin' at all, sir. Only the time a day. No witness and no physical evidence except the two .40 slugs and Michael Saddicks's wee gun. And the stiffs a course. I put Doc's initial report in the murder log, but he won't have better till tomorrow. Should have the photos then, too."

The Chief nodded and looked at Frank. "Frank? What do you make of it?"

"It's just conjecture, like the Detective here said, but dollars to donuts. It's our boy tryin' to distract us. Get us lookin' at somethin' else."

O'Dell answered next. "He's right, Chief, bet me last fiver on it. Early mornin, no witnesses, no real evidence. Gotta be him."

Chief Lee thought for a moment. "Cill, you said that Eric's gun was fired?"

"Michael's gun, Chief, the other victim." Cillian O'Dell, like many homicide detectives, was in the habit of referring to the victims of crimes by their first names. It made the case more personal, more urgent for them. It gave the crime a face rather than just a number. The Chief continued.

"Right, Michael's gun. What if he hit Mr. Forty-Caliber with the shot he fired?"

"Thought a' that could be too. But there was no other blood at the scene. Not surprising though, bein' such a small gun."

Bass offered, "Worth checkin' the doctors in town and the hospital, I guess. We're due to get lucky with this thing."

The Chief mentioned, "Some time ago, I asked all the doctors in town to report gunshot wounds of any kind, but it's voluntary. Most doctors want to protect the doctor-patient confidence, I guess." Bass said,

"that's a good idea, but until it's a law, we can't count on the Docs following through. Best to still check ourselves," Cillian added.

"Right, you are, sir. I'll assign a couple a trainees for the leg work. Oh, and I've heard from the two hoofers that I asked to look into mortuaries and the medical college . . . both came up empty. Nobody new to any of the mortis, and the medical school doesn't buy no cadavers. Never has."

Bass asked Cillian O'Dell. "Tell me Sarge, when you talked to Marion Gilmore, what was your overall impression of him?"

"*Hah*! The man's a bloody creeper if you ask me. Got a feelin' he wanted me outta there fast from the way he acted."

"I got the same notion." Bass looked at his watch. "Either of you boys hungry? We can walk over to the Capitol Club. 'Ate there earlier, and it weren't too bad."

"Nah, that place is full a politicians and hangers-on. 'Rather eat at the Nightstick with people, ya know," Cillian said.

Bass smiled. "Fair enough, Chief buys; he's got a per diem."

All three left the Chief's office and walked to the Nightstick.

7:30 p.m., May 18, 1888
Benoit's Boarding House
225 Neches St.
Austin, Texas

"*Goddamn* the luck! One little pop from that pipsqueak pistol when he hits the ground, and it gets to my leg."

He sat with his right leg hooked over the basin, collecting the blood slowly oozing through his bandage. He'd set the basin on a chair and then laid on his bed looking out the window as lamps were being lit along Second Street. The horse-drawn trolley bell tolled as the tracks made the turn from Second Street onto Neches and then again when it turned on Third Street. He was warm, very warm, and he'd already sweat through his bedding. He felt the small bullet still stuck in his leg just above the knee. He knew what he had to do; he had all the necessary implements. *Ha! God knows that, too.* He needed the pain to be subdued further so he didn't cry out uncontrollably.

No, that would end everything. The police aren't fools; I have to remember that. He took another swallow of the laudanum he'd been given to treat his "condition," as the asylum doctors called it, and just the one swallow gave him some relief. He also had a bottle of *One Night Cough Syrup* that he would use for sleep when his mind became too active to rest on its own. *Yes, the doctors at the hospital thought of it all and provided well for my release.*

He grew dozy from the laudanum and took a swallow of the cough syrup. *I have got to get past this . . . there are still two . . . two of* them *working their evil, casting their spells, their witchery. Two of* them . . . *two . . . two.*

He was asleep and didn't hear the rap on the door. Mrs. Benoit had supper ready, and since Mr. Hunter never missed a seating, she decided to call on him. She opened the door with her key and saw the man sleeping with his leg over a chair and assumed he was simply *resting his good leg, poor dear.* In the dark of the room, she couldn't see the basin filling with blood or the stain on his trouser leg.

He awoke later in the evening, near 11:00 p.m., and calculated that he'd been asleep for almost four hours. *Or did I lose a day? One can never tell using these drugs. I don't know how many days I lost on the farm because of them.* Then, the pain caught up with his nervous system, and he had to hold a pillow to his face to scream out the agony. He began sweating, and his stomach rolled as he tried to light the candle at his bedside. When he did, he saw that his leg had swollen to constriction by his trouser leg, and he reached for his folding scalpel and cut the pant leg away. He took another swallow from the laudanum bottle and waited for the opiate to work. Once the pain had dulled, he sat up to observe his wound in the candlelight. No one would suspect a candle at this hour. *He's probably reading one of his trade magazines*, is all they'd think.

The wound was angry, no doubt about that, and it meant it could wait no longer. He used his sheet to mop the area until he saw the small opening in his leg caused by the conical piece of lead from that damned little gun. He had laid out on the bed what he thought he'd need first thing on returning early this morning. *Yesterday morning? Damn, it didn't matter, the bullet has to come out now.*

He took the small scissor-like retractors in his left hand and the hemostatic forceps in his right. He knew the bullet had not penetrated the muscle deeply, so the hemostatic forceps could be used. Working with only the one candle, he carefully retracted the flesh from the wound. This caused excruciating pain, which he could only squelch with force of will. He breathed more quickly now and knew he had to guard against hyperventilating. Sweat blurred his vision as it seeped into his eyes, but he could not use his arm to wipe his brow. He inserted the straight ends of the forceps until he felt the metal object, and now, nearly delirious with pain, his eyes closed to focus on the feeling of his tools, he managed to grasp the projectile and withdrew it slowly so as not to rupture the blood vessels any further.

Finally, he doused the area with his laudanum, trusting the alcohol in the mixture would work as an astringent. He struggled to maintain consciousness as he wrapped the leg in clean cotton and gauze, taping the bandage closed just before blacking out.

When he regained consciousness, it was dark outside. He checked his watch, but it had stopped for want of winding. He felt better, generally. The swelling in his leg had receded and the fever had broken during his sleep and was gone. He was hungry and thirsty all at once. He decided to risk a trip to the kitchen to try to find something to eat and drink. He stood for the first time in possibly two days, he had no way to judge the time he'd lost, and using his cane for support, made his way carefully down the stairs and to the kitchen. There were baskets of biscuits and fruit set out on the dining table, so he filled his pockets and then drank deeply from the water pitcher left out for nighttime thirsts. He returned to his room, quietly making sure to lock the door behind him.

He ate methodically, carving an apple and a biscuit into exact quarters and eating each in sequence. When he was finished, he straightened his bedclothes, swallowed some laudanum—his leg was pained by the activity on the stairs—and lay fully clothed on the bed. He would have to think how to explain the bloody bedsheets to Mrs. Benoit, but he was confident he'd come up with something she'd believe. He was asleep ten minutes later.

Chapter 13

8:45 p.m., May 19, 1888
Winslow Hotel
Congress Ave at Ash Street
Austin, Texas

Bass put up Dotty in the same stall he used the night before, filled her water bucket, and pitched some barley hay into her trough to keep her digestion regular. He had no idea what she'd gotten at the livery barn, but when quality fodder was available, he always used it. Dotty would be no exception. He brushed her down and noticed a little girth gall on the left side of her rib cage. It was minor now, only some hair worn away, but it would get worse if left alone. He decided to put a folded-up piece of blanket between the horse and the girth strap. He decided if he could find some, a wool wrapping would be best. Less likely to move around.

Bass walked through the back door and down the hall along the stairs to the lobby. He wanted to see if a late newspaper was available and check for messages. He hoped Sally might have responded, but he'd only sent his wire yesterday, so he wasn't disappointed when there was no wire. There was no message from Gandy Dave Lomax either, but there was a message for him in a plain envelope addressed to him as Marshal Bass in care of the hotel. He assumed that it would be local and decided to wait to open it when he got to his room.

The papers were out and available for sale, so he bought one and headed for the staircase. Once in his room, he removed his gun belt spurs and hung his hat and coat on the rack by the door. He poured himself a whiskey and sat in the chair by the window. The signature surprised him when he read the message.

Dear Marshal Bass,

You don't know my name, but you beat me up yesterday at the asylum. I'm not writing to carp or complain, though I could wish your fists were not so hard.—Bass chuckled at that—*I'm writing to make you aware of things Doctor Gilmore does to some of our female patients. He is pragmatic and insatiable in his sexual appetite for them and does so much damage to vulnerable and fragile minds that it's difficult to conceive.*

I am not the only one who has noticed this, and perhaps you have heard from others before me. I am a medical student at the state university, and I wish to specialize in Psychiatry. Along with the terrible impact he has on his patients, he discredits the Psychiatric Care Community as well.

I will do anything I can to assist in bringing him to justice.
—Lawrence Ratcliff

Now Bass felt bad about thumping the youngster. The letter proved that he was only doing what he'd been told to do: keep people away from Gilmore's office. It also showed him to be a young man of integrity and moral character. *Probably make a good deputy. He sure had the size for it.*

Bass could only imagine the grilling he caught from Gilmore for letting Bass through.

If, as the letter stated, the situation was bad enough that others had noticed, action was called for sooner rather than later. Bass made plans to visit Marion Gilmore in the morning. He checked his Elgin: 9:30 p.m. Time enough for another whiskey, and look at the paper before bed.

7:15 a.m., May 20, 1888
Winslow Hotel
Congress Ave at Ash Street
Austin, Texas

Bass rose early. Usually, he slept light anyway, a habit he established while following the trail of outlaws on the dodge. It wasn't so much a case of the early bird catching the worm as it was the early bird staying alive in case the worm doubled back on his trail during the night.

Bass was eating breakfast in the hotel café when a page came to his table with a note. He glanced at the signature and called the page back. "Who delivered this? Did you see?"

"Yes, sir, a policeman, sir. He left right away. Shall I try catching him?"

"No, no, but I need to write a response, have you a pad and pencil?"

The page produced a sharpened pencil and small tablet, and Bass wrote, *In by 11:00 a.m. I have an arrest to make. Keep it under wraps till I get there. —Bass*

Bass asked the page to deliver the note to Chief Grooms Lee at police headquarters and tipped the boy a dollar. The youngster was off like a shot. Bass paid for breakfast and went to the barn to saddle Dotty for the long ride to the State Asylum.

The morning was clear and breezy, with a slight chill unusual for mid-May in Texas. He rode the same route as before and admired the lawns all neatly cut and the trees and shrubbery, which were all starting to green up. The flowering trees and bushes added perfume to the breeze, and the sun became warmer as it climbed to its zenith. The roads were dry but not yet dusty. That would come later with the summer heat.

It took nearly thirty minutes to reach the asylum entrance. Bass tied Dotty to the same rail he used before and climbed the same marble steps. Once inside, he looked toward the information desk, but it was unmanned. He'd fully expected to see Lawrence Ratliff sitting there. A lamp light glowed in Gilmore's office, so he climbed to the second floor once again.

Bass knocked on the door and listened. From the other side came faint sobbing and quiet cursing behind the door and, finally, the sound of someone tripping or falling over furniture.

Bass pushed his weight into the door, and it gave easily. The glass pane with Gilmore's name and station shattered. There was no one in the anteroom, so Bass kicked open the office door. There, he found Gilmore half naked on the floor, his trousers around his ankles. The young girl couldn't have been more than fifteen, was crying and partially dressed, and she took the interruption as her moment to flee. Gilmore was still on the ground, but this time, he was meek and withdrawn as Bass approached.

"See here now, officer, I know how this must appear, but it's all part of advanced therapy, you see. The girl was . . ."

"Get dressed!"

Gilmore looked away as he buttoned his trousers and rearranged his shirt. "Officer, I know what you must be thinking; of course, I would . . . that is, perhaps I could make a donation of cash to your retirement fund, yes, yes, say a thousand dollars, *hmm*?"

"Gilmore, you're under arrest. There'll be a laundry list of charges when I get you back to police headquarters, but child molestin' will do for now. You know what they do to child molesters in the penitentiary, Gilmore?" Marion Gilmore could only stare at the floor. "Believe me, you're gonna wish your ma and pa never met. Now get your things, and let's go."

Gilmore appeared resigned to his fate. He walked slowly back to his desk and gazed at a picture propped against a lamp. He took a deep breath, reached into the top drawer, withdrew a two-shot derringer pistol, and aimed it at Bass.

"Officer, I can't go to prison; I won't let you take me there." Tears flowed as he spoke, and he finally whispered, "God forgive me . . ." Gilmore quickly put the barrel of the pistol into his mouth and pulled the trigger.

Bass was startled at first but immediately understood the action. *By God, the world's better off.* Bass then thought. *He knew he was wrong but couldn't stop. I guess that's what's call an obsession.*

The sound of the shot attracted a crowd outside Gilmore's office. Bass walked out and spotted Lawrence Ratliff right away, he was the one with the black eye and broken nose. He approached first.

"Was it Doctor Gilmore?"

"Yes. He shot himself rather than be arrested."

Ratliff was silent for a moment. "I'm sorry it ended like this; he was a very knowledgeable man. I've read many of his papers. Some are brilliant."

"What's the old saying? Physician, heal thyself?"

"Yes, it's a proverb . . . in Luke, I believe."

"Do me a favor, kid, close the office door and don't let anyone in till the city mortician gets here, will ya? It might be a little while; I have to ride into town to find him."

"Alright, I have reading to do anyway."

Bass smiled at him and turned for the stairs. Just as he did, he overheard Ratliff quietly say, "Maybe I can switch to Theology."

Bass stopped at Doc Flotter's on the way and then continued on to the police station. When he arrived at police headquarters, he tied off Dotty and strode into the station house, past the desk sergeant, and into the Chief's office unannounced. He tossed his hat on the divan and plopped down in one of the chairs at the desk next to O'Dell.

"*Welp*, Gilmore's dead, 'shot himself just as I was arresting him. I suppose he saved the state a bunch a money, but I can't help but feel just a bit sorry for him. He knew what he was doin' was wrong. He just couldn't stop. Maybe like our Annihilator fella. I wonder if he thinks deep down what he's doin is wrong?"

Grooms answered. "Not likely, Frank. I believe he's convinced himself that what he's doing is right like he's protectin' us all from some kinda menace. Read this; it came just 'fore you left this mornin."

To the Worthy Officers of the Peace in our Fair Austin,

You don't know me and likely never will, not as long as you keep fumbling about with meaningless clues (most of which I've left on purpose) and counting on the memory of that darky I let live. I suppose that may have been a mistake. I am human, after all, but should the situation recur, I will not be so hasty. I imagine you're wrestling with the crucifix tattoo and the salt I employed, or perhaps you're wondering about my little keepsakes, haha, or the timing of my actions. If I wanted to be remembered as a martyr, I suppose I should explain them all, but alas, I have no such desire. I might suggest, however, the "Malleus Maleficarum," or even the histories of dark disciples, like Mary and Elizabeth Hicks, Janet Home, and Catharine Repond. I shall leave it to your own device as to locate and interpret, and maybe a trip to the old Greenwood Cemetery might enlighten you.

Until the first of June, then, I remain society's benefactor.

"Holy Mother of God, Grooms. Did anyone see who left it?"

"No. It was on the duty desk when the Sergeant noticed it. Obviously, it's authentic. He knows about the salt and the forehead crosses. I assume that quip he made about keepsakes refers to the missing hearts. None of that has made it into the papers."

Cillian O'Dell added, "And who the bloody hell is *Malleus Maleficarum*? And them women listed, who in God's Holy name are they? Where do we start on somethin like 'at?"

"The University. *Malleus Maleficarum* sounds like Latin to me. And those women's names? Well, maybe we start at the newspapers, or the library. Maybe there's been a story 'bout 'em. And let's find out where Greenwood Cemetery is at, by God," Bass said.

8:00 a.m., May 21, 1888
E. P. & S. W. Terminal
Austin Texas

By the end of the next day, the three men had broken down assignments from the information in the Annihilator's note. Cillian would check out the newspaper and library for any reference to the women listed in the Annihilator's letter within the last five years. Newspapers rarely kept editions passed that period, though occasionally, for special, wide-interest stories, the front pages were retained for a longer time.

Grooms would check out the meaning of *Malleus Maleficarum* at the state university. He had a passing acquaintance with a nursing instructor there and it seemed to him as good a place to start as any.

And Bass discovered from the Coroner's records at Doc Flotter's office that Greenwood Cemetery was in Weatherford, Texas, about thirty-five miles west of Fort Worth. He decided to pay a visit to the Sexton of the cemetery and was waiting to board the 8:15 mail train, northbound.

The distance between Austin and Fort Worth is a bit more than one hundred and fifty miles and Weatherford is an additional thirty-five. He'd have to travel to Fort Worth and then take a second train to Weatherford; there was no direct service. The trip would normally require travel time of five and a half hours. However, as this was a mail train, travel time was extended by two hours to accommodate a one-hour stop in Waco, where the mail and passengers were boarded and discharged. Then, there were several small stops at mail stations that did not use 'mail cranes' or 'catcher pouches.' These devices were not meant for oddly shaped packages and large items that would not fit in the pouch or might be too bulky for the crane.

Bass settled himself for the expected seven-hour journey on one of the cushioned, forward-facing benches next to the window. The conductor advised that "since this is a Thursday there won't be near as many kids aboard," students from Baylor University in Waco going home to Dallas or Fort Worth would always crowd the train.

Bass spent the first half of the trip reading the latest *Austin Statesman*, front to back, top to bottom. In particular, he studied the sports section that featured stories about a new baseball team in Houston called the Buffalos. He liked to keep up to date on the Texas League in general, and his favorite team was the San Antonio Cowboys. He also followed the St. Louis Browns, but only because they'd recently overtaken the New York Giants for first place in the Major League and, as a result, received regular press coverage. He was also becoming interested in the college sport of football, but except for championships, the games rarely received any coverage by the press. He really didn't know the rules of the game yet, anyway.

At Waco, he ducked into a café next to the station for a bite to eat. It was 11:15 a.m., and he hadn't eaten before boarding. He had a ham sandwich with fried potatoes and a slice of day-old apple pie that went particularly well with the bourbon he ordered—they had no rye.

He slept for an hour during the second half of the trip but was awake as the train pulled slowly through Fort Worth to the station there. He couldn't remember the last time he was in Fort Worth, or Dallas for that matter, either for business or pleasure. He wasn't even sure of the local sheriff's name, though the Federal Marshal was Bill "Red" Angus. He knew that because Angus had just been appointed.

He brought no luggage, planning only for a day or two, and knew that any personal items he might need for an overnight could be bought at a general store. He asked a porter if he knew when the train for Weatherford left, and the man said, "Four-fifteen, same as usual 'cept it's runnin' half an hour late . . . same as usual."

Bass walked to the ticket counter and bought a seat for Weatherford for one dollar and ten cents, and took a seat on a bench outside to smoke a small cigar and wait.

The train to Weatherford and points beyond was right on time, which is to say it was thirty minutes late. Bass took a seat next to the window again and watched as a part of Texas he wasn't familiar with slid by. They went through a small town named Aledo, and the rest of the countryside seemed ripe for farming. They passed several livestock watering tanks along the way and crossed the Clear Fork of the Trinity River, arriving in Weatherford just at 3:30 p.m.

Bass had never been to Weatherford, Texas before, so he asked a porter as he stepped down where he might find the Town Marshal's office or the City Police?"

"Yessir. Be right down yar on Trinty Street and turn . . . which is it now lef' or right, I forgets. *Hmm.* It's lef' I belee, sir, you turns lef' on uh what's it? One a' them tree streets, Elm it is, sir . . . den it be down a piece on yer right."

Bass thanked the man and had a good notion from the directions where he was going.

The Town Marshal's office was on Elm Street, and the Marshal's name was "Tully, Don Tully, and it's a right honor to make your acquaintance, Marshal Bass. Now, how can I help you?"

"Don, I'm working on the Annihilator killins' down in Austin, you maya heard."

"Oh indeed, sir, indeed. So horrible, so gruesome."

"Yes, I'm following a lead that takes me to a nearby cemetery, the Greenwood Cemetery in Weatherford, in fact."

"Yes, of course, y'all want I should take you there?"

"Not just yet Don, see, I don't really know what I'm lookin' for or what to expect. I sent a wire to the cemetery's sexton yesterday, but I never heard back from the fella. Do you know him?"

"Small town, Marshal, Athol Porter, I know him to say howdy. But say, he's a weird old duck, that one."

"I suppose to spend your days caretakin' a cemetery you'd hafta be a might touched, don't ya reckon?"

"Yeah . . . it's more 'n that. He claims he's a spiritualist, got no idea what that is, but it sure ain't God-fearin', I can tell you that."

"Oh, how do you mean?"

"It's kinda like every day is Halloween to him, and I don't mean jack-o-lanterns and tricks or treats. He gets into things like Devil worshippin' and spells and all. 'Takes it real serious. Not my cup-a-tea a' all. It's spooky, is what I mean. So I'll take you out there, but I don't plan on visitin' too. I'll wait in the buggy."

"Alright. 'Guess I'm prepared enough." Bass checked his Elgin. "It's nearly 4:00 p.m. still time, let's take a run out there. Oh, and it's Deputy Marshal, actually."

The Greenwood Cemetery was due north on Elm Avenue to Front Street and then east one block. The sexton's cabin was just inside the gate beneath several towering black oaks. The cabin was larger than Bass thought it might be, and he noticed several outbuildings as well. One looked like a large brick-and-mortar kiln with a tall chimney on one side.

Bass rapped on the door, and Tully, true to his earlier statement, remained in the one-horse buggy. The door opened, and Bass got his first look at Athol Porter as he opened the door.

"Who're you?"

Porter was a small man to start with, and he looked smaller because he was hunched over in a stooped position with a pronounced curvature to his back. His white hair hung straight and long, covering his shoulders as he stooped, and it appeared dry and straw-like. He was clean shaven, but his brows, also white as snow, were thick and steeply arched. His nearly colorless gray eyes gave the impression of blindness, though clearly he was not. His voice was high-pitched and nasally and had a sing-song quality to it. He sounded more like a woman than a man.

"Are you Athol Porter, the sexton here?"

"I am, he. I repeat, who're you?"

"My name is Frank Bass; I sent a wire yesterday. May I come in?"

"No, stay where y'are. Whadaya want?" The intonation of his voice rose in pitch at the end of each question and was disconcerting to Bass. He wasn't sure if the man had finished speaking.

"I'm a US Deputy Marshal, and I'm investigating the 'Annihilator' killings in Austin. Your name was mentioned as one who might help us out."

A grin appeared on Porter's lips that grew into a crooked smile. Bass noticed that he only had teeth on the right side of his jaw, and those that he saw were yellow and cracked. Bass assumed that the man was in constant pain.

"Come into the cottage then and tell me what you know."

Bass had to bend low to enter, but once inside, he marveled at the space. The cabin, or *cottage* as Porter called it, was a single large room with three long tables placed in rows. It smelled first of mold, and then the musty odor of decay became predominant. Beakers and glass tubes, labeled brown jars, magnifying lenses, and lamps covered three tables four to a table. Bass assumed the tubs of water and bottles of liquids on each table were chemicals of a sort. Bookshelves lined the walls of the cottage, filled with books of varying sizes: some were enormous tomes, and many could fit into your hand. Scrolls of parchment laid about, and a few looked like skins that had the appearance of great age. In a corner near the hearth, a wooden pallet seemed to be the old man's cot.

"Mr. Porter, what is all this? What's it for?"

"Young man, do you know what a magus is?

"No, I guess I don't."

"I am a third-order magus of the Golden Dawn, which is meaningless to you, but it is an impressive rank. What you see about you is my work, my life, in fact. The oldest known histories of my craft."

"The craft? Are you a warlock?" Bass wasn't sure what a Warlock was himself, but it seemed a knowledgeable question to ask.

"Warlock? Ha! No, boy, no. Warlocks serve the Dark Lord, like his sisters. A magus is one who is opposed to the black arts. Their followers are a selfish, self-serving public menace whose practice only promotes death and the Evil One. I, as a magus, am a healer of sorts and mortal enemy of the Dark Crafts. I am a master of both arts but promote only life. Now tell me what you want to know."

Bass was mystified and, at the same time, impressed. From the old man's words he could imagine an ages-long battle between the two forces fought in secrecy, underground, out of sight of the . . . what was it called? Non-spiritualists? He looked at the old man bent by age.

"Mr. Porter, the killer, this Annihilator, gave us your name as someone we should consult. Can you think of a reason why he would do this?"

The old man thought for a moment. "He mentioned the Witches' Tomb here, then? 'Not surprised, it put our little boneyard on the map, so to speak. 'Course, there's nothing to it, you know. A supposed witch named Anna Katalin, a Hungarian was buried alive along with her consort whom she supposedly bewitched. *Nonsense,* of course, but people still come to see the edifice."

"No sir, he didn't mention a tomb. Can you think of a reason why he would want us to see you?"

The old man looked at the floor and stroked his chin.

"I think perhaps, and you may disbelieve, you would not be the first; I think that he sees himself as my disciple. I assure you he is not, and I do not know the man. He is delusional in his thinking, and his methods are obscene. Still, I believe he sees his role as a righteous one according to the order and in another time, another less enlightened age, he may have been lauded. But not today. Tell me, does he use water?"

"Water, sir?"

"In his cleansing, does he use water? Wiccans hate water."

"No. He covers his victims in salt, is 'at what you mean?"

The old man slumped and nodded. "Yes, salt is repugnant to the creature and considered a cleansing agent as well.

"He also carves a cross in the forehead."

The old man looked up. "The forehead, huh? A Cross. That's a nice touch. There is an archaic rite, a playful saying from the witchery of the Middle Ages. It goes, 'First of the month, a pinch and a punch.' The pinch is, of course, the reference to salt. The first of any month has significance to Wiccans, and the pinch of salt, well . . . the reference is to keep the creatures away. The punch . . . no idea really. Playfulness, perhaps?"

"I think you've hit something there. His killings are always on the first of the month, right after midnight. Perhaps he sent me here to find that out?"

The old man looked incredulous. "I suppose it's possible. His thinking is certainly deranged, so *anything* might be possible."

"So does he believe he's killing . . . witches, sir?"

"Oh yes, of course. Haven't you been listening? He believes he is doing humankind a service by slaughtering these poor women, and he must be stopped. If for no other reason than he gives us all a bad name."

"Alright, then. I agree. Can you help us find him?"

Again, the old man was silent for a long moment. "I'm afraid not. He is completely unknown to me, and I dare say to the orders in your area. He is obviously well-studied. His methods are from the very early days, the Middle Ages when clerics like Thomas Aquinas and Emperor Charlemagne applied tortures and disembodiments of suspected witches. Later, by centuries, eradication was done by fire." The old man spoke more slowly now. "What you are facing, I have never seen the like. In my one hundred forty-two years, young man, I've never seen the like."

The old man collapsed into a chair and appeared to be asleep.

Bass took it as his sign to leave. He closed the door and walked back to the buggy, where Tully smoked a cigarette. As he walked, he thought to himself, *one hundred and forty-two?*

Nah. He climbed into the buggy and nodded for Tully to whip up.

"Well? What'd he say?"

"Tully? You wouldn't believe it if I told you. But you're right to stay away from there."

Bass contemplated all he'd just heard and wondered if he should discount it because the guy thought he was a hundred forty-two. *Nobody lives that long. Right?* He thought at some length about the killer being a disciple and thinking he was doin' us all a favor by killin these "witches."

He was silent in thought all the way back to the Town Marshal's office, and as Tully reined up, Bass said out loud, "Damnit, what if he is!?"

Chapter 14

6:45 p.m., May 22, 1888
The Junction Hotel
815 Spring Street
Weatherford, Texas

The Junction Hotel was handy to the City Jail, so Bass decided to take a room for the night. He wasn't sure of the return schedule on the E. P. & S. W., but he assumed it would be similar to his trip today, only in reverse. His room was like a hundred other rooms he'd stayed in, a cotton mattress over steel springs, worn linens, an armoire or chifforobe, and a basin table with a pitcher and mirror. The price for the night was six bits paid in advance. As he had no horse, there was no livery charge.

Tully had gone home to his family. He'd not invited Bass, and it was just as well because Bass was too tired to be social. He'd had a very long travel day and a mentally taxing encounter with a bizarre old man and only wanted a drink, a steak, and a drink in pretty much that order. He also decided he might need a shaving kit and toothbrush, maybe some witch hazel for his face after shaving. The sun was beginning to set when he left the hotel in search of a sundry's seller somewhere nearby. He found an apothecary on the next corner and purchased what he needed, including a tin of Floriline's Toothpaste, something he'd never tried before.

There was no café or dining room in the hotel, but there was a saloon that served "hearty gentleman's fare" at reasonable prices. Bass decided he'd try it out.

The Bearded Beast Saloon was an all-in-one establishment. Food for the hungry, drink for the thirsty, and gaming tables for the foolish—or simple-minded. At least Bass saw gambling in card rooms that way. He'd never won a dime in one, never knew anyone who'd won a dime in one, and allowed anyone who went back a second time deserved what he got. As a lawman, he'd seen the results of cheap whiskey and high-stakes card games too often and had a strict habit of avoiding them if at all possible.

Tonight, he sat at a corner table in the saloon, near the piano and banjo players, and ordered a T-bone steak, boiled greens, potatoes, and a pint bottle of Overholt Rye Whiskey. He sipped his whiskey, listened to the music, and ate well when his plate was delivered. The waitress was a sturdy-looking middle-aged woman, handsome, he thought, with short dark hair, hazel eyes, a green dress to below her knees, and a bright red apron with a few kitchen stains around the middle.

"You stayin' in town for business, Marshal?" Bass looked at her, wondering if they'd met before.

"I 'seen your badge when you opened your jacket. 'You on a manhunt? That's what brings most of the Marshals into town."

"Oh, no, I'm not . . . uh Trina"—Bass read her name tag—"actually I'm here from Austin following a clue."

"Holy Jesus, the Annihilator, right? Is it someone from here? God, I hope it ain't no one from here."

"No, no, it's just a clue I'm looking into, nothing like what you might be thinking."

"Good. There's crazy folks in town, but nobody like that devil down there. Who'd you come to see then?"

"Well, I don't think it has to be a secret. I saw the sexton out at the city cemetery, Athol Porter."

The woman's expression changed from light to dark just that quickly. "Oh, and did he tell you anything of interest, Marshal?" Trina's eyes moved furtively from one table to the next.

"Yes, he did, Trina. Why? Do you know him?"

"*Ha*, well enough to hate the ground he walks on. He's dangerous-crazy that one is, Marshal. I don't think you should believe anything he said." Trina had a kind of glow in her eye Bass had not seen before.

He assumed most of the folks in town were like Tully, cautiously fearful of the man. But Trina's reaction was so hateful and so quick that Bass assumed she must have had some unpleasant experience with the old timer in the recent past. Trina left the dinner bill and didn't return to Bass's table, so he paid, left a generous tip, and went to drink at the bar.

He was intrigued now with Trina's reaction, so he asked the man next to him, a tall, lanky fellow if he'd ever heard of Athol Porter.

"Oh, the crazy old man at the cemetery, right? sure I heard a' him . . . never met him though. What'd you go see him for?"

Bass explained he was a US. Marshal, looking into the Annihilator killings and a clue led him up here.

"Oh, I see. I live in Dallas I just have a construction site here in town, so I've been here off and on for about a year. Building a new hotel and saloon just down on Parker Square near the courthouse. I go home every couple weeks or so . . . just to check up on the missus, you know."

Bass thought for a moment and said, "Say that reminds me, I ought to send a wire to mine in El Paso, let her know I'm all right."

"Yeah, I guess you're investigatin' that lunatic down there. You'll be visitin' the local asylum then. Good reason for a wife to worry there, I guess."

"Yeah, you're right . . . we only have the one though in Austin, and I've been there a few times asking questions."

"Oh? Then you don't plan to see the state asylum in Terrel outside Dallas?"

Bass now took a keener interest in what the man was saying. "There's another state asylum up here?"

"Yeah, biggun too. Lotsa loonies in that bin, brother. *Welp*, 'believe I'll head on to my room early day tomorrow. Good luck to ya. Hope you find that madman sooner than later."

"Yeah . . . me too. Hey, thanks for the information." Bass finished his rye and went to his room.

It had been a long, tiring day, and he had a lot to think about.

8:15 a.m., May 23, 1888
Junction Hotel
Weatherford, Texas

Bass was up and out of the hotel after a pot of coffee and two biscuits. He walked down the street to the City Jail and walked in as Don Tully swept out the cells.

"Mornin', Marshal, sleep okay?"

"Yeah, slept fine. It was a long day."

Tully set his broom aside and smiled. "I meant, after seein' that old spook, you didn't have no night terrors?"

"Oh. No, no bad dreams or boogeymen in the closet. But I did want to ask you somethin' I heard last night. Is there another state lunatic asylum outside Dallas?"

"Uh, yeah, in Terrel, 'bout twenty-five miles east of Dallas. You wanna go there?"

"I believe so. I can take the train back to Fort Worth and rent a pony to get to Terrel. Have you ever heard anything about the hospital at all?"

"No, but it's a lockdown, same as the one down your way. I ain't never been there, though. 'Never sent nobody there neither, thank God. I heard them places can be downright hellish, folks screamin' and whatnot. No sir, I'll stay right here where there ain't a lot goin on."

"Alright, can't say I blame you. You have a family?"

"Yup, my wife Susanne and two little girls."

"I see. Well then, you stay close, Don, and watch your back."

"Will do, Marshal."

Bass was about to say *it's Deputy...* . but decided to let it slide. "Do you happen to know the next eastbound train?"

"No, I don't, Marshal. The best bet is to check at the station. You want a lift?"

"Thank you, Don, 'preciate it."

Bass stepped out of the buggy, and Sheriff Tully made a U-turn in the freight loading area. He checked on the train and was told he'd have an hour wait, but after that the trains east ran pretty regular. Bass took the time to hunt up a map of the state and found the town of Terrel almost due east of Dallas. It showed up on the railroad map as a mail stop, so Bass figured he'd just ride the train all the way. Bass had gotten used to train travel on his last big case, the kidnapping in the panhandle up north. He was starting to appreciate it over long days in the saddle on manhunts. Of course, nothing could improve on riding horseback for tracking, but if you were pretty sure of your man's location, and there was a train depot nearby . . .

He also took the time to send a wire to Sally just to keep her up to date on his whereabouts. He'd tell her about Athol Porter when he finally got home.

The wait for the train seemed longer than the hour delay he expected, but when he got on the eastbound mail train, it was exactly 9:15 a.m. He sat at a window and watched the scenery move by for the short ride to Fort Worth, and upon arrival, he went to the ticket window again to check on times for his return to Austin from Fort Worth.

He found that the same train he came up on ran in reverse order every day as well so that he could take the same train at the same hour tomorrow. It would mean an extra night in Fort Worth, but he didn't feel he'd be missing much in the Annihilator case. However, he considered it possible that Gandy Dave Lomax might be trying to contact him and would not know about the trip to Weatherford. He couldn't send a wire to Grooms about it. That would violate Gandy Dave's secrecy. And asking the hotel to forward the contents of the note carried the same penalty. He would just have to wait until his return to check on contact from the disguised Pinkerton detective. The discovery of another lunatic asylum within a hundred and seventy miles of the murders was too significant to disregard.

As was his habit whenever arriving in a town outside his jurisdiction, he went first to the office of the local Federal Deputy Marshal to advise him of his presence and the nature of his call. The marshal's name was Bill Red Angus, a man Bass had only heard of and never met. He was supposedly a hard man, quick to his temper but also an honest one. Bass knew that final commodities were becoming more and more scarce, primarily in local law enforcement. Communities were starting to catch on and many had begun to offer proper wages for their town marshals.

Angus's office was at the corner of Main Street and Market Street. When Bass knocked there was no response even though the window shades were up and the lamps all lit. Bass decided then to try the local Police Chief, another man he'd never met and never heard of either.

The police department was half a block west on Market and Bass was forced again to wait his turn at the front desk. Several minutes later, a large uniformed Black Officer asked Bass about his business there.

"Wanna see the Chief. Name's Frank Bass, Deputy US Marshal, just a courtesy call, really."

"Alright, Marshal, come this way; I'll take you to the Chief's office."

The nameplate next to the door read R. M. Kitts, Special Officer. "This is him, sir. We ain't got no Chief yet. Ol' Ricky is fillin' in." The man knocked on the wooden door jamb and opened it for Bass. "Go on in, Marshal."

"Officer Kitts? My name is Frank Bass. I'm the US Deputy Marshal for West Texas."

"Yes, Marshal, I've heard of you, of course. What can I do for you?" Kitts was a fit-looking older man Bass pegged as late forties. His thinning brown hair was combed straight back, he was clean shaven, and his uniform showed the creases of starched laundry.

"Actually, this is more of a courtesy or duty call, Officer Kitts. I'm investigating the Annihilator killings in Austin, and I plan to visit the asylum in Terrel. Do you know it?"

"Yes, as a matter of fact, I do. Sit down, please. Would you like coffee?"

"Yes, thanks, kind a' you to offer."

Kitts signaled a young officer, and a few minutes later, a tray with coffee and cups appeared. "Now, what is it you will be looking for?"

"I got a pretty good idea of the man I'm looking for; I plan to ask the chief physician there if he's released anyone that might match up."

"I see. You do know the hospital is a locked-down facility? Not too many inmates ever leave?"

"Yeah, I know, but it's a natural question, and he may have some additional information on the kind of madman we're after."

"Just so you know, Marshal, the superintendent, there is a woman, Dr. Agatha Waters. She was appointed by the Governor."

"Oh? Well, thanks for the notice, then."

Kitts smiled. "And, *uh* . . . she don't really care for men. 'Might as well know in advance. She's run me outta her office more 'n once for asking personal questions 'bout residents. She's mighty protective, I guess you'd call it."

"Well, again, much obliged. Say, can you recommend a livery nearby? I'll be needin' a horse for the ride out."

"No need, no need, take your pick from the department's stable across the street. You know it's near half a day's ride, right?"

"Do indeed. Thanks for the use of your horse, Officer Kitts, pleasure meetin' you."

"Likewise, Marshal, do be careful, won't you? The horse I mean, they're very valuable. Well trained."

Bass was nearly out the door, but he turned with a concerned look on his face. "Good to know." And he closed the door behind him.

The stable was actually in the next block on the other side of the street. Bass showed his badge and ID card to the liveryman at the corral gate and picked out a tall, muscular-looking gelding. The department had nothing but English riding saddles available, so Bass had little choice in that area. A slight rise for the cantle, barely anything for a pommel horn, and slight pieces of leather for fenders. And the nickel stirrups were nothing more than thin bars of metal to catch your bootheel on. *How them fancy English folk stayed on a spirited animal is beyond me,* he thought as he rode out of the barn and turned east onto Ackard Avenue.

His ride took him through a fertile-looking range land around the North Fork of the Trinity River. Once he crossed that stream, he encountered several other smaller creeks and streams he assumed were all part of the natural Trinity watershed. The land was flat, with green belts located along the small waterways, and Bass was impressed with the natural appeal of the landscape. He pushed the tall gelding when he thought proper, recalling Officer Kitts' admonition to take care of his horse.

It was just before 3:00 p.m. when the Victorian facade of the state asylum loomed into view. *Even on a bright, sunny day, these places look gloomy.* He dismounted at the front door and tied the horse off near a trough. He climbed the steps to the entry and found himself inside a similar looking rotunda to the hospital in Austin. The light from the dome's skylights seemed filtered to a yellowish color, and Bass assumed it had been a while since anyone thought to clean the things.

He scanned the second floor, thinking there might be a similarity to Austin on the inside as well, but there were no offices on that level. 'Only numbered rooms of indeterminate size. Above that level, he spotted several official-looking rooms with glass entrances and names painted on the doors. He saw no information desk, so he decided to climb to the third floor and walk until he found Dr. Agatha Waters.

By the time he reached the third level, the second level was labeled The Mezzanine. He was a bit winded, so he started walking slowly to his left. Finally, in the center opposite the staircase, Bass found Dr. Waters' office. He knocked politely, and when there was no offer, he entered the antechamber.

He heard a lady's voice say, "Serena? Who is it?" she appeared shortly after speaking and seemed startled at seeing an unannounced man.

"Good Lord. Who're you?"

"Marshal Frank Bass, ma'am. 'Didn't mean for to scare you just now. You alright then?"

"Yes, yes, I'm fine . . . what do you want? And please be quick, will you?" Agatha Waters was a middle-aged woman with short dark hair, spectacles, and a snug-fitting skirt that barely passed her knees. It appeared that she wore a man's shirt beneath a tight vest that displayed modest cleavage. Bass thought she was dressed in a provocative style and did his best not to stare.

"Ma'am, I'm here to ask a few questions about the Annihilator killin's in Austin. It's agreed that he's certainly a lunatic, and I hoped you might have an idea or two to help us out."

"You thought . . . yes, he's a lunatic, and from what I've read, *a very capable one*. He certainly has powers that've stymied you lawmen down in our state Capitol. Evidently, you 'fellas' have met your match."

"Yes, ma'am, he's a clever rascal, but preventing more victims is what we're tryin to do. Now the theory we have is that he's some kinda witch hunter, thinks he's doing humankind a favor by killin' off witches. Have you ever run across any patient like that?"

Agatha Waters sat on the edge of a divan in the anteroom and answered quickly, almost without thinking. "No, I don't recall that kind of syndrome in this hospital, ever. Certainly, we have quite a few residents who hear voices and believe they see things. We've just begun using the drug paraldehyde, and that seems to quiet the disturbed imagination. But the answer to your question is *no*. Now, if you're finished, I have—"

"Just one or two more, please, Doctor Waters. Where do most of your, er, *residents* come from? How do they get here?"

"Most are committed by loving families who cannot cope with their behaviors, who recognize the need for round-the-clock care. Others are sentenced here by the courts after committing crimes of bizarre or peculiar natures. Is that all?"

"Ma'am, I know I can find this out from your registrar or record keepers, but can you recall releasing anyone lately that might've been of a dangerous nature? To himself and others?"

The Doctor smiled as best she could. "Marshal, the hospital releases several patients a year whom we deem competent enough to return to and function successfully in society. Now I'm through. I've answered enough of your questions. Please see yourself out of my hospital."

Bass tipped his hat and left. Shaking his head as he descended the stairs, he decided to ask Kitts a question or two on his return.

Chapter 15

6:45 p.m., May 23, 1888
   Dallas Police Department
   Market Street
   Dallas, Texas

Bass arrived back at the Police Stables a little before 7:00 p.m. and, after caring for the gelding, went directly to Officer Kitt's Office. Kitts was preparing to leave for the day.

"Officer Kitts, glad I caught you. Time for a quick question?"

"Well, I'm a bit late as it is . . . alright, go ahead."

"Obliged. I chatted with Dr. Waters at the asylum; I think she wanted to be helpful, but she musta been in a hurry to get to something else. I asked if any of her residents had been released within the last year. Lady didn't seem to want to answer, and I didn't wanna push."

"Ah, well, off the top of my head, I don't recall, but if you can wait a day or two, I can look it up in our records department."

"Yeah, sure, Officer. Can I ask you to wire the information to me at the Winslow Hotel in Austin? I'll pay for the service if it's a problem."

"No, no, let me make a quick note here. Alright, I'll send you what I find out, Marshal Bass."

"Many thanks, Officer Kitts."

"For God's sake, call me Ricky like everybody else."

"Thanks for all your help, Ricky, and thanks again for hangin' around for me."

Bass left Ricky Kitts's office and decided to look for a hotel for the night. Since he didn't see one nearby, he decided to walk back down to the livery and ask the attendant for a recommendation. "It don't have to be fancy, but I'd like it to have a café or saloon handy."

"Sure-nuff, Marshal. If you goes down round that corner yonder, you'll see some signs for what you're lookin' for. I never used one, 'cause I lives nearby, but I heard tell the Sanderson's a good one."

"Thanks, I'll take a look."

Bass walked down to the corner and looked up Commerce Street and saw three or four signs for hotels or boarding Houses. The Sanderson was the second one up, about halfway into the next block, so Bass started walking.

The Sanderson Hotel was perfect for Bass: clean, bigger rooms, electric lights, and an electric Otis Elevator that dropped you off on your floor. The building itself was narrow, but it rose six stories, and Bass imagined there might be a pleasant view from up there. His room was on the third floor, and he received another happy surprise when he opened the door. The room had a separate sitting area with two chairs and end tables for each. There was also an actual closet rather than the stand-alone armoire, and the basin had a cold-water tap and drain.

His ranch house at TwainHeart had a commode built into the first-floor privy under the stairs that his friend and carpenter Silas Pratt installed for him, but aside from the pump at the kitchen sink, that was all the plumbing TwainHeart could boast. There was a tub room at the end of the hall that had chilly water piped in and there was a gas water heater attached to the tub to heat the cold water. The desk clerk said it was like a fancy hotel in Boston. And the best part of all this comfort was the price was reasonable: only a dollar and fifty per night.

Bass grew hungry, so he deposited his toothbrush and Floriline's toothpaste in his room and headed down to the dining room on the second floor. He went down the staircase rather than wait for the elevator and went into the long, narrow room alone. A portion of the dining room was opened to the lobby below, and Bass took a table along the railing. A waiter came by in a black vest, black trousers, white starched shirt, and green apron to take his order.

Bass started with a whiskey and then selected the pork chops, boiled greens—collards mostly—and fried potatoes. He said for dessert, he'd like whiskey. The waiter slid his pencil behind his ear and snapped his pad shut. He smiled when he returned with Bass's first whiskey and asked, "Are you stayin' in the hotel, sir? I can put it on your bill if you like?"

Bass thought that'd be just fine and would he please bring a pint of Overholt's when he finished eating.

The saloon was just that. No card room, no café on one side, just a good old-fashioned saloon with mirrors behind the bar and horse paintings on the wall. Of course, behind the center of the bar was a painting of *Lady Fatima* reclining naked with her legs crossed and just a gossamer-thin veil covering her rather small breasts. Bass thought, all in all, Sally would love the place.

He finished his plate and signed the bill where the waiter indicated, "One dollar and eighty cents."

"Say that's a good price for a fine meal and a pint."

"Thank you, sir, I'm glad you enjoyed it."

Bass picked up his hat from the empty chair and went up to his room. He decided to review the complimentary newspaper left in his room even though it was getting late, and his train left at 8:00 a.m. He poured himself a final whiskey and dozed in the chair next to the window, letting the paper fall to the floor.

The sun poked its way through the window shade and woke him up just after 6:00 a.m., and Bass was surprised he'd stayed asleep in the chair all night. He must've been more tired than he realized. He'd taken his gun belt off and hung it up with his hat, but otherwise, he'd spent the night fully dressed. He saw the wrinkles in his shirt and trousers as a result. Bass wasn't a real fastidious man, but he always wanted to make a good impression. He decided since he had some time, he'd walk down to the end of the hall and take a bath, he'd hang up his shirt and pants and let the steam in the small room loosen the wrinkles. He locked his coat, vest, boots, and gun belt in his room and went down the hall to the tub room.

The tub room was functionally small. On the opposite wall from the door was a Mosely Self-Heating Folding Bathtub, a floor-to-ceiling cabinet that, when opened, allowed a tub to be folded to the floor, like a Murphy bed. The water heater tank, fixed to the cabinet, was attached to a cold-water pipe, which allowed the tank to be filled. The water was then heated by a small kerosene burner, and hot water was expelled directly into the tub.

Bass was fascinated. The instructions for the tub's use were printed and attached to the door of the tub. As he read, he pulled the tub down, turned on the water tap, he heard the tank fill, and then he ignited the burner using the long match provided. The instructions said it would take up to thirty minutes to fill the tub adequately, and if the water was too hot, a cold-water tap could be opened. He hung his shirt and trousers above the tub as it filled with steaming water and he sat in the little room, wearing only his drawers and socks, amazed at the modern age he lived in. When the water temperature was to his liking, he moved the clothing to hooks on the wall and sat in the tin-lined tub, adding heated water when necessary. He was in heaven and wondered what one of these Moseley contraptions would cost to install at home.

Bass finished his tub just in time to check out of the Sanderson Hotel and get to the train depot for the 8:00 a.m. train. Again, he sat on a wooden bench seat next to a window. It was Saturday and the train was more crowded than he expected it would be. He mentioned it to the conductor and was told that most of the travelers were heading to Fort Worth, and from that station and beyond, the train would be less crowded.

Sure enough, about an hour after leaving Dallas, the train pulled into Fort Worth, and at least half the riders got off. Once the train left Fort Worth, the time to Waco would pass slowly as there were mail stops to make along the way in Itasca, Abbot, and the little town of West, but the conductor advised it would be faster going from Waco south to Austin as there were no mail stops to make.

Bass decided that even with the stops early on, the overall time on the train would be less than his trip north. He spent most of the morning in the dining car, where he had the breakfast he skipped to enjoy his modern bathing experience. The seats in the dining car were also more comfortable, so after eating, he picked up a periodical, *The Saturday Evening Post*, from April fourteenth and read excerpts from novelists Rudyard Kipling and Herman Melville. He had started reading Melville's seafaring novel *Moby Dick*, and though it was not terribly popular, he enjoyed it. Bass was not a fast reader. However, he took time to analyze those certain passages he found interesting, so he never finished the book. Still, the notion of a white whale intrigued him, and he decided he'd like to see one of the creatures someday.

Finally, the train pulled away from the small town of West, the last stop before Austin, and Bass had returned to his regular seat. Since he wasn't eating, and people would be coming back for lunch soon, one of the porters politely asked him to give up his table for other passengers. He found a cushion that was not being used, sat back in his window seat, and watched Waco slide and sway past his window. The train took him directly through the Baylor campus to the bridge over the Brazos River and finally into the open countryside, flat and green. The day was warming up so Bass tipped his hat forward and stretched out as far as the seats would allow, dozing off and on and finally sleeping about an hour into the three-hour trip.

He woke to the sound of brakes screeching and the strong odor of black smoke from the coal fires beneath the engine's boilers. The train was coming to an unplanned stop. As he looked out the window, the conductor walked hurriedly down the aisle.

"Marshal? M-Marshal, sorry, sir, but it looks like we're bein' robbed."

"Oh? What's on the train worth stealing?"

"Well, there's always the mail, sir, but this time, we have a receipt from Abbot Mines in the safe up front in the mail car. S'posed to go to the bank in Austin."

Bass looked quickly around the passenger car and asked, "How many riders on the two coaches?"

"Twenty-four, sir, fourteen men, and ten women and children."

"Okay, I want you to get them all back into the dining car and ready to get off at my signal. I'm gonna go back now and see how many are watchin the back a' the train."

The conductor went to each row and asked the passengers to move to the dining car slowly. Bass drew his Colt and walked as casually as he could to the open vestibule aye the rear of the dining car. He was counting on most of the gang being up front in the mail car, opening the safe. The train was elevated on the right of way, so no one might have been able to see into the coaches.

When he got to the door leading out to the open platform, he saw two riders sitting their mounts on the starboard side of the tracks, no doubt watching the action at the mail car, waiting for a signal to board the train and rob the passengers. Both men had sidearms, but their weapons were holstered.

Bass knew his first obligation was to get the passengers to safety, away from the probably heavily armed robbers. Slowly, he opened the door and stepped out onto the deck of the vestibule. Thanks to the roof overhang, he was still in the shadows. When he was in earshot, he quietly spoke to the two riders, "Don't move." Naturally, both men looked to see the tall man pointing his pistol at them.

"If either of you moves, I'll shoot you both. Now, very slowly climb down from those horses."

The men looked at each other and then did as they were told. One of the men was older, perhaps forty, and the other looked like just a kid.

"Now, walk slowly to the tracks and get behind the train."

The horses remained where they were, cropping the green prairie grass that had sprouted with the last rain. The two men had to climb up to the roadbed and take their position behind the train.

"Now, both a' you, using two fingers, slowly toss them pistols down this side of the hill."

Under Bass's gun, they did as they were told and looked back at Bass. "Now lie face down between the rails."

"Hey, wait a minute, mister, now we done all you said, we ain't gonna let you run us down with no train."

Bass climbed down from the platform and walked to the young one who'd just spoken.

"Yeah? Weren't my idea fer y'all to rob the durned train, buster."

And Bass knocked the young man out with the barrel of his gun. He crumbled at Bass's feet. Next, he looked at the older man standing next to the boy.

He started to look scared. "Weren't my idea to rob nothin' neither."

Bass looked at him and said, "Then why are you standin' here?"

And he knocked the older one out as well. Before going back inside the car, he arranged the two men so they were well between the rails. Then he bounded into the train and found the conductor in the second coach.

"What's your name, friend?"

"Samuel Potts, Marshal. It's my second robbery."

"*Oh*, a veteran. Then you'll know we gotta get the folks off. You take 'em back through the cars and get off through the dining car. You'll see a couple of the gang layin' unconscious between the tracks. If you can find somethin' to tie their hands, I'd appreciate it."

The conductor reached over and tore two pieces of twine from the window curtains. Bass smiled at him as he went on. "Make sure the people stay on the track or down on the left side so they can't be seen walkin' away. Try to get 'em into 'em into them cottonwoods yonder. Now, how do I get to the mail car?"

Samuel Potts explained how to get to the roof of the car, and as Bass headed back to the front, he passed two passengers with small pistols in their hands.

"You two be the last ones off, alright?" Both men nodded. "And if anybody who's not me shows their face, you shoot 'em."

Bass continued through to the first coach and then out onto the coupler platform and the ladder to the roof of the mail car.

The mail car had a sliding door entrance on the starboard side for accepting larger packages sent via mail rather than freight. There was also a standard railway door on that side for regular use by employees. Access to the coupler levers and ladder was at either end of the car via a doorway that could be locked from the inside and was covered by a grate to keep from losing mail when moving.

Samuel Potts had told Bass that the safe was located near the forward-end doorway between the string of mailbags that lined both sides of a central aisle. Bass thought his best bet for total surprise would be the forward doorway . . . if it wasn't locked.

He climbed the ladder next to the rear doorway of the mail car and crawled along the top of the car to stay as silent as he could. The engine was still making noise as it sat idling, but not enough to cover the sound of a boot step on the roof of the car. As he passed ventilation slots, he made out two separate voices but not the words being spoken. He assumed there were at least two armed men in the car. When he reached the end coupled to the tender, he tried seeing if there was a gunman in with the engineer, but he couldn't get an angle to see down into the cab. If there was a man there and he heard shooting, he'd have to jump from the cab and run outside to the mail car. Bass figured whatever he was about to do had to be done quickly.

Slowly, carefully, he eased himself down the ladder and stood on the forward doorway platform. The door was open; only the metal grate covered it. Bass saw several men inside. At least three were workers, and two more were lying on the floor, possibly shot. Perhaps they were guards sent along by Abbot?

Two men with guns drawn stood over a clerk, who was obviously shaken. He was having trouble opening the safe. One of the gunmen moved, blocking Bass's view but also shielding him from the other man with the clerk by the safe. Slowly, Bass opened the hinged grate and stepped inside. He timed his next move with the engine's rhythmic steam huff and cold-cocked the gunman in front of him with his pistol. The gunman did not fall immediately but staggered enough to allow Bass a clear shot at the other man standing at the safe. He recognized the man standing opposite him as Brack Cornett, who was startled at seeing Bass and fired his pistol. The shot missed and thudded into a mailbag.

Bass fired just as quickly and struck Cornett in the forehead, eliminating the need for a second shot. The man he'd struck was still stumbling and trying for an angle to shoot when Bass shot him in the upper chest. A fine red mist flew from his back and stained the mailsacks along the wall. The smaller man kneeling at the safe had his hands raised instinctively. His eyes were wide, and a thin line of drool escaped the corner of his mouth.

Bass asked, "Are you hurt?"

The man couldn't speak, only shake his head. Bass turned his attention to the open sliding door, expecting a man from the engine cab. He appeared a few seconds later, believing the gunshots had come from his partners. When he recognized Bass, he aimed his gun but was hit in the chest by Bass's third shot. He tumbled backward and rolled down the railroad embankment.

The two other men on the floor were both dead, shot in the back, and as he turned each body over, the gold badge of a private security company pinned to each man's vest gleamed. The clerk, still kneeling at the safe, lowered his hands. As he stood up, he asked, "Who are these bastards?"

Bass answered, "That one there is Brack Cornett, and the one outside was Bill Whitley. Don't recognize this other fella, but the Cornett-Whitley gang's the most notorious train robbers in Texas." Bass was replacing the spent cartridges in his Colt. "Unfortunately for these two boys here, they're also the most lethal gang in Texas, too." Bass jumped from the car and went forward to the engine. The engineer and fireman were unhurt, and Bass told them to sound the whistle. It was time to get going again.

Chapter 16

1:30 p.m., May 24, 1888
E. P. & S. W. Station
Austin, Texas

The train was an hour late arriving at the station; Bass learned there was another southbound train on the main line ninety minutes behind them. By the time they reached Austin, the second train had nearly caught up. Bass finished the trip in the dining car alone with the two men he'd left tied up on the tracks. It turned out the two were brothers Rube Burrow and his younger brother James. Both men were well-known train robbers in Alabama, and more than one railroad offered a reward for their capture. Upon arrival at the Austin depot, the twine that Conductor Potts had used was replaced with nickel-plated manacles, and the two men were taken to the city jail by the beat officer and a sergeant. Bass went straight to his hotel for a change of clothes. The close work in the mail car had left blood stains on his shirt and vest.

As he walked into the Winslow Hotel, he stopped at the desk and checked for messages. There was one from Sally.

My Love— All's well here. Lillian is happy and getting big. We both miss her Daddy very much. Please be careful. You pursue a madman with no sense of humanity.— Love Sally

The wire was dated the morning he left and before she would have gotten his last wire. He paused for a moment on the stairs to think of his ladies, and his throat began to tighten as he continued to his room. Behind the closed door to his room, he cursed his involvement in the absurd nature of the Annihilator Case and the people he'd met in trying to bring the thing to a conclusion.

He changed his shirt and transferred his badge to his silver vest. Then he washed his face and hands at the basin and decided he'd need a drink before meeting with Grooms Lee and Cillian O'Dell. He went back downstairs and into the saloon, where he took a seat at a table in a quiet corner. No sooner had he sat down than the two men he'd just been thinking of walked into the saloon, spotted him and sat down.

Cillian was smiling when he said, "Boyo? Ere ye tryin to win the lawman a' the year award? Saints, at was some fine work on the train, my dear. Proud to call you friend, I am."

"That really was something, Frank," Grooms added. "The Cornett-Whitley Gang all in one arrest. I heard you shot three . . . did you get Brack? He was supposed to be the toughest."

Bass nodded and took a swallow from his glass, "Yup, and Bill Whitley, and a fella I didn't know, Fitch, somethin'. The Burrow brothers are coolin' their heels in the city slams. I believe."

"You know," said Grooms, "this ain't your territory. You can claim the rewards for yourself."

"Well, I ain't one to collect on blood money. Let's let the city of Austin have that. Horses and weapons, too. I will take whatever's comin' on the Burrow Brothers, though. Set it up for Lily's schooling.'"

"Aye, some good'll come of it all then. By the by, there's a cailin reporter, who's much too fair a maid to be single, wantin' to talk to you, bein' the hero that you are. Now, as a favor to my friend, I can relate the tale as well as any. You bein' a married man with a wee babe might not want to trouble your good self," Cillian offered.

Bass smiled at him. "Just make me sound good, and it's all yours."

Cillian excused himself and primped in the saloon mirror before walking into the lobby. Both men chuckled, watching him go.

"So, hero, what'd you find at the Greenwood Cemetery?" Grooms asked.

"Chief? It's the damndest story ya ever heard. The local Marshal took me out to the cemetery, but he didn't want to sit in on the interview 'cause he'd heard stories and had some experience with the old man, the sexton that looks after the place. And believe me, this ol' bird is somethin else. His place is filled with old books and scrolls that prob'ly he knew by heart. Spells, potions, curses maybe, and histories of witchcraft, the like. And that's the bottom line.

"He says that the fella we're lookin' for is thinkin he's savin' the human race from the witches of Austin. The old man said that's what the salt's about. Witches hate salt 'cause I guess it cleanses the witchiness outta folks. And the cross on the forehead? Same thing. S'posed to mean the woman's been cleaned a' witchery.

"He said the culprit thinks he's a magus, not a warlock, which is different, I guess. The old man said, and he was old, all bent over, long white hair, said he was a hundred forty-two years old . . . and he looked it. Anyway, the old man said that he himself was a magus of some high degree in the Yellow Dawn somethin'. I tried to take notes, but he went too fast. So . . . that's the gist.

"Oh. *Oh*, and the old man said somethin about why he commits his crimes on the first of the month. It goes to an old ritual that says, *a pinch and a punch, it's the first of the month*. The pinch part refers to a pinch of salt. I don't know, but it seemed Weatherford is a hotbed for witchery 'cause they have a tomb someplace in that cemetery where they buried a witch and her sweetheart alive. Now, the old man said all that was hooey, but it shows that some folks believe that guff. The local man told me about another state asylum just outside'a Dallas in Terrel. I went out there and talked to the Superintendent, a lady I'd just as soon never cross paths with again. Anyway, I told her what we were lookin' into and what we found out about witches, but she had nothin to offer. That's about all I got."

Chief Lee had been listening intently, and when Bass finished, he raised his eyebrows.

"That sounds like it dovetails with what I found at the University. I went into the library and asked if anyone could tell me what *Malleus Maleficarum* meant. The girl at the desk had no idea, but she found a professor in the library that had some Latin and he said it meant *the hammer of witches*. Yeah . . . so with that, I asked if I could take a look, not that I'd be able to read it, but I'd never seen a four-hundred-year-old book. Anyway, they ain't got one . . . but the girl said she could cross reference it and see what she found, see? Well, this little girl came back with a what-a-ya-call-it. . . abstract? Excerpt? I don't know, but basically, it's a book about Heresy. How to recognize witches, and how to run a witchcraft trial. Then it talks about torture and punishment and burning people at the stake . . . and basically that's when I figured out it was just our guy's way of rationalizing the crimes he's committing."

"What about Cill? Did he say what he found out?"

"Not yet, I guess he was waitin' till we were all together."

"Yeah, I'm gonna get another drink, be right back."

On his way to the bar, Bass was able to see the handsome mick Sergeant pitchin' the train story to the reporter. He was smiling as big as Sunday, and Bass noticed she was, too. He also noticed she was too young for him.

When he sat back down, he told Grooms again about the fancy bathtub in the Sanderson Hotel, about how it folded down from a cabinet against the wall and heated the water right there from an inside pipe. Grooms said he'd heard two of the hotels in town had 'em, the Diplomat and the Congress House, but that he'd never seen one himself. He said he was still impressed with the electric lights goin' up downtown. Bass then told him about the 'crapper' his friend Silas Pratt had installed downstairs at his house, and Grooms seemed impressed with that, too.

Just as Bass finished his second whiskey, Cillian O'Dell sat down with one for himself and another for Bass.

"Tanks to you, friend Frank, for lettin' me charm the sweetest darlin I ever saw. Fiona's her name, and it sounds like sweet music just to say it. Here's to you and yer heroics."

"So it went well with the reporter, did it?" Grooms asked.

"*Ach* such a one as herself. And she's doin me the honor of supper tomorrow night."

"And you don't think she might be a little young for you, Sergeant?" Bass asked.

"Young, is it? Why, she's fully twenty-tree and a recent graduate of newspaper school, so let's have no more a' that." O'Dell smiled again. "She's cast her spell on me she has, and it's thankful I am, she did."

Bass looked at Grooms, and they both started to laugh.

Finally, Bass said, "Then I guess the interview was a success?"

"Indeed it was. Especially when I told how you single-handed dispatched ten villains with your blazing pistols and saved two old ladies from losing their life savings."

Bass stared at O'Dell straight-faced and said, "I did what, again?"

Grooms leaned into Bass. "They prob'ly won't print it cause they all know Cillian O'Dell . . . but if they do, it'll be good publicity for ya. Think about it. Could be another one a' them little dime books written about it."

They all chuckled at the reference.

"Cillian, old man? I hope supper tomorrow works out well for you both. Now, I'm hungry . . . let's get somethin to eat."

The Chief hailed a waiter, and they all ordered dinner. Grooms said he'd pay 'cause he got a daily stipend, and if he didn't use it, the City Council might take it away.

During and after dinner, Bass and Chief Lee explained to O'Dell what they'd found out about the subjects they'd checked on as per the Annihilator's letter. When they were finished, O'Dell began his report on the three names in the letter. He opened his notebook.

"Them women . . . *witches*, they were, it said, who were all accused and tried for witchery in Britain hundreds'a years ago. Fifteen and sixteen hundreds. Tried they were for everything from child murder to cannibalism, and the ones found guilty was executed. Some was burned at the stake or drowned. 'Interestin' thing is this Mary Hicks had a daughter Elizabeth, and they was both executed. The one Catharine Repond . . . she was strangled, and den burned, in case the strangling didn't take. And that, my friends is what I found in there. Bunch a guff, ya ask me."

All three were silent when O'Dell finished, trying to find some hint of the murderer's identity in what had been learned.

Bass recapped. "It's obvious here we're dealing with a madman who thinks he's doing Austin and the world a favor killing witches. I think the exercises we've been through seem to indicate that he feels justified in his actions. Serial killers aren't new boys, but this one, I think, is different. It seemed at first he was targeting hookers, like many of those killers in the past. And whores are easy targets, let's face it. They get close and personal with men they don't know for money, usually at night and, often as not, in secret. Is there something in all this that might help us set a trap for him?"

Grooms thought for a moment. "It seems to me that, from what you said, we shouldn't expect to hear from him again till midnight on June 1st. Makes sense, right?"

"Aye, but we mustn't drop our guard though. He may find a witch that he thinks needs fixin' before then, my dears."

8:45 p.m., May 24, 1888
Winslow Hotel Lobby
Austin, Texas

Chief Lee and Sergeant O'Dell left the hotel for the night, and each went home. Lee was still suffering, but only mildly from the effects of alcohol withdrawal, and Bass wondered, had it been himself, would he have handled it so well. He'd seen firsthand the effects of prolonged laudanum use, weight loss, sleep deprived, and eventually sinking into the restless oblivion from which many never recovered. He'd needed laudanum himself, and recently too, but he limited his use.

The stuff was cheap, effective, and easy to find, and those with prolonged pain and limited means had no other alternative. With morphine, the addictive effects were less severe, but supply was limited and required a doctor's care. Doc Spalding had used morphine early in Sally's delivery to ease some of the pain. And he carried a supply with him when he traveled on manhunts or recently on the short cattle drive at home. He'd asked for it after his most recent episode involving the kidnapping of two young girls. During that rescue, he'd been stabbed while on the prairie in winter and was disabled for a time when he might have been in pursuit.

The wound had become septic, requiring the use of a bromide solution, which caused nearly as much suffering as the wound itself. Had he the morphine, he may have gotten to a doctor before the infection began. All these considerations flooded Bass's thinking and increased his respect for the fortitude of Grooms Lee.

Bass finally got to bed around 9:30 p.m. and read for a brief while. The day had been full, and he was starting to realize that train travel could be as tiring as the trail. By 10:00 p.m., he was sound asleep.

11:15 p.m., May 24, 1888
Benoit's Boarding House
225 Neches Street
Austin, Texas

He lay on his bed in the darkened room, sweat streaming from every pore and excruciating pain erupting each time he tried to move. *Damn, damn, damn. Bloody hell to the peasant and his popgun. Infected? Of course, it's infected, you damn fool. Look at it . . . swelled up tighter than a hatband. There's no question now . . . it's been nearly a week, a week?*

How would I know? The notches, of course, the notches on the nightstand, hmm . . . six. But is it really six? The hallucinations, the dreams, are so real. How can I be sure?

Did I send to C. C.? Think, blast it. The last thing you need is your boss to come looking for you. Two notes. I remember now one to C. C. and the other to the police, ha!

That's right, two notes.

So that means then, six days makes it . . . God help me! It's the twenty-fourth! I must see a doctor, any doctor, it can be any doctor, but I must solve this infection. I have so little time, so little time to finish. In the morning, then another note to C. C. and a doctor.

He swallowed the last of his second bottle and fell into fitful sleep.

7:15 a.m., May 25, 1888
Winslow Hotel
Austin, Texas

Bass wished he was an early riser by habit; he wished it almost every morning. The plain fact was he did not wake up easy . . . everything about early rising was hard and uncomfortable. Winters were the worst, of course, when the bed was warm, and the floors were cold. Especially now with Sally back to her old playful self, early mornings, working mornings were a strange subtle punishment. Paulo could wake up at any time and happily whistle a merry tune, but Bass on an early day needed a solid hour to be coherent at all.

That's why today, this morning, he relished the extra time in bed. He had thought about it last night and decided that this morning, he would take the morning off. He'd loll in bed till nine or so, and then once the sun had warmed the room, he'd wash up and head downstairs for breakfast. He'd treat himself to a big breakfast with an extra pot of coffee and then sit in one of the easy chairs in the lobby and read the paper. Later, he might stroll to the hotel veranda, where he'd claim one of the wicker-made rockers, and he'd sit and watch Austin go by.

He enjoyed the days in El Paso when he and Bart Mariany would sit on the boardwalk, feet on the hitch-rails, sip coffee, and talk about outlaws, criminals he could understand. Outlaws that could be found and arrested for crimes like cattle-rustling, horse theft, or bank robbery. Like his work on the train yesterday, outlaws gunning to get rich and needing to be stopped before they hurt a bystander or someone innocent.

He checked his Elgin again, 7:32 a.m. And the bastard was still at large. They knew what he was doing now and had a good idea when he'd do it again. Just not where or to whom. *'No idea how to figure this one out. By God, we need a break. We need him to slip up. What was it Gilmore said? He'll be wicked clever? He has to mess up somewhere; they always do. We just have to be able to see it when it happens . . . be able to recognize it.*

He looked at his Elgin again, 7:35 a.m. Bass leaned back onto his pillow, his mind racing with the possible mistakes their madman might make. He glanced out the window and shook his head slowly. Then, he threw off the blanket, washed his face and cleaned his teeth, dressed, and went downstairs for coffee. As he walked down the stairs, he thought to himself, *that's the problem with time off. Your body might be ready, but if your head ain't into it, 'might just as well go to work.*

7:45 a.m., May 25, 1888
Benoit's Boarding House
225 Neches Street
Austin, Texas
This one will be perfect. Open on Saturday, and I can take the trolly almost all the way. He wrote the address on a note pad and closed the *Austin Physician's Registry* he'd gotten from his mother before coming to town. He was to see any of the members in the registry as a condition to come here. Fortunately, she did not ask for proof of his visits. And the money kept appearing regularly, which he did appreciate. *The pittance I get from C.C. wouldn't keep me in razors.* The one downtown had been accommodating, though, providing an ample supply of laudanum, the tincture of powdered opium and alcohol that he was supposed to use "to ease my mind." *Well it certainly was useless in preventing infection, that's for certain.*

He was dressed as any other worker would be in this part of town: dungarees, a stained linen shirt, and steel reenforced work boots that rose above the ankle. Fortunately, the loose-fitting leg of the dungarees covered the gauze and cotton bandage he'd applied before leaving.

He used a bamboo cane and limped only slightly, not enough that anyone would notice. His only concern was the look of his face, gaunt and gray . . . slick with sweat. He pulled the twill newsboy cap as far over his face as he could and left his room. As he eased himself down the stairs, the widow Mrs. Benoit—a lovely older lady—said good morning. He tipped his hat and smiled, asking that she send over another note to C. C. that he was seeing a doctor and should be back next week.

The woman's eyesight was not what it had been, and she didn't notice the grimace on his face or the sweat stain at his collar. He thanked her, and she wished him a pleasant day. He closed the door behind him and walked as regularly as he could to the trolley stop and waited. Thirty minutes later, he entered the waiting room of Doctor Lawrence Procket, *Internist*.

9:30 a.m., May 25, 1888
Doctor Lawrence Procket's Office
588 San Jacinto Ave.
Austin, Texas

"Can I help you, sir?" The nurse was not one of *them*. She did not have the wanton aura of the sisterhood, the blasphemous harlots of Satan. His senses were still acute to *them*. Though his body had been corrupted by infection his brain had remained alert and his senses keen. It explained why the pain was so intense, so invasive.

"I'd like to see the doctor, please. It's quite urgent."

"Are you one of his regular patients?"

"No, I'm new. I was impressed by his credentials in the Physician's Registry." She smiled at that. Doctors were always susceptible to professional acknowledgments.

"Please have a seat and let me see if he can see you. Can I have your name?"

"Yes, of course, it's Brian McDougal."

"And the nature of your complaint?"

"It's terribly foolish, I'm afraid, but I shot myself in the leg when cleaning my pistol."

"Oh dear, when was this?"

"A few days ago. Please, I'm in serious discomfort." She closed the door to the doctor's office behind her and emerged a few minutes later. "You can go in now, Mr. McDougal."

The doctor's examining room was the same as every other one he'd been in, and he'd seen more thana few when he was in the hospital.

"Good morning, . . . Brian, is it? Edna said you have a gunshot wound, yes?"

"That's right, a silly thing, embarrassing really. I was cleaning my pistol, and it went off. I removed the bullet myself, it' wasn't very deep, I hoped it would heal on its own and with God's Grace."

"*Uh-huh.* My God, that must have been quite painful. Why in the world would you not see a doctor right away?"

"I should explain, I am originally from Boston and my religion, I declared for the Christian Science Fellowship some years ago, requires complete faith in God's healing power, so I stopped seeing physicians at all. However, the extent of infection and severity of pain has made me question my faith, which is why I'm here."

"I see. Yes, I've heard of Faith-Based Healing in religions denying even the simplest of medical care to children. Many such children die of disease that could have been prevented easily with modern medical intervention, you know."

"Yes, I have heard that from other disillusioned members."

"Very well. First, I must advise that, as a matter of form, I report all gunshot wounds to the police. The local Police Chief has requested it, and almost all doctors comply. If this is a problem for you, I'm afraid I won't be able to treat you."

"Yes, that's fine. It only adds to my embarrassment."

"Let's have a look then, shall we? *Hmm,* that's quite an infection that's developed. You must be in terrible pain. The infection is quite advanced, but I don't believe it has reached sepsis. Normally, I would apply sulpha, but I believe your infection is too advanced for that alone. I think one of the mercurials would work best, yes, and fastest. Wait here a moment."

The doctor went to a storeroom and returned with a tray of syringes and a packet. "First, I'm going to give you an injection of morphine. This will kill the pain you're experiencing and allow for the application of Sulpha to the wound. This would ordinarily cause severe pian. Finally, an injection of a mercurial drug to kill the infection, even if it has entered your blood. This will make you disoriented and perhaps dizzy, but that will pass. I'll give you two bottles of laudanum for the pain when the morphine wears off. The

Sulpha is applied locally, and the injection of the mercury should have an affect by oh . . . tomorrow evening. So, are you ready?"

"Oh yes, doctor. *Quite*."

The doctor gave him first the morphine injection and waited several minutes for the effects to begin. Then, he applied a sprinkling of Sulpha powder to the wound. Though Sulpha was primarily a preventive drug, it would serve to guard against further infection. Brian McDougal cried out despite the morphine but slowly recovered as the pain subsided. Finally, it was down to the mercurial injection. Brian felt nothing from that, though he expected he might later in the day.

"Now, Mr. McDougal, will you give me your date of birth for my report?"

Brian McDougal feigned incapacity by shaking and moaning as if the final injection was too much for him.

The doctor approached him to see to the problem, and McDougal grabbed the man's smock with his left hand and pulled the doctor's throat close enough to be reached by the folding scalpel in his right. There was a swift swipe of the blade, an explosion of blood, and Doctor Procket was eased to the floor, clutching at his throat by McDougal's left hand. A few spasms shook his body and then the good doctor was still.

McDougal took a position behind the examining room's door and called to Edna the nurse. "Edna! Come in here. Quickly!"

The door opened, and Edna saw the body of her employer on the floor, blood seeping from his wound. Before she could scream, McDougal had covered her mouth with his left hand and again applied his scalpel with his right. He held her upright until he felt her body sag and then dropped her to the floor alongside the doctor.

Brian McDougal cleaned the blood from his face and covered his stained clothing with a lightweight evening coat. He limped out of Doctor Procket's office and into the sun, carrying his bottles of laudanum to the trolley stop. He didn't have to wait long.

Chapter 17

7:15 a.m., May 26, 18887
Doctor Lawrence Procket's Office
588 San Jacinto Ave.
Austin, Texas

It was Saturday. The cleaning service that Doctor Procket employed was fifteen minutes late arriving at his office. The two women were Mexican laborers and didn't speak English, so when they discovered the bodies of the doctor and his nurse, they ran screaming from the building, hysterical with fright and speaking rapidly in Spanish.

Their supervisor had left to go to another job and, it being early on a Saturday, there was no one else in the vicinity to help. The area was predominantly offices which were generally un-occupied early on Saturday. It was obvious by their expressions and agitated state that something was terribly wrong, but because no one was about at that hour, they did not know what to do.

Between them, they decided to find their supervisor. The other job she was going to was somewhere in the area, so they began searching the nearby buildings and calling her name, hoping to find her and make a report.

8:00 a.m., May 26, 1888
1250 Fourteenth Street
Austin, Texas

Roland Vasquez, the beat officer for the Fourteenth Street area, was hailed by an attractive lady standing on her porch. The house was not large, but it was recently painted, and the shrubbery and lawn all looked nicely manicured.

"Yes, ma'am, how can I help you?"

"Officer, my name is Maryanne Procket, my husband is Doctor Procket. He has an office south of here on San Jacinto. He didn't come home last night. He didn't come home for lunch yesterday as he promised, either. Have there been any accidents reported? I just walked up to the hospital, and he's not there; they know him. I'm afraid something has happened to him, and I'm worried."

"Of course, I understand. No, there've been no accidents or serious crimes reported yesterday or last night. Where is his office, did you say?"

"588 Trinity, he has a sign out front. I have an awful feeling about this officer. It's so very unlike Lawrence to stay away like this."

Officer Vasquez tipped his hat and mounted up for the ride to San Jacinto Ave. He turned his horse's head to the south and spurred the animal to an increased gait. It took only ten minutes to find the office, and when he entered, he found, first, two mops and a pail in the anteroom and then the same horrible sight in the examining room that had frightened the cleaners.

Officer Vasquez's mouth went dry, and his stomach rolled so that he had to use the pail in the anteroom. His senses caught up with him shortly after that, and he ran outside, hoping to find someone to send to headquarters for help. Still, there was no one to be seen, so he mounted his horse and galloped all the way to Congress Avenue and Peach Street to make his report to the desk sergeant.

"Slow down a bit, Rolly, slow down, or you'll bust. Now, what did you see?"

"I'll say it again, two bodies in the doc's office, throats cut, blood everywhere, flies . . . I'm getting sick again thinkin' about it."

"Well, good God, don't think about it, then." The weekend desk sergeant was a retired County Sheriff named Eli Doud. He was nearing sixty, but was still spry and lean enough to pass for younger.

"Here's what you do. Go to this address and ring Sergeant Cillian O'Dell. He's workin' the Annihilator killings, and this sounds close enough." He handed Vasquez a note with O'Dell's address, and the officer took off on his horse again.

Cillian O'Dell lived only a few blocks from headquarters on Peach Street. He was able to afford the nicer neighborhood because he still received his pension from the City of Brooklyn back east.

When he got to O'Dell's address, he twisted the ringer on the front door and waited. From inside, he heard, *The bloody goddamn is it this hour of a Sattidy?*

Vasquez yelled back, "It's another killin', Sergeant. Doud said to get you."

"Bloody, bloody, damn. Alright, den, wait where ye are . . . I'll be right out."

After five minutes or so, the front door opened and out stepped Cillian O'Dell, dressed in a tailored suit of clothes, with a very pretty redheaded girl on his arm.

"Darlin? This officer, see how fine he looks. He'll see you home safe. Duty calls, you know."

"You will tell me all about it, though, won't you Cill?"

"Well, a' course I will, darlin'. Alright then. Be off with ya. Officer, I'm takin' your animal, hail a cab, and I'll see you back at headquarters. When ya get there, send a couple a hoofers and the doctor . . . oh and the picture guy, too . . . now where is she? Where's the stiff?"

"It's a man and a woman, Sarge. 588 San Jacinto Ave. Doctor Procket."

"A man too, you say? Ain't dis novel then."

11:55 a.m., May 26, 1888
Police Headquarters
Congress at Peach Street
Austin, Texas

Bass had spent the morning at the office of the *Austin Statesman*, reading and rereading the accounts of the Annihilator's killings right after they occurred. He verified that no mention had been made of the salt, the missing heart, or the cross tattoo. He'd read each account over and over, looking for some difference or discrepancy in the killer's modus operandi. Still, aside from the locations being different, everything, every detail was the same. The conditions of the body, the implements used, the size and location of the indentation in the skull.

Everything, damnit, everything except the location, which would always be a matter of chance and opportunity. The locations. The location. Where did Heeltap say he found the dog? By a lumber mill or lumber yard. What was the name?

And that's why he was at police headquarters at noon on Saturday. He knew he couldn't reveal how he knew about the dog, but he wanted to know the name of the lumber yard Heeltap . . . Gandy Dave had said was nearby. He knocked on Groom's office door, but there was no answer, so he went back to the front desk.

"Still lookin' for the Chief, Sheriff, got any idea where he might be?"

"Yeah, Marshal, as a matter of fact, he might be in with Sergeant O'Dell, been another murder."

"What!? This is, this is . . . what the hell day is it, anyway?"

"Saturday."

"The date, man, the date?"

"Oh . . . the twenty-sixth."

"Damn . . . he's early. Jesus, what happened?" Bass trotted down the hall to the interrogation room where the Chief and O'Dell usually met.

He walked in without knocking, "What the hell, what the damn hell, boys? Why didn't you come get me?"

Both men looked, and Cillian said. "Good mornin' then to you too, boyo. Please, take a seat."

"We sent a hoofer to your hotel, but you weren't there, Frank," Grooms said.

Bass looked sheepishly at his demands. "Oh . . . yeah. I was at the newspaper readin' over the accounts of the first three killings. What about this new one Doud just told me about?"

"Relax, darlin'. It ain't one a' the ritual killin's. It must be the same bastard, though, but it seems he's branchin' out," Cillian said.

Grooms began, "That's right, this time he's killed a doctor and his nurse over on Trinity. Throats slit. I'll let Cill tell you about it."

Bass looked at the Sergeant. "Well . . . what?"

"Marshal, sit down, will ye? Hurts me neck to talk up to anyone."

Bass sat in the third chair at the table and took a deep breath.

"So it's like this. Sometime yesterday, 'ccording to our good Doctor Flotter, a patient named Brian McDougal went to see the doc and left him and his nurse dead. Throats cut bled out on the floor."

"How do you know it was a patient?"

O'Dell leaned back. "It's an informed guess, the doctor had started writing a report on a man of that name but never finished. There were also needles and medicine packs on the floor under the bodies."

"What kind of medicine?"

"Morphine, mercury, and a package of sulpha."

"How about instruments? Were there any instruments around?"

"None. Looked for 'em too."

"Okay. So the name is an alias, but whoever he is, he's hurt. Hence, the morphine. His wound must be infected, hence the sulpha. I don't know about the mercury. We'll have to ask Doc Flotter what it might be used for. Oh, say while I'm thinkin about it, what's the name of the lumber company on the southeast side?"

"That's Gardiners, right along the tracks," Grooms answered.

"And where was the doctor's office?"

"588 San Jacinto Avenue, a couple blocks away. What 're ya getting at?" Cillian asked.

"Just a hunch. A long shot. Probably nothin.'"

"You will keep us appraised, though, right?" Grooms asked.

"Oh yeah, yeah. Like I said a long shot, a hunch. If anything even remotely connected comes up, I'll let you know. Anybody want lunch?"

"Not I. The scene's a wee bit too fresh in me mind," Cillian excused himself.

Grooms begged off, too, explaining he had a Council meeting.

"Okay, guess I'll head on down to the Nightstick for a quick bite. See you guys later." Bass stood up and left the room. Just before he got to Doud's desk, he stopped short. "Holy . . . *of course* he is." Bass dashed back down the hall and into the interrogation room again. "Boys? Try this out. Go back to the Willow Street shooting. The little gun, what was it?"

"A 6mm Flobert," Cillian said.

"Right, it was fired once. Suppose it hit our boy in the arm or leg and went through. Then suppose our guy wraps it up tight so we see no blood leavin' the scene, and he goes home. Let's also suppose, since he'd rather not walk around in broad daylight, that he treats it himself at home, and it turns septic. It's the end of the month. He's got a deadline, right? Forgive the pun. He has to go out on a Saturday morning to get the wound treated. And he picks a doctor; what's his name?"

"Procket," Both the Chief and O'Dell said together.

"Right, the poor SOBs in the right place at the wrong time. I'll bet Doc Flotter says mercury is used to treat infections."

O'Dell thought for a moment. "I like it, Marshal."

Grooms nodded his head, too. "So what does that give us?"

Bass smiled. "Location. Think about it, if you're hurtin real bad, so bad you'll risk seeing a doctor, how far from home would you travel?"

"Not too bloody far, boyo. You're right. It feels right," O'Dell said.

"It's a very likely scenario, but . . . I think it's thin," Grooms said.

Bass agreed. "You're right, Chief, but it's a start. Show me where the lumber yard and the doctor's office is."

Cillian put red dots on the city street map that hung on the wall. Bass drew a red circle around the two. "It's a start."

8:45 p.m., May 26, 1888
Benoit Boarding House
225 Neches Street
Austin, Texas

He woke from a protected sleep, a peaceful, restive sleep. His leg still hurt, but the swelling had gone down, and he no longer noticed the smell of dying flesh. His laudanum was next to his bed, but he decided to forgo the treatment and ask Mrs. Benoit for a tray. It was the first time he'd felt hungry in a week.

"Mrs. Benoit? Mrs. Benoit, dear."

She was downstairs cleaning up after dinner. Her hearing was not the best anymore, so she went to the landing to find out what he wanted.

"Yes? What can I do for you? Are you feeling well?"

He answered in the pleasant tone she had come to expect, "Oh yes, much better, thank you for asking. I wonder if I may have a tray of leftovers. I don't wish to put you out."

She smiled and said, "Of course you may. I'll bring it right up."

He closed the door, saying, "Just leave it on the table as usual. I'll pick it up once I've straightened up my room."

Mrs. Benoit liked to hear that her rooms were being cared for. She did as she was instructed and left a tray on the hall table outside his room. After he was sure she'd left, he brought the tray into his room and ate ravenously.

When he had finished, he felt exhausted again and after putting the tray back on the hall table, he drank some of his laudanum and fell into a deep sleep.

9:15 p.m., May 27, 1888
The Winslow Hotel
Austin, Texas.

Bass finished eating at 8:30 p.m. and went to his room directly. He had spent the whole day and part of the previous one canvassing the neighborhoods that were circled in red on Cillian O'Dell's map of Austin. Working with him was Sheriff Eli Doud, the only man the police department could spare. With summer coming and this being an election year, many of the politicians in Austin were holding or planning rallies for supporters to recruit volunteers for campaign work. This meant increased pressure on the police department for crowd control, and the extra help could only come from the beat officers.

Bass and Doud worked methodically canvasing the twelve square blocks in a grid pattern. By necessity, the work was on foot pretty much and door to door. By the end of the day, both men were exhausted. They reported directly to the Chief and assisted Cillian O'Dell whenever necessary, but in essence, they were a two-man Annihilator Task Force.

When Bass got back to his hotel he had received a note from Gandy Dave Lomax.

The note was short and to the point. It read, *The hell you doin roustin' about in my territory? Be careful you don't queer my play.*

Bass remembered that Gandy Dave had isolated that area because of the dog he'd found with its throat cut. As it had turned out, Gandy Dave wasn't too far from the target. He decided that tomorrow, he'd leave a note on the bench and suggest a meeting. In fact, Bass was a little surprised he hadn't heard from Gandy Dave sooner.

Chapter 18

8:30 a.m., May 27, 1888
   Dining Room
   Hotel Winslow
   Austin, Texas

Bass had just finished his breakfast and walked out of the hotel to Congress Ave. The morning was bright, sunny, and cool, the perfect spring day, so Bass decided to walk to the park. He left his note under the foot of the bench they'd agreed to use and then decided to sit for a bit. The sun was warm on his face, warm enough to make him a little dozy. He closed his eyes and ran through all the directions and locations this case had taken him.

He'd been away from Sally and Lil for almost two weeks now, and in that time, he'd been to Dallas, Fort Worth, and Weatherford, Texas, for interviews. *What? What were they?* Porter was a weird old duck but certainly no suspect or even a witness, and the Waters woman at the other asylum, she wasn't much of anything. Only two things with any societal benefit had happened during that time.

One was that Marion Gilmore, a scourge if there ever was one, was no longer a threat to the vulnerable young women in his charge, and two was the removal of public enemies Brack Cornett and Bill Whitely and their gang of train robbers.

They were still no closer to apprehending this Annihilator bastard, who was the real threat to public safety. Aside from the three women he'd slaughtered, he'd also killed four innocent people to cover his tracks. The man had no soul, no conscience. He was the closest thing to pure evil that Bass had ever encountered, and he was due to act again in four days. Surely, a man that depraved would have to be known somewhere to someone. But where else to check? The only practical advantage that law enforcement had generated was his probable location, which was really only a theory anyway. Time was running out for the next victim, and there wasn't much he could do about it.

Bass recognized the frustration building inside him and knew it would do him no good. His thought processes had to stay clear and open to anything that might present itself. He thought, hoped, that maybe Gandy Dave could have something to add. Anything would be welcome. For now, it'd be checking back in with Grooms and Cillian and then back to pounding the streets with Eli Doud.

Bass walked back to the hotel's barn and saddled Dotty for the ride first to the police station and then out to Gardiner's Lumber Yard. It was a hunch he wanted to check that maybe the guy had a day job at Gardiner's. He'd ask for anyone who might have missed work lately or was walking with a limp.

At the station, he stopped in first at the Chief's office.

"Hey, Grooms, what's goin on today?

"Frank! Glad you're here. Just the lawman I need today."

Naturally, Bass became wary.

"Whatdaya want, Grooms? You don't say stuff like that less'en you want something."

"Frank, I'm hurt . . . *no;* actually, we have a family disturbance goin on right now, well, it's been goin off and on since last night. The beat officer just came in and said it flared up again this mornin. I was hoping, what with your knowledge of married life, you'd take a ride out there, see if you can't settle the couple down before they hurt each other or somebody else."

"*Uh-huh.* Where Grooms?"

"Oh, nearby, easy to get to."

"Where Grooms?"

"I told you, practically right around the corner."

"Where Grooms?

"Alright, it's out toward the asylum on Marcos Street."

"Jesus, Grooms . . . take me a half hour just to get there."

"Yeah, I know, but I got a meeting with Mayor Nalle this morning, and Cill's working on three cases. It needs someone senior, Frank. Will ya do it for me?"

"Yeah, I guess, but I won't get to meet up with Eli till this afternoon. Can you send somebody? He'll be working the Second Street area."

"Sure, sure. Anything you want. Thanks, Frank."

Bass scowled at his friend, put his hat back on, and went back out to Dotty.

Emmaline and Henry Rouche were arguing. They started last night, went to bed, woke up this morning, and started up again over breakfast.

"You know you haven't even tried to hold a steady job since you hurt your damned toe. Now we're bein' evicted, you lazy ol man."

"Emmaline, please find somethin else to whine about. You know I can't hardly walk right since that draft horse stepped on me. Doc told me he might hafta cut my toe off if it don't heal."

"And maybe if you'd get off your fat keister and go back to work like they asked ya, we'd have money for the rent. Ain't nothin wrong with your toe."

Emmaline picked up Henry's pistol that hung on a hook near the door.

"No, and there ain't nothin wrong with my aim neither . . . come here and stand still. I'll fix your damn toe."

"Put my gun down now, woman. That's my gun and ain't to be handled by no woman folk. You're liable to hurt someone."

"I'm a sight more than liable to Henry. Now get out the door and go to work!"

"I already tol' you. I can't nearly walk . . . how 'm I s'posed to work? You crazy old woman."

"Old? I wer'nt half as old then as I am living with you. Look what you've drove me to."

Bass heard them a block away. Once he'd tied off Dotty, he slowly approached the front door. It was wide open. "Excuse me, folks . . . I'm with the police . . ."

"The Police?" Emmaline said, "We just chased one a' you boys away about an hour ago. You're a bigun though . . . maybe you can tell this worthless old man he's gotta go to work, lest we be 'victed."

Henry turned to Bass. "I've tried tellin' her I can't work cause I gotta bad toe. 'Draft horse stepped on it."

"That so? You can't walk?"

"Not hardly. Doc said he'd amputate it if it didn't heal. I don't wanna live my days with an amputated toe."

"No, I suppose not. Mrs.—what's the last name again?"

"*Rouche*, Emmaline Rouche, and he don't have no trouble getting down to that gin palace on the corner and comin home smellin' a' whiskey."

"Is 'at so, Mr. Rouche?"

"No, I gimps my way down to old Marley's house and keep him company on his sick bed. And yes, I do have a taste while I'm there, but I never get too waggly, and I comes home early."

"That's right, comes home smellin' a' whiskey and expects me to slave for him makin' his supper."

"I may be off base here, but ain't that what you're s'posed to do, Mrs. Rouche?"

"Well, not if he don't bring home nothin to cook, so I'm starvin' right along with him."

"I see. Henry, where do you work?"

"I work out here for C. C. Slaughter. His pens are out here, and I work carin' for his animals, feedin' 'em and what not. We grain 'em out for a month before they go to the meat packers."

"Oh? What happens there?"

"We bring 'em down to his processing plant for to make steaks, whatdaya think?"

"And where is this plant?"

"Down by the railroad yard, crossed the river, cause a' the smell."

"Okay . . . Henry? I'm gonna go see your boss and ask him to give you a sittin' down job. And also to advance some money to you so you can pay rent. Emmaline, how much do you need for rent and food shopping?"

"Well, twenty dollars oughta do nicely."

"Alright then. Emmaline, you put that gun away; it ain't legal for you to be wavin' it all around . . . especially with me bein' here. I see it again, and I'll arrest ya on the spot."

"*Oh.*"

"That's right. Now, I want you both to come out here on your porch and sit in these two chairs. I want you both to sit and enjoy the sun and not say a word to each other till I get back. Agreed?"

Both of them agreed, and Bass went out to Dotty. "So Henry. Where do I find this C. C. Slaughter's feedlot?"

Bass rode to the feedlot and explained the situation to the foreman there, Al Kaminsky. He had no idea about Henry's toe and wondered why he hadn't been to work.

"He's normally a reliable guy, takes instructions well, don't shirk. His job'll be waiting for him when his toe heels."

Bass asked, "Is there somethin maybe he could do while sittin' so he could get outta the house and back to work?"

Kaminsky thought for a moment. "I guess in the meantime, if he wants to come back, I can find somethin that don't require a lotta movin' about."

Kaminsky had the bookkeeper give Bass the twenty dollars as what he called 'tide money.' It was meant to tide Henry over till he could get back to work again. Then Bass asked a couple of unrelated questions.

"You folks have a meat packing plant down by the railroad?"

"Sure do. C. C.'s got two others like it in Fort Worth and Amarillo."

"I suppose he hires folks to do the actual meat cutting, though, huh?"

"Well, a course. C. C. don't get his hands bloody. He hires people . . . hires or trains 'em."

"Alright, Al, Thanks for bein' so understandin' about Henry. I'll see his Missus gets the money.

"Sure thing . . . Say, you the Frank Bass they write them little books about?"

"Me? *Nah* . . . it's a common name."

Bass dropped off the twenty-dollar bill and explained everything that Al Kaminsky had said. Henry seemed anxious to get back to work and held his head a bit higher as Bass left, going back to the police station. He was more than a little miffed that Grooms didn't tell him about the slaughterhouse and packing plant.

"Grooms, Goddamnit. There's a meat packer in town down by the railroad. C. C. Slaughters."

"Yeah, I know where they are, but I thought they just shipped cows from there."

"No . . . they slaughter and process cattle there, probably pigs too. You ever been there?"

"No. Technically, they're not in the city. It's county jurisdiction. Never paid much attention to 'em really."

"Yeah? Well let's pay some now, whatdaya say?"

Bass left the Chief after telling him he was going to take a ride out to the processing plant. He wanted to meet with Cillian O'Dell and the Chief once he'd finished at the C. C. Slaughters and had a chance to check in with Eli Doud. The Chief reminded him that it was county jurisdiction, but Bass told Grooms that as a Federal Officer, wherever he happened to be his jurisdiction.

11:15 a.m. May 27, 1888
C. C. Slaughter Animal Handlers
Grimsby Road
Travis County, Texas

Bass Spurred Dotty into Gallop across the Congress Avenue Bridge and for nearly a mile after until he saw the sign for Grimsby Road. He slowed the horse and turned her to the east onto the

rutted dirt road that had been worn wide by passing cattle. He saw in the distance a large building with varying roof lines which indicated more than one building at the facility. As he got closer, he began to smell the stench of blood, bone dust, and offal, and he heard the bawling of cattle coming from somewhere behind the buildings.

He reigned Dotty in and tied her off at the buggy stand in front of what Bass assumed was the front entry. As he walked inside, he noticed the odor and noise were less prevalent, and he approached an attractive young woman at a desk. She was busy on her Remington number two typewriter, and he waited until she was finished.

"Yes, how can I help you?"

"Ma'am, my name is Frank Bass. I'm United States Deputy Marshal, and I'm helpin' out the Austin Police with a couple of investigations. I wonder, could I speak with the foreman, please?"

"Would you like coffee, Marshal? Roger Most is the foreman on duty. I'll see if I can find him. He's likely on the floor somewhere."

"No, thank you, ma'am. I'll just wait for Mr. Most."

"Are you sure, Marshal? I make a really special cup?" She smiled at Bass as she rose from her chair. "My name is Adelaide Winston, Marshal. Won't you reconsider?"

"Well, all right, if it ain't no bother."

"Oh, no bother at all, Frank . . . was it? I enjoy doing things for men. I'm quite hospitable." Again, she smiled as she filled a cup from a pot warmed on a stove in the corner. "Are you married, Frank?" she asked as she walked back to Bass.

"Yes, I am, Miss Adelaide. I have a baby daughter at home, too."

"Oh, well, it doesn't really matter. It never has *with me*." At that point, she opened the door to the plant, and the smell and noise returned. After a few minutes, she returned with a large man wearing a white duck cotton duster with blood stains on the sleeves.

"I'm Roger Most, Marshal. Adelaide said you're doin some investigatin'?"

"That's right, Mr. Most, I wonder do you have any employees who've missed some work recently or perhaps walk with a limp that might be recent?"

"As a matter of fact, I do. Devin Smith has missed four days of work. He just sent another note indicating he'd be back next week. Why? Is he in some kind of trouble with the police?"

"Oh, we'd just like to ask him a few questions is all. What's his job here at the plant, Mr. Most?"

"He's a meat cutter, a damn fine one too. The line's runnin' a lot slower without him, I can tell you."

"I see. Do you happen to have his address?"

"Yes, we do. Adelaide, give the Marshal Devin Smith's address, will you?"

"Of course, Roger." Roger Most said, "if that's all you need, I have to get back to the floor."

"Yes, a course, obliged for your help." Adelaide Winston handed Bass a slip of paper with Devin Smith's address written on it. Below his address, she had written hers too. Bass took the paper and tipped his hat as he walked back through the door. The address written was Benoit's Boarding House, 225 Neches Street, Austin. Bass knew just where the house was. It was in the grids he and Eli Doud were to work today.

11:45 a.m., May 27, 1888
Benoit's Boarding House
225 Neches Street
Austin, Texas

Eli Doud tied off his buggy and walked from one house to another, knockin' on doors, identifying himself, and asking the same questions.

"The Austin Police Department is looking for anyone, probably a young man who may be walking with a limp or using a cane." Only one person came to the door that limped and used a cane, and it was an old man, with a pegleg from fighting in the War for Southern Independence. Doud began chatting with the veteran and wound-up spending most of the morning with him, comparing war stories.

When he left he decided he'd check one more house on the corner of Neches. It had a sign out front, Mrs. Benoit's Boarding House, Clean Rooms, and Hot Food. He knocked on the door and was about to leave when an older lady opened the door and politely bid the man to enter. "Why yes, our Mr. Smith, Devin Smith, upstairs limps from an injury when just a child."

"Is he in? May I speak with him?"

"Oh, I don't believe so. He works, you know."

"Of course. May I see his room, please? It's police business, ma'am." Mrs. Benoit led Eli upstairs to the second room on the right and unlocked it. "I wouldn't do this if it wasn't police business. I believe in allowing boarders their privacy." Eli opened the door and was immediately struck by the smell. It was an odor he recognized, and he turned to Mrs. Benoit. "Perhaps you could do me a favor, ma'am. Would you go downstairs and see if you can find a police officer in the area, please. Just as a precaution."

"Why, oh my, is something amiss? Mr. Smith is a very good boarder, pays on time . . ."

"I'm sure he is, but please, if you wouldn't mind?"

Eli Doud walked carefully into the room, and as he did, the putrid odor of rotting flesh got stronger. As he approached the bed, he noticed the widespread bloodstain on the blanket and sheets. He saw empty bottles of laudanum on the nightstand, and as he examined them, he read, *for refill, see Doctor Lawrence Procket, 588 San Jacinto Street, Austin, Texas.*

Eli Doud swallowed hard. The realization that he'd found the Annihilator frightened and relieved him all at the same time. He took a step away from the bed and felt the floorboard sag under his weight. He looked down and saw dark stains in the hardwood planking around a one-foot section of planning. Slowly, he kneeled down and lifted the board. Between the framing beams of the floor, he saw three small, dried-out pieces of sinew and muscle about the size of a fist. He knew, of course, what they were, and the ghastly recognition transfixed him so that he didn't hear the footsteps until it was too late.

The folding scalpel was drawn smoothly across the old man's throat, and he fell forward, covering the Annihilator's keepsakes, bleeding into their hiding place between the beams above the room below.

Damn . . . damn . . . holy damn. Now I'll have to find another place to live. Devin Smith wiped his folding scalpel on the comforter and picked up his remaining bottle of laudanum. He took a last look at the room, decided there was nothing he truly needed except his cane, of course, and backed out of the room. As he walked slowly down the stairs, he thought, *what a lovely time the Police will have rummaging through my things.*

When he reached the landing, he carefully stepped over dear Mrs. Benoit. Outside, he casually closed the front door, gently brushing her apron as it swung shut.

Bass arrived at the Benoit Boarding House at a little past noon and recognized Eli's horse and buggy standing at the curd on Second

Street. Bass hopped off his horse while tying her off and ran to the front door. He saw, as he approached that the door was slightly ajar, and as he opened it fully, he saw Mrs. Benoit lying on the plank flooring, her life's blood pooled around her head and shoulders. He saw the blood-stained boot prints on the stairs, and he followed them up to the second floor. Bass withdrew his Colt and pressed his back against the wall, trying to make himself as small an ambush target as he could be. At the top of the stairs, he saw the door to the second room on the right was open, and he began to smell the fetid odor of blood and decaying flesh.

As he walked into the room, he saw the lifeless body of Eli Doud on the floor beyond the bed, and as he got closer, he saw the blood, Eli's blood, that had congealed on the floor. He squatted down to turn Eli over and saw the three shriveled hearts, each in its place under the flooring. They had dried and turned brown, shrunken from exposure to the air. Bass looked down at Eli, and his throat closed . . . tears began to well as he gently reached down and closed Eli's eyes.

He was thinking of all the lawmen, the unknown heroes in all the small towns who'd given their lives in the line of duty, now dead at the hands of those they were trying to capture, to put away. He dwelled on this for several minutes and used his kerchief to wipe his face. Then he became angry.

How do ya catch guys like this in a city? On the prairie, you can read sign, the signs of fearful men beginning to flee, but in the city, there was nothing to find. Any sign a killer may a left behind is covered, erased by the endless foot traffic and carriage trade of a modern city. The people who walk about on the streets avoid making eye contact. It's a part of their desire to protect themselves from intrusion from the outside world, from having to get involved in something they don't want to see. 'Don't want to know. And the killers know it, the outlaws, they all know it.

They know it and count on it. What was it Gilmore said . . . Wicked clever.

Bass had no idea where to go from here. He had no toolset he could use to capture the man. The tools he knew weren't working. The city required new skills. He didn't have them yet, but he was learning.

Chapter 19

2:15 p.m., May 27, 1888
> *Benoit's Boarding House*
> *225 Neches Street*
> *Austin, Texas*

Bass walked slowly down the stairs and out into the sunny front yard that Mrs. Benoit had taken such pride in. He stood in the middle of the lawn and looked up Neches Street and down Second Street, following the horse-drawn trolley as it moved slowly through the next intersection. A voice called his name from behind, and when he turned, a ragged derelict approached. As the man came forward, Bass recognized the face beneath the dirt and grime. Gandy Dave Lomax had seen Bass go into the house and then come out a few minutes later.

"Was it him, Frank? The man in this house?"

"Yes . . . it was."

"I saw him leave maybe thirty minutes ago; he didn't seem in a hurry."

"The woman who runs the house and an old lawman who was helping me track down the . . . both dead. Inside."

"I had been watching this one, Frank. This one and two others fit the description. All three limped to the right and were the right age. This one hadn't been out, must've been sick I thought."

"No, he was shot by a man he killed trying to divert our attention. I'd say it worked."

"Frank, I'm sorry about the old lawman. I can see you're upset."

"I am Heeltap. I had him. By God, I had him, and I was too late. Now he's gone, and I have no idea where. Another town? Another state? 'No way to know. In the wind."

"How's that, Frank?"

"The Comanche say that when a spirit leaves this life, it's in the wind. Gone . . . like our man here."

"Then I'd suggest, old friend, that you go back to the beginning. Paint a new picture with what you've learned." Gandy Dave paused for a moment and said, "I've had enough of these hobo shenanigans. I'll get cleaned up and meet you at police headquarters. We'll think this thing through together."

Gandy Dave Lomax walked back toward the lumber yard, and Bass looked around again. He raised his Colt in the air and fired it twice. Before he had the gun back in its holster, the beat officer rode up from another street, his pistol drawn, ready for trouble.

"It's alright, officer, it's all right. My name's Frank Bass, Deputy US Marshal helping Chief Lee with the Annihilator case."

"Yeah? You got a badge?"

Bass showed the officer his badge and identification card and the officer relaxed some. "Listen to me now, officer. There are two dead folks inside, both victims of the Annihilator. I want you to stay at the door and let no one enter. I'm going back to police headquarters, and I'll send another officer out to assist. Doc Flotter and the picture guy will be out, too. It's vital that nobody gets in. Nobody enters the house, not even you. It must stay as it is until Doc Flotter gets here. Got it?"

"Yeah, I got it. Did ya get him, Marshal?"

Bass was walking to his horse when he heard the question. "No, I didn't."

Bass mounted up and rode the mile or so back to the police station. He unsaddled Dotty, left her with the stable hand, and walked across the street to the police station. He walked directly to Grooms Lee's office, walked in without knocking, and sat in one of the chairs across from the Chief's desk. When he looked up, the Chief had a puzzled look.

"He's gone," Bass said. "Eli and the old woman who owned the house where he lived are dead. We need to send the Doc and another officer out to the scene at 225 Neches Street."

The Chief was silent for a moment. "I'll see to it, Frank. I'll take care of it." He rose and stepped out of the room.

Bass helped himself to a whiskey from Grooms's drawer and sat back down. He began thinking, *when that guy at the feed pens told me about the meat packing plant, why didn't I drop the squabblin' couple and ride straight out to the slaughter plant? Why'd I have to stop back here and lean on Grooms? By God, it as much as fell into my lap, and I didn't see it.*

Grooms Lee walked back into the office and sat down at his desk. He watched Bass for a few moments and said, "You wanna tell me about it?"

"Ain't much to tell, Chief. I rode out to see that married couple was fightin' and callin' each other names, and by chance, the husband worked at the feed lot for the packing plant. Shoulda gone there direct 'stead of stopping back here."

"Aw Frank, hell, you wasn't here more 'en a couple minutes. Sure wouldn't a' made any difference to the Widow Benoit or Eli. No, ain't no reason for you to take this on yourself. We'll catch the bastard . . . sure as Texas lives and breathes . . . we'll get him."

"Well . . . better do it quick. It's only four days till the bastard strikes again."

Chief Lee sat back. "You really think after all this he's still gonna hang around Austin? I doubt it, Frank. I think he knows how close he came to the gallows . . . don't believe he'd stay."

"No, at first that's what I thought too, but remember his letter? He said somethin' 'bout wait till the first of June. Oh, he'll stay alright, Grooms. He knows how much smarter he is than us, and he's close to another killin. He's here, Grooms. I know it."

"Well, let's get back to work on it then. We have a name, though I'm sure it's an alias, but he's been usin' it around town. He's gonna need somebody's help sooner or later, so we'll put his alias and description in the paper. Somebody'll know him, Frank. We'll get him."

Bass had been thinking all the while Grooms was talking, remembering what Athol Porter said. H*e thinks he's a Magus. 'Opposes the black arts.* "Chief, I know it's a weird question, but are there any witchcraft or sorcerer's type shops about in Austin, do you know?"

"Hell, Frank, I don't know. Ask me about gin palaces, something I got experience with. Witchy shops? No idea."

"You know, Chief, I think we should look at this guy from those he's opposed to. People who practice witchcraft. Maybe there's shops or bookstores or the like that cater to that kinda customer."

Grooms was interested in Bass's direction. "Alright, how do we find these places?"

Bass looked at Grooms Lee and smiled. "It's simple, Chief. We ask a priest."

Just as Bass was talking, Cillian O'Dell walked into the Chief's office.

"Hello, mates. What's the good word?"

Bass said, "Hey Cill, well, we was real close today. I picked up on a lead today, remember? You were here, but by the time I'd talked to people at C. C. Slaughter's, he'd already killed his landlady, and when poor Eli Doud arrived as part of our neighborhood canvassing, he killed Eli too. I got there too late to do anything but set a guard."

Cillian's thick red eyebrow curled up. "Aye . . . well, he knows we're close, that'll put a fear into him. He'll make a mistake, and we'll nab the bugger then. Chief? The shootin' down to Zimpelman's was a love triangle between Eileen Zimpleman, Katharine Morger, and Dooley Stain. Dooley was shot, but Doc tinks he'll make it, and

Katie Morger's under arrest. *Ah,* springtime and love's flowers are in bloom. 'Assault with a deadly weapon' is the charge, Chief, unless the City Lawyers want to make more of it."

Grooms smiled at Cillian and said, "Well done, Cill. We'll leave it at that for now."

"Cillian, with your vast knowledge of the city of Austin, would you have any idea 'bout a shop for witchcraft, maybe sells books, special candles, stuff like that?" Bass asked.

The Irishman leaned back in his chair, thinking. "A shop for witches, is it? No, I can't tink a' nuttin' like 'at. Public library's where I found that stuff from the madman's letter, but even at that, there weren't much a' all. But a shop, you say? Can't tink a' one."

"*Welp*, I guess I'll try a priest then. Where'll I find one a' them, boys?" he asked.

"Church of Immaculate Conception." They said in unison.

3:00 p.m., May 27, 1888
350 Bowie Street
Austin Texas

The sign outside the single-story house read: Room to Let—$20 Per Month— Home Cooking. And then, in smaller letters, Inquire Within. He knocked on the door, and after a few moments, an older man opened and said, yes? You here 'bout the room?" He was stooped over and leaned on an old Hickory cane that was nearly as bent as he was.

"Good afternoon, sir. My name is Harleigh Jones, and indeed, I am interested in your room to let."

"Okay, sonny, tell me where you work.

"I'm employed at C. C. Slaughter as a meat packer, though I have missed a few days' work due to injury. If it's a question of rent, I'll gladly pay two months' rent in advance."

The old man's ears perked up at hearing that. He'd be able to get his teeth fixed with the extra money. "Two months, ya say? Well, come on in and have a look at the room, and if it suits ya, fine, well, and good."

The young man was dressed nicely, he was polite and cheerful looking, and he seemed to have money available. The two men walked to the rear of the house, where a spare bedroom was furnished just off the kitchen area. "My poor wife, rest her soul, lived here till she passed last year. It's just me in the house now . . . might be nice to have someone to chew the fat with."

"Yes, of course, we'll be pals. Well, I like the room very much . . . I see a back door here, so I can come and go without disturbing you?"

"Yes, yes, certainly. The commode is out back. It's brand new this spring."

"Enticing indeed. Here's the forty dollars for the next two months, and I'll get my things moved in as quick as a wink."

"That's fine. My name's Ed, by the way. Ed Landick 'retired from the railroad. Worked thirty-five years from Yard Bull to Brakeman, yup . . . full pensioner."

"I'm sure you have many fine stories, Ed. Now, if you'll excuse me, I'll fetch my things."

"Oh, 'course. Say, uh, how'd you hurt your leg?"

"An accident at work, my fault actually, twisted it real bad. My other leg has been weak since birth, and I'm missing several toes, actually. Well, goodbye now."

The old man watched Harleigh Jones walk back down Bowie Street to the Trolley Stop and then counted out his cash. He was excited about getting his teeth fixed.

4:30 p.m., May 27, 1888
Roman Catholic Church of
Immaculate Conception
Mulberry at Brazos Street
Austin, Texas

Bass tied off Dotty at the buggy rail in front of the church and walked up the marble steps to the tall double doors that opened to the Narthex with the Nave straight ahead. There were quite a few rows of pews set up in preparation for Evening Mass, and he passed by the choir's position on either side. There were beautiful stained-glass windows behind the choir seats, catching light and projecting colorful images on the floor. He continued to walk forward to the altar and noticed a small doorway on the left between four confessionals. He knocked on the door, and a voice asked, "Yes? Who is it, please? I am cloistered this hour."

"Excuse me interruptin' your prayer, Father. My name is Frank Bass. I'm a US Deputy Marshal investigatin' these Annihilator killin's."

Again from behind the door, "Oh dear, oh my, a moment please, Marshal."

When the door opened, a small, round man in a dark wine-colored robe emerged. He was clean shaven and balding, and his ears stood out from his head by at least two inches. He wore sandals and a gold sash that gave his robe a little shape. His smile was bright and infectious, and Bass liked him immediately.

"You're the famous lawman, aren't you? Oh my, I've read several of your exploits, you know, such dashing stuff. A welcome release from my daily recitals, yes, yes."

Bass found himself unable to stop grinning. "Well, thank you kindly, padre. I had no idea that such devout . . . *er* religious . . . well, you know."

"Oh yes, indeed, I do. And when you shot that desperado's hand off . . . I can't tell you how smashing it was. Good triumphs over evil again. *Hoorah*! I'm Father Noel. How can I help your investigation?"

Bass nearly chuckled; he was so tickled by the man's demeanor. "Well, Father Noel, I'm workin' with the Police Chief in tryin to find this fella they call the Annihilator. Maybe you read about it in the papers?"

"Oh dear me, yes, quite. Horrible business, the Devil himself at work, I think."

"Actually, the way he sees it, Father Noel is kinda the opposite. He believes he's doing the people of Austin a favor by killin witches."

Father Noel's face screwed up into a disbelieving question. "My goodness, how can anyone believe that witches exist in this day and age? So then, what can I do?"

"Father Noel, have you or maybe anyone in the church ever heard of a shop or maybe a bookstore that might cater to this kind of . . . of witchery?"

"Oh my. Oh dear, you know it's funny you should ask but a penitent in confession made mention of such a place and what an affront to Our Lord it presented."

"Father, can you tell me the name of the place or its location?"

"Oh no, dear me no. A violation, you see, of the confessional. No, I'm afraid not, no."

"I see, and a course, I wouldn't want you to violate any kind a trust with your parishioners. But simply from your own knowledge, would you say the shop was in Austin City limits?"

"*Hmm*? Oh yes . . . yes, I see what you're doing, yes. Ah, well, from my knowledge, I can say yes, it is."

"Excellent, thank you, Father, is it on the north side? Or the south side?"

"*Um*, No, no, on the very near north side. Ah, in fact, if I were to go to the University Chapel on Elm Street, I should walk right past it."

Bass smiled at the little priest and shook his hand. "Thank you, Father Noel, I believe we have enough of your knowledge for today."

"Oh, splendid! This is exciting. I hope I've been able to help you find this demon, Marshal Bass."

"I believe we have a good start, Father. Thank you. Oh, and it's Deputy Marshal, actually."

Bass returned to Grooms Lee's office, but the Chief had already left for the day. Bass checked his Elgin and discovered it to be after 6:00 p.m. and decided that even if he found the place that Father Noel referenced, it was probably closed for the day anyway. He decided to leave Dotty at the police barn and walk back to the Winslow Hotel. It was less than a mile, and the evening was cool and pleasant.

The clouds on the western horizon promised a colorful sunset, and Bass considered that it might help to witness some of the world's natural beauty. He'd been wading through the filthy business of the Annihilator so long a short respite to renew his spirit was certainly in order. He would send another wire to Sally and the baby, too. That always lifted his heart.

It was nearly seven o'clock when he walked through the doors to the Winslow Hotel lobby. He stopped at the front desk to get paper and a pencil and then went into the dining room area to find a seat where he could write. It was just twilight now, and the days were getting longer. He chose a table at a window along the boardwalk on Ash Street and ordered a whiskey when the girl stopped at his table. He began writing:

My Dearest Sally and My Treasure Lil,

This case of all the others puzzles me—I've seen and heard things that are hard to imagine—when this is finished, I will happily leave them behind— Thinking of you both safe at home is a comfort— I miss you both very much— I may be home soon— will write if I must stay longer.

—Your Frederick

Bass asked the waitress to send a messenger to his table, and within moments, a boy of twelve or thirteen appeared.

"Take this to the telegraph, son. It's a long message and I'd like it delivered special." He gave the boy a five-dollar bill to cover the cost of the wire and delivery charge and an extra dollar for the boy's transport to the Western Union Office and back. There should be enough left to provide the boy with a handsome tip as well.

He ordered dinner, a Blue Plate Special, meatloaf and collards, and another whiskey to replace the first. Once he'd finished eating, he sipped the second whiskey and watched the end of the sunset. His Elgin said it was 8:25 p.m. and time to go upstairs and read before bed. He bought a newspaper that flashed headlines in bold print: Annihilator Kills Officer Who Discovered His Lair. Then below in smaller print, Madman Still At Large In The City, Police Baffled.

Bass read the headline over again and couldn't wait to get upstairs to read the article. He also noticed a headline just below the center fold of the paper. It read, Federal Marshal Thwarts Train Robbers, Local Detective Instrumental In Arrests. Now, he was also anxious to read about all the help he had on the train.

3:30 a.m., May 28, 1888
350 Bowie Street
Austin Texas

The early morning hours of May 28th had become quite chilly, and Harleigh Jones decided to light the small stove in the corner of his room. The tinder was dry, and the wood lit quickly. Soon, a small fire burned in the stove, and the room warmed up. Jones went back to bed and was asleep in short order.

After fifteen- or twenty-minutes, smoke belched from the stove door and the wall gasket where the flue exited the house. Evidently, it had been some time since the stove had been used, and the flue cap was blocked on the outside of the house well above the roof. Jones immediately threw open the window and the back door to vent the smoke and then used water to extinguish the blaze in the stove. The fire was extinguished, but the smoke and soot remained, along with the smell of whatever it was that had blocked the flue.

Naturally, Ed Landick had been awakened and was apologetic for neglecting the maintenance of the flue, but the damage was done. One of the neighbors woke up from the commotion and came over to investigate, concerned that a fire might spread to his roof. Once he saw the nature of the problem, he was reassured and returned to his home. This was not the kind of attention that Harleigh Jones wanted at all. In addition to the neighbor seeing his face and learning his name, Jones's clothes, bedding, and window shades now reeked of smoke.

When the neighbor left and Ed went back to bed, Harleigh Jones returned to his bed and decided he'd have to replace his wardrobe in the morning. Anything that caused him to stand out among other people, such as the odor of woodsmoke, was a senseless risk to his avocation. He reconciled that he must go to the bank for funds, a task he dreaded since it took him outside during the busiest time of the day, at the busiest part of town. There would be people around, milling about, watching him, judging him, scoffing as they always did in the bright daylight. He slept only briefly in the hours before dawn.

7:00 a.m., May 28, 1888
Winslow Hotel
Congress Ave at Ash Street
Austin, Texas

Bass was awake and dressed early this morning. Surprisingly, he'd slept very well and felt eager to begin his day of sleuthing by stopping at police headquarters and advising Cillian and the Chief of his meeting with Father Noel and that he'd gotten a solid lead on a shop for witches, warlocks, and spells. As he walked downstairs to the lobby, he recognized a man sitting in a chair by the front door—James McParland, a.k.a. Heeltap in Fort Stockton and Gandy Dave Lomax in Austin.

"What name are you using today, Mr. McParland?"

"Why, whatever do you mean, Marshal Bass? I don't know you as anyone other than US Deputy Marshal Frank Bass and have met you and your—much too lovely for you—wife Sally only as myself, James McParland of Chicago, Illinois."

"I see. The wind blows a bit differently this morning, I suppose. Have you had breakfast?"

"No, I haven't, and since I am not on *per diem* as some marshals I know to be, I will not embarrass you by refusing to dine with you at your expense."

"I swear, Heeltap, you get more mystifyin' every time I see you. Come along then."

The two ate relatively quickly as Bass wanted to get the preliminaries of his day over with. McParland was anxious as well to introduce himself to the chief of police so he could be advised of everything the department knew. On the walk over to see Grooms Lee, Bass told McParland about Cillian O'Dell, his trip to Weatherford, Marion Gilmore, and the Brack Cornett Gang of train robbers. He also relived his frustration and remorse at the death of

Eli Doud and now his renewed enthusiasm for finding the "witchy shop" Father Noel mentioned . . . without actually mentioning.

"My word, Frank, it sounds as though you have a day laid out for you. I believe I will spend it reading the murder log you mentioned that Mr. O'Dell keeps if he will allow it, and I'd like to visit the killer's rooms. I'll tell you why. The Pinkerton Agency has been experimenting of late with a technique that our English compatriots are trying, called fingerprinting. It seems that no matter what we do or how old we get, our fingerprints, the swirls and ridges, stay the same. And they are unique. No two sets of prints are alike.

"Now, in this case, the culprit's prints will not help us identify or locate the madman, but they might serve to positively identify whoever we apprehend as the guilty party. His prints will match those we have from the crime scene of his room, you see. Now, the courts are not accepting fingerprints as an exact identifier, so they can't be admitted as evidence. But we don't have to tell our suspect that. Just having the prints as a match may be enough to elicit a confession. It has worked well this way, up north."

"Fingerprints. By God, that sounds so modern and scientific. 'Like matchin' bullets to a gun based on rifling. Can we get fingerprints from off a knife or a saw?"

"Absolutely. We have been using exceptionally fine talcum powder, which adheres to the natural oils left behind when a subject touches something. It works best if the surface is hard and flat, like glass or metal. Then we photograph the impression, and *bingo*, an impeccable record that an individual was there at the scene. The technique has been used in the courts of South America and Europe for several years, so I'd like to visit his room with that process in mind. I don't see how anyone might object."

"Me neither. Let's run it by Grooms and Cillian and see what they think."

Chapter 20

9:00 a.m., May 28, 1888
   Police Headquarters
   Congress at Peach Street
   Austin, Texas

"So you're the Pinkerton man the Mayor called for, huh? How long you been in my town mister, sneakin' about, peekin' in windows?

"I understand why you're angry, Chief, but please recognize that the Mayor engaged us because he thought a little more professional help was needed. Had the Mayor known about Frank Bass bein here, he might not a been so hasty. And as to peekin' in windows? I get results, buster. And in this case, especially, the end to this maniac justifies any means. Now, I've come in today with a new technique that might assist in finding this bastard. If you'll table that attitude of yours and listen, it just might help."

McParland and Bass explained the nature of fingerprints and the way they're obtained. McParland also spoke of the photographic resolution needed.

"A fella named Eastman has produced some new kinda photographic invention that means you don't need to use wet plates anymore . . . makes the picture better and faster. It also means the camera can be smaller. He's made some handheld camera models . . . calls the company Kodak, I believe. I'd like to talk to your department photographer about getting him one a' these cameras. 'Shouldn't be too difficult. I'm sure they sell 'em someplace around here."

Chief Grooms agreed to the purchase of the camera following a demonstration using the talcum powder in McParland's kit. The photographer, Bill Breitwish, was also excited about the prospect of getting a camera he'd only read about in his trade journals. A wire to

Rochester, New York, produced the name of a retailer in Fort Worth, and they ordered the camera the next day.

While this was going on, Bass and McParland continued their search for Devin Smith. O'Dell had other police work that required his expertise, so Bass set out to find the store near the University Chapel that Father Noel had suggested, and McParland went back to the existing photographs of the murder scenes already taken by Bill Breitwish. He also made it a point to review the murder log that Cillian O'Dell had started.

11:00 a.m., May 28, 1888
The Magic Hat
1200 San Marcos Street at Elm
Austin, Texas

Bass had ridden Dotty up and down the streets and alleyways around the University Chapel for nearly a half-hour before finally expanding his search to San Marcos Avenue. There, on the corner of San Marcos and Elm, he spotted a little hole-in-the-wall shop called The Magic Hat. Bass tied Dotty off at the hitch rail and walked in. The first thing he noted was a sweet, musky smell, unlike anything he'd ever scented before.

The shop itself was dark, with low ceilings and candle sconces on the walls for light rather than oil lamps. Various fabrics and readymade clothing hung on hooks and hangers about the room and quite a few books on shelves against the back wall. Two glass counter cases ran parallel to each other in the center of the room with an odd-looking assortment of bones, strands of hair in diverse colors, and dried frogs and other lizard-like creatures. Brown jars—like what he'd seen in Athol Porter's Cemetery Cottage— lined the shelf of a locked glass cabinet standing in a far corner. A wide assortment of what appeared to be cooking utensils in bowls sat on top of the counters alongside other bowls, holding crystals, rocks, and vials of oil. As he approached one of the counters, an older woman with very long black hair and dark eye makeup approached him.

"My Lord, how can I help you?"

"'Scuse me?"

"I asked how I could serve, my Lord."

"Oh . . . the Lord part threw me, well I ain't never been in one a' these stores before and thought I'd drop in."

The woman's shoulders dropped, and she smiled knowingly. "Is it something for a young lady, my Lord?"

"*Hmm?*"

"A potion, an aphrodisiac, we have several that when applied, will make you irresistible to her."

"Oh, oh no, it's nothin' like that, ma'am. I mean, actually, I'm lookin' for somethin' that might repel a warlock."

"Say what?"

"Ma'am, I'm a deputy US Marshal, and I'm tryin to catch this fella they call the Annihilator. He believes he's killing witches, ma'am, and I thought, maybe foolish of me, I thought there might be somethin in your store 'could help me identify him."

"Ah, I see. Marshal, I should explain. There are very few things in this world that we of the craft fear. Hence there is little in the line of defense that we need. We are more often on the offensive if you take my meaning. However, I possess a book of incantations and charms that will outline for you the type of spell you may wish to cast. It was written centuries ago by a Welsh physician. It is quite complete and inexpensive at four dollars and fifty cents."

"How much?"

"It is an ancient text, my Lord. Few exist today. However since you are a guardian of the peace, today only it is three dollars."

"Well, thanks anyway . . . can I just look around here?"

"Of course, my Lord."

Bass walked up and down the glass showcases wondering at some of the artifacts displayed. He came upon a display that read Bones of Infants, and he stopped where he stood.

"'Scuse me again, but are these uh . . . uh real infant bones?"

"Oh yes, my Lord, a most popular item and, I'll say, one of our most costly commodities."

"But . . . but, they're—are they real?"

"Oh indeed, my Lord. We sell no false components."

"But where do you, how do . . .?"

"Stillborns, my Lord, from the hospital. 'Perfectly legal."

Bass was incredulous. He'd had enough of the ghoulish paraphernalia on sale in the store and decided if there was anything of value to the investigation in that place, he'd just as soon find it elsewhere.

"Believe I'll take my leave, ma'am," he muttered and walked out the door.

Bass rode slowly back to the police department. Though he'd never say it, he knew Grooms secretly hoped the killer had moved on after so narrow an escape. Of course, that would only mean that another community would eventually have to deal with the homicidal maniac that had plagued Austin for three months. He decided to stop at the hotel on his way back. It was only slightly out of the way, and he was hoping for a response from Sally.

When he got to the Winslow, he walked inside and stopped at the front desk, "Is there anything for me?" The clerks had become familiar with Bass.

"Yes, this wire just came for you from Dallas, sir."

"Thanks." Bass stood at the desk reading and began moving toward the door as he finished.

The clerk behind called out, "Any reply?" but Bass was already aboard Dotty and galloping to the police department.

2:30 p.m., May 28, 1888
Police Headquarters
Congress at Peach Street
Austin, Texas

Bass strode into Chief Lee's office waving a telegram and calling out to no one in particular,

"Well, goddamn, the fools."

He sat in front of Grooms Lee and said, "Read this, Chief. It's from your colleague in Dallas."

The Chief picked up the half-page wire and read:

From Special Officer R.M. Kitts, Chief Pro Tempore,

Dallas Police Department, Dallas, Texas.

Sir, I write to advise that following your visit, I discovered an unauthorized release of a patient from the state asylum in Terrel. The patient's name is Develin Waters. He is the son of former superintendent Agatha Waters, who is now in custody. I have tried obtaining the son's location, but the prisoner only identifies Austin. I will advise any development; Dr. Waters will be vigorously prosecuted. Patient Waters is criminally deranged and should be considered quite dangerous. As interim Chief, I was only recently made aware of this criminal behavior.

—I am yours truly —R.M. Kitts

"So," Grooms Lee stated, "now we know who we're chasing. Obviously, the man has a close personal knowledge of the workings of the police in general. His mother has seen to that."

Bass added, "And I talked to the woman as much as told what we were doing. Stood right in front of the old bat and asked her pointed questions, which she naturally dodged."

Bass was quiet for a moment, then Grooms asked, "So what does this do for us?"

Bass stood and walked to the front of the desk, "Not much, I'm afraid. It gives us his name, but we already know he's not using his real name. And he's still on the loose. Austin's a big place, lotsa people. I'm afraid it doesn't give us much at all."

Grooms nodded. "Oh. I meant to ask, how did your trip to the witch shop go?"

"Ha! There's nothing of value to us there . . . unless we wanna cast a hex on someone. Then they got everything you need, including the bones from infant babies."

"What!? How is that possible? We must arrest them for it?"

"Said it was legal . . . bones are from stillborn babies they get from the hospital. Don't sound right to me either, but I got other stuff on my mind. 'Sides, they could be bones from small animals for all I know."

"Yeah, well, even so, dead bodies from the hospitals are to be used only for medical research and then only with permission from the families. 'Find it hard to believe a witch shop has 'at kinda permission. When this is over, I'm gonna look into that myself."

A few minutes later, a commotion was heard in the hall outside the Chief's office. It was O'Dell and McParland arguing over O'Dell's murder log.

"You fat-fingered oaf . . . I can barely read your scrawl on these pages, and while the photographs seem to be in order, I can't make out a date or location. And the clippings? No date at all! I know there's only one paper in town, but you gotta show the date of the story!"

"Say listen here ya Scottish dobber, if ya had any education in the detective arts, the murder log would be clear as a sunny day. But a backwater like Chi-ca-gue don't give no education a 'tall, I see. And it ain't my fault that yer eyes are crossed so that ya can't read American newsprint! I imagine it's that childish Scottish whiskey that's addled ya so."

"You big dumb clobber-headed mick, the Pinkertons have been solving crime since 'fore your birth. Look it this here, is it an *L* or a *T*? Is this a *W* or a *U*? And ya can't misread the date on this photograph . . . cause there ain't none!"

Bass and the Chief were enjoying the banter but called a halt at this point. "Gentlemen, gentlemen, let's try to remember where we are and that we're all on the same side here," said the Chief.

Bass added, "Yeah, let's quit the squabbling and get back to findin' the maniac, okay? I'd like to go back to the Benoit house and see how this fingerprintin' stuff is done. I imagine the old lady's family will want the place cleaned up soon, so there ain't no time to lose. Chief, you wanna have the photographer to meet us there?"

"Will do. I'll tell the desk sergeant. Give me a minute or two to finish this report, and we'll go."

3:30 p.m., May 28, 1888
Benoit's Boarding House
225 Neches Street
Austin, Texas

The four men arrived in two Gurney cabs and made their way into the Benoit house. Bass was surprised to see that there was no uniformed officer present protecting the quality of the crime scene.

"Grooms, there really ought to be an officer on duty here to keep people away from the scene. You know how folks like to gawk."

"I suppose you're right, but our visit today is due to the fingerprinting demonstration, 'the doctor and photographer finished up last night. Normally, once the bodies are removed, we allow the owner to reenter. In this case I believe Mrs. Benoit had a sister who would inherit. I don't believe she has arrived in town; she lives in San Antone."

"Then I guess we'll find things as the doctor left them," Bass agreed.

Just as the four men entered the house, the photographer arrived. Bill Breitwish was a young man of twenty-three, Bass judged, who'd had some little experience with his camera. Along with his work for the Austin Police Department, he had his own portrait shop on Congress Avenue and lived in an apartment above. He was a handsome young man with chiseled features, long blond hair that curled over his collar, and a keen wit. He also was experienced enough that the blood and gore of crime scene photography didn't upset him, though at the first Annihilator scene it had.

As he got out of his cab, he called out, "Yo, there, Gents, hold up a bit." He grabbed his camera and plate case and dashed to the front door just as the four men walked in.

"The banister and railing might be a good place to start. They're varnished to a gloss and should retain prints." McParland opened his kit and produced a small rubber bellows and a large tin of talcum powder. He sprinkled the banister liberally and then used the small bulblike bellows to blow the residue away. All five men watched as the powder adhered to the oils left behind by a touch, revealing the grooves and ridges of many fingerprints.

Bass spoke first. "That's amazing; you can see the hand grip on the railing. But how do we know whose it is?"

McParland smiled. "We don't know because this stairway would be subject to various traffic. When we get to his room, we can safely assume that most of the prints will be his. We'll ask Bill here to photograph them as accurately as he's able, and then we'll compare the pictures. Let's go upstairs."

The five men walked up the staircase and entered Devin Smith's room.

"We'll get the best results from hard, flat surfaces. Glass is a good example, but varnished wood, metal that sort of thing gives the best image. That empty laudanum bottle, for instance, without touching the body of the container, set it on the dresser. We'll dust them both."

Bass took hold of the bottle by the tip of its neck and set it on the dresser. McParland then, again, lightly sprinkled talcum powder on the front of the bottle.

"If you think of how you ordinarily hold a bottle, we should get a thumb print from the front."

As he blew the dust away, several smeared thumbprints appeared. McParland spun the bottle around and dusted the back. A perfectly formed thumbprint emerged when the powder was blown away.

Everyone was suitably impressed, and finally, McParland said, "Bill, take a close-up image if you can."

Then, they proceeded to dust and photograph every likely spot that a print might appear. On the enamel basin they found another thumbprint and forefinger from the right hand. On the marble table top an entire handprint from the left hand. And on the mirror, they found prints of the fingertips of all five fingers of his left hand. Photographs were made, and the men left the house at five o' clock.

On the way back to the station, Grooms asked Bill Breitwish how long he'd need to develop the prints. He said he'd do them overnight and have them ready in the morning. Once they arrived at police headquarters, the men dispersed, each going in their own direction, after agreeing to meet first thing in the morning.

Chapter 21

7:45 a.m., May 29, 1888

   350 Bowie Street

   Austin Texas

The sun woke Harleigh Jones slowly, but he began coughing as soon as he took a deep breath and inhaled the remnants of the lingering smoke. The fine new clothes he'd bought hung on the pole in his closet with the top hat in a box on the shelf above. He reflected on yesterday.

He'd first gone to the bank to replenish his funds and then went shopping at Keough & Son's haberdashery on Congress Avenue. There, he purchased nearly a new wardrobe, daily work clothes, casual shirts and trousers, underwear—of course—and a complete suite of evening clothes, from the patent leather ankle boots to the three-quarter black cape and top hat, finely made of beaver, of course.

His leg had begun healing, and he assumed the mercurial medicine was having its effect. In any event, he was able to walk short distances and ride the trolley to get wherever he wanted. He was also fortunate, on one trolley trip up Congress Avenue, to spot another of the local covens. He couldn't believe his good fortune spotting one out and about so near the first of the month. *She ought to be in her room in the covenstead reviewing her Wiccaning rites and practicing her spells for the High Priestess or Crone.*

He was pleased, though, when he spotted her watching him. *She knows what I am, certainly, and like the moth to the flame, so is the witch to the Magus.* He noticed her Trolley stop was near the Ballinger Building, and as the trolley pulled away, he watched her enter one of the several office doorways in the block south of the Capitol Building. Number 312 Congress Avenue. He also noticed it was nearby to the Capitol Club and though he'd never been there, he imagined it to be a fine meeting spot.

He got off the trolley two blocks later and during his shopping at Keogh & Son's, he continued visualizing her.

Quite young, perhaps twenty or so, a lovely face, fresh an' eager, auburn hair in soft waves and curls, a stunning figure, I'm sure, under her shawl. And all of it concealed a cunning soul, apprentice perhaps, to the black craft and handmaiden to the Dark Lord. Even at her age, how many has she corrupted by using her vile willfulness against them? And she thinks she will do the same to me . . . ha! In her blind overconfidence, she thinks the Magus has no chance against her. She plans to convert me. Of course, she does . . . I know it, like all the others. She has no idea how powerful I am . . . but she will find out. Perhaps this evening, I'll be at her building on Congress Avenue and offer a drink, sure a drink on a Tuesday evening after a hard day's work? Why not? And the saloon is so handy. From there, nature will take its course.

9:00 a.m., May 29, 1888
Police Headquarters
Congress Avenue at Peach Street
Austin, Texas

Bass arrived at Grooms's Office in desperate need of coffee. He had slept late this morning and skipped breakfast to be on time to review the fingerprint photographs. He drank the whole pot that was first offered and beseeched the clerk who brought it to the Chief's office for another.

By 9:20 a.m., everyone was assembled, and Bill Breitwish said he'd lay everything out on a table in the Chief's meeting room. He opened his large folio case and spread out twenty-four black-and-white photos and copies in sepia tone.

"So you can see the contrasts. Black-and-white plate prints sometimes display grays too darkly, and it's hard to identify some things."

The men gathered around the table, and each examined the pictures one by one.

"I see what you mean about the brown color. What did you call it?" Chief Lee asked.

"Sepia." Breitwish answered, "it treats shadows differently, too."

"I can see definite ridges and swirled curves in the fingerprints in these pictures of the bottle, and they look very similar to the ones from the mirror in another part of the room," Bass said.

McParland answered, "That gives us a pretty good notion that the similar prints we see in the photos belong to our guy. Look at these over here from the banister. They're identical to both the mirror and the bottle. This is how fingerprinting can be used in identifying suspects. No two fingerprints in all the world are the same."

"Aye, that's the part that boggles me, you know. O'Dell said. That nobody on earth has prints of a similar kind."

At that, McParland interjected, "Wouldn't take much to boggle your mind anyway."

O'Dell turned to McParland. "Say then, ya bandy Scotsman, if yer race hadn't just crawled outta the peat bogs, I might hafta punch yer nose. Guess I can allow for the less advanced."

While they bickered, Bass continued examining the photos. He stopped and picked up one. It was a photograph showing a close view of the mirror over the dresser. Bass noticed something else in the photo.

"Grooms? 'You got a magnifier lens? I wanna look at this closer."

Grooms walked across the hall to his office and returned with the glass while Bass continued to look at the picture. McParland and O'Dell had closed in to look also.

"Look here in the corner. Is that a slip of paper?"

Everyone agreed and commented that they hadn't noticed.

Bass went on, "You know what I think that is, boys? I believe that's a bank withdrawal slip. Gimme the glass, Grooms."

Bass moved to one of the lamps along the wall and examined the picture using the magnifier. Bass looked up at the others.

"Damn, it's a banking slip from the First State Bank of Texas. Is there such a bank in Austin?"

Bill Breitwish, who'd been quietly enjoying accolades for the quality of his work, said, "Well, yeah. It's on Pecan Street between Brazos and Congress Avenue. That's my bank."

Bass looked at Grooms Lee and said, "Chief? We're gonna need a warrant."

"On my way," Lee said and left the room immediately while the other men looked satisfied and relieved that finally they had something real on the man they'd been searching for so long.

Bass took Bill Breitwish aside and said, "You know, don'tcha that if we catch this guy because a' your camera work, you'll be a hero in this town."

Bill smiled and said, "Camera, don't lie, Marshal. You guys'll get him. I know you will."

It took two hours for Chief Lee to find a judge willing to sign a warrant to examine bank records. Most judges found the privacy of bank accounts to be almost sacrosanct, and considering who might be making contributions to specific judges for reelection, the Chief understood why. He didn't have time, however, for election reform matters now, and he took his Financial Search Warrant back to the office to collect Bass and Cillian O'Dell. McParland said he wanted to take Breitwish and his camera back over to Doctor Lawrence Procket's office for additional fingerprinting.

"If this ever gets to court," McParland said, "we want to have as much evidence as we can find to actually put him at the scene of those killings."

Bass agreed and decided to take the picture of the banking slip with him, thinking it might be of some use at the bank. It was clearly from the First State Bank of Texas, and it could be seen as a withdrawal slip, but the date was not visible. There was another object on top of the paper that hid the date.

The three men arrived at the bank just before noon and climbed out of the Gurney Cab onto the cobblestones of Pecan Street. They entered the bank purposefully, striding through the bank's lobby to a desk at the rear of the room.

"My name is Grooms Lee. I'm the Chief of Police, and we'd like to see the bank manager now, please."

The clerk was a small man in a tweed suit that Bass thought looked too warm for near-June weather. The clerk did not stand but wrinkled his nose and removed his spectacles, carefully sliding them into his breast pocket.

"I'm terribly sorry, gentlemen. Mr. Hanover is at lunch and can't be disturbed." He smiled politely and folded his hands on his desk. "If you'd like to have a seat . . ."

At that, Bass interrupted and leaned over the man's desk. He said quietly, "You'd best go fetch him sonny, else you may wind up in the city slams for obstruction. Savvy?"

The clerk smiled again through a nervous twitch and said, "I believe I can find him for you gentlemen, if you'll please wait here?"

"That's the spirit we're looking for, pal. We'll be right here," the Chief replied.

The clerk dashed to the very back of the room and up a flight of stairs. The three men heard a door open and close, then some muffled talking followed by an abrupt door slamming and finally the appearance of a rotund older man as he rumbled down the metal staircase. He was dressed in a dark colored business suit and red bow tie and carried with him a practiced scowl of discontent.

"See here, what's the meaning of this interruption that couldn't wait until I'd finished my sandwich?"

Chief Lee listened. "What's your name, sir?"

"E. A. Tolkar, I'm 'President of this bank."

"*Uh-huh*. What's the *E* stand for?"

"Edwin. Edwin Alloysius Tolkar."

"Edwin, I'm Chief of Police Grooms Lee, and these two men are detectives working on the Annihilator case. We have reason to believe that our primary suspect does his banking with you folks, and we want some information from you about his activities."

"With us? My God, the scandal, to have business dealings with a crazed a . . . uh madman like that. Activities, *hmra,* I don't know, naturally we want to cooperate, but we have rules .. promises made to depositors, you understand."

Bass nodded and smiled at Edwin Tolkar. "Of course ya do, we understand. But now the Chief here has this Financial Search Warrant signed by, who was it again, Chief?"

"Judge Larkin, Joseph Larkin." Chief Lee responded, and Bass continued.

"Signed by Judge Larkin, which basically says he'd be personally offended if you didn't help us out."

E. A. Tolkar had lost some of his starch and was wringing his hands at what he'd heard.

"I see. *Hmm,* yes, quite. Well then, what information do you wish to see?"

Chief Lee smiled. "Good, good. Let's go someplace more private, shall we? Be better able to discuss things."

"Of course, of course. Follow me then." Tolkar led the three men to his office, which was in the rear corner of the building on the first floor. Cillian O'Dell sat on a leather divan along one wall, and the Chief and Bass each sat in two chairs at Tolkar's desk.

Chief Lee began. "Edwin, our suspect has a history of using aliases so we can't just give you a name and ask for a banking history. Let's just start with recent banking records for Devin Smith. He was an employee at the C. C. Slaughter packing plant. What we're looking for in particular is an address, Ed."

"Certainly, yes . . . but if I may suggest, it would be best if you gave all the names you have at once. What happens is I'll assign a teller to review transactions for the names for the last . . . How long?"

Bass answered, "say for the last ten business days. That should give us a good sample."

The Chief agreed. "Sergeant O'Dell, what other names should Edwin here be looking for?"

"Well, let me recollect now, we have Devin Smith, then he used the name Brian McDougal at the poor Doctor's office, and it's possible he may be using what we tink is his real name, Develin Waters. Let's try those, shall we?"

The Chief added, "I'd start looking for withdrawals, though he may have made deposits from his employer. And again, we're most interested in getting an address."

"Alright, alright. I'll be right back."

Edwin Tolkar excused himself for several minutes and returned indicating it might take some time to go through the receipt stubs for each day. Some had been moved to a partition of the vault where bank records were kept. Bass suggested the three of them go to lunch and leave Edwin to his day-to-day banking duties.

"We'll be back after an hour or so, Ed. Hopefully, you'll have some information for us."

Edwin Tolkar nodded and smiled weakly as the three men left his office and exited the bank.

Cillian recommended the Trinity Saloon and Café, which was just around the corner on Congress Avenue. As it turned out, the saloon was actually a gambling hall, noisy with a low-hanging cloud of cigar and cigarette smoke covering the room. The men opted for the café side of the business, which advertised free lunch for big losers from the saloon side, along with Blue Plates for a dime and sandwiches for nickel. Bass recognized that the café was there to keep gamblers in the building and reckoned if that was the case, the food would probably be good.

At Cillian's request, the three were seated at a table farthest away from the noise in the saloon, at a table near a window with light enough to read by. Bass and Cillian each ordered a whiskey, and Chief Lee asked for coffee.

"You know, boys, the back a' my neck is startin' to tickle me," Bass said. "It only does that when I've missed something, and it's never been wrong before."

Cillian said, "I don't know what it could be. We have evidence linking him to the old lady and Sheriff Doud in his room, and them three hearts he had stashed in the floor ought to be enough to get him for the Annihilator killings. What are we missing, then?"

The Chief added, "Cill's right, Frank, the picture of the bank slip was a real lucky find . . . All we need now is an address from the bank. Should be easy enough, don't you think?"

Bass sipped at his rye and stared through the window at the people walking by.

"No, no, there's somethin else. It'll come to me, always has. I just hope it hits me sooner than later."

Lunch plates came, and the conversation turned to McParland and the fingerprints. All agreed they'd be a valuable tool in placing people at the scene of crimes and it was only a matter of time before the US Courts began allowing them as evidence. It was almost 2:00 p.m. when they returned to the bank.

This time, Tolkar came out to meet them. He was flushed, and a light sheen of sweat had formed along his forehead.

"Gentlemen, please come back to my office. I'm afraid I have bad news."

They followed E. A. Tolkar back to his office and sat in the same places they'd left before lunch. "Gentlemen, I'm terribly sorry, but we've found nothing under those names, no withdrawals, no deposits. I had the teller even try different spellings and she still came up empty. She's our floor manager, so I believe her search was thorough." He paused, watching all three for a reaction. "I'm sorry, really. I know it's not what you wanted to hear."

Chief Lee answered, "Well, you're absolutely right about that. We were certain he'd done some banking here recently; we have a picture of a receipt of some kind that was taken in his room."

Bass handed Tolkar the photograph across the desk. Tolkar looked at it and said, "Yes, that is our withdrawal slip . . . I don't see a date . . . that would surely help. Also, all our deposit and withdrawal slips are numbered, and we keep carbon ink copies of all of them for two years by law. In this photo I cannot see either the date or the number sequence. I'm truly sorry, gentlemen. I want the devil caught just like everyone else."

There was a long pause as the bad news sunk in. Finally, Cillian spoke up.

"Edwin, me dear, ya done your best for us. I can see the stymie in it now. We'll just have to find another way to catch the bugger, is all."

The other two men nodded and voiced their agreement, and all three stood to leave. Tolkar walked them to the front of the bank, and the Chief said as they left, "Be sure to thank your teller for us. I'm sure she gave it her best."

All three got into a cab for the return ride to headquarters. It was a quiet trip back.

Chapter 22

3:30 p.m., May 29, 1888

Police Headquarters

Congress Avenue at Peach Street

Austin, Texas

Upon arrival, all three went directly to Grooms Office, where they found James McParland and Bill Breitwish waiting for them.

"By your expressions, I'm afraid to ask what happened at the bank," McParland said.

"A waste of time, I'm afraid. The folks at the bank were trying to be helpful but they couldn't find any record at all for the names we have. Damned frustrating," Grooms answered.

Bass added, "And on top of everything else, we got two days until he's likely to strike again. We have an idea of his appearance, but we can't guard all the dark alleys and empty streets in Austin."

"Aye, it's a bloody pisser it is," Cillian said.

Bass went on, "And we have no idea who's gonna be his next victim."

A few moments went by. "Well, boys, the day wasn't a total loss. Young Bill here, and I found several clear and matching fingerprints at Doctor Procket's office. They may not be needed, but we got 'em," McParland announced.

They gathered around the pictures that Bill had just processed and agreed the match was exact.

"That's good work there, Bill. I bet when you get that new camera, it'll be even better," Bass said.

Bill Breitwish beamed at the accolade. "I imagine it'll take some time to learn how it works. Gotta be a new way to process that kind of photo bein' so different from wet plates. 'Be a challenge."

"You know, as fast as things change, we gotta make sure we take advantage of the most modern ideas in crime fighting. Boy, it wasn't that long ago that ballistic evidence was admitted by the courts, but with advances in magnifying lenses, the differences in rifling become clear. We're at the same place with fingerprinting and photography. The newest advances by fellas like Eastman make our work better, faster, and maybe safer. I can see a time comin' when evidence from all over the country gets stored in a massive filing facility, kinda like a library, and law officers have access to it. I bet it'd make discovering our guy's identity much easier," James McParland said.

Their discussions went on for some time but always ended in frustration, and finally, Chief Lee said, "Boy, it's getting late, and I still have to do my daily reports. Gotta keep showin' the town council we're worth the money I keep asking 'em for. Let's brainstorm again tomorrow. If Frank's right and the bastard's still in town, we got some decisions to make before midnight, Thursday."

They nodded and solemnly filed out of the Chief's office. Bass decided he'd go back to the hotel and get a bath before dinner. Then maybe send another wire back to Sally and the baby.

6:30 p.m., May 29, 1888
350 Bowie Street
Austin, Texas

Harleigh Jones had tried on the clothes he'd bought for the third time, admiring himself in the mirror each time he placed the beaver hat on his head. He had just taken the last of the mercurial that Doctor Procket had given him and still had two pint bottles of laudanum remaining in his dresser drawer.

His left leg felt nearly as strong as before the shooting, and as he examined the wound, he thought it looked so much better than it had just four days ago. Of course, it was still red and a bit puffy . . . and it itched terribly, but he knew that to be a sign of healing. There would always be an indentation from the bullet, but that was neither here nor there. His trousers covered that, and the overall effect of his new suit and shoes, he acknowledged, was devasting.

She won't be able to resist . . . like all the others. I think, though, I'll need to bathe and shave tomorrow before meeting her in case any of that vile smoke still adhered to my person.

6:45 p.m., May 29, 1888
Winslow Hotel
Congress Ave at Ash Street
Austin, Texas

Bass had stopped in the hotel saloon for a whiskey where he struck up a conversation with the bartender. Bass always found bartenders and servers to be excellent sources of information and stories of noteworthy events. They remained sober while all those around them became intoxicated and generally more talkative.

The bartender's name was Steven Coe. Bass, remembering his encounter with the Coe brothers earlier in the month, naturally asked if he had any relatives in west Texas or Las Cruces in the New Mexico Territory.

"What, out in the sticks? Hell no. My family's all from Baltimore. I'm actually the first of all of us to head out here in the frontier."

Bass smiled to himself hearing that. He reckoned that a frontier was relative to where you came from. "That's good to know. I had uh . . . issues with a family named Coe out in Las Cruces. So then tell me, Steven, do you have a family?"

"I do. I have a wife and a little girl. We do not yet have a home, but we do alright."

"Oh? Where do you live then? In town?"

"Oh no, we can't afford to live in the city. We have rented a cottage on the far west side. It's small, but it's enough for now."

"How old are you, Steven? Bass sipped from his dram.

"I'm twenty-two, and my wife is nineteen. She takes in mendin' and sewin' work so she can stay home with Elizabeth. We save every dime a' course. Someday, I hope to have land enough to farm."

"To farm, you say? Out here on the frontier?" Bass smiled as he said it.

"Well, maybe a bit closer to Waco, but here in Texas, yes."

"Well, I wish you luck, young man. And your wife and daughter, too. I have a wife and baby girl at home in El Paso on the Rio. 'Been here about three weeks, I think. I miss 'em so bad I can taste it. Say, give me another rye, will you? Then I'm off for a bath, a good supper, and a soft bed."

Steven poured an extra deep dram for Bass and went about his business behind the bar. Bass laid a dollar on the bar, picked up his glass, and went out onto the hotel porch overlooking Ash Street.

The weather was changing, threatening with heavy clouds in the west and the scent of rain in the air. A pleasant spring day had turned into a cool, gusty evening. It was 7:15 p.m., according to Bass's Elgin, and the sun sent its last rays through the dark clouds and across the Texas prairie. Sally was seeing it. She would be on the front porch overlooking the Rio, holding baby Lil and watching the same sunset. What he wouldn't give to be with them now.

After a few minutes Bass recognized the symptoms of melancholy settling over him, so he finished his whiskey and went into the hotel for his bath. Later that night, after a good supper, he went upstairs and got ready for bed.

He doused the lamp, and as he lay on his back, he thought about Steven Coe and his family. He thought of his own family, too, and how much parents want for their children. He lay with his head on his pillow, his eyes slowly closing in the dark, when suddenly, the back of his neck began to itch again. His eyes flashed open, and he sat bolt upright in bed, thinking. After a moment, it all became clear to him.

"I'll be damned! Of course . . . that's it!" He felt himself smiling like an idiot in the darkened room, and he laid his head back down on the pillow. The itch was gone, and he slept like a child.

6:50 a.m., May 30, 1888
Winslow Hotel
Congress Ave. at Ash St.
Austin, Texas

The storm that Bass had seen in the evening arrived overnight, dropping several inches of rainfall on Austin and the surrounding area. The cobblestoned streets shed rainwater into drains, but the dirt streets on the outskirts of town were quagmires of mud and debris. The cloud cover was still heavy, and occasional downpours drenched traffic in the metropolitan area.

Bass felt better than he had since the day he arrived, believing that the solution to finding and identifying the Annihilator was quite possibly at hand. He sat in the hotel café drinking coffee and reviewing his plan, wondering if he should check it out himself in case it proved another frustration for everybody. Then he recalled that the bank wouldn't be open till after 9:00 a.m. anyway, so he decided to have another pot of coffee and a substantial breakfast. While he waited, he wrote out a wire to Sally and his daughter.

My beloved family,

I can't say how important you both are to me or even explain how much I miss you. I don't know the words, I guess. Anyway, I've been away too long, but with luck, I may be coming home within days. Writing wires like this makes it seem more likely.

I love you both,
Frederick

He signaled for the waitress and asked that a messenger be sent to his table. He arrived just as his breakfast was being served.

"Young man, I want you to take this to the telegraph office for me. See that it gets sent special to be hand delivered today. I believe the charge will be near to four dollars, so here's five dollars, you can keep what's left. I know it's stormy out . . . you got a slicker? Er, a poncho? Somethin' against the rain to wear?"

The boy may have been twelve and was used to running all kinds of errands for guests. "Yes, sir. A goodun too. A goose grease poncho and a wool crusher with a wide brim."

Bass smiled at the boy's eagerness to run out in the rain. "All right, boy, I'm countin' on ya."

The boy took the bills and said, "Yes sir!" and dashed into the lobby. A few minutes later, he ran out through the front doors and turned left on Ash Street. Bass checked his watch; it was near eight-thirty—time to go to police headquarters.

9:00 a.m., May 30, 1888
Police Headquarters
Congress Avenue at Peach Street
Austin, Texas

"Good morning, Grooms, good morning. Ain't the rain refreshin'?" Bass was smiling again, and Grooms Lee had no idea why. The rain did nothing for him.

"What?"

"You know, a nice change from the constant sunshine. A man can only take so much, you know."

Still confused, the Chief butted in. Sit down, Frank, take a load off and also maybe take a coupla deep breaths."

Cillian O'Dell walked into the room just then his normally cheerful mood turned surly, "The bloody hell you smilin' for Mr. Marshal? You look like ya won at bingo."

Bass only shook his head. "Boys, boys. You remember when I said yesterday about the back a' my neck itching?"

"Yeah, so what?" Grooms Lee said.

Bass sat back in his chair. "It stopped itchin' last night. I think I found another way to use his bank info."

Now, the other two were all ears, focusing their attention on what Bass would say next.

"Look, we know his mother sprung him from the asylum up in Terrel, knowin' full well she was breakin' the law, right?"

"Aye, that's right, a mother's love and all," O'Dell answered.

James McParland walked in before Bass could start. "Sorry I'm late, damn rain's slowed everything down." He looked at the faces in the room, all intent on what Bass had to say. "What? What'd I miss?"

"Sit down, Heeltap. I got an idea." Bass said. "I believe that our guy here has been more than needy of his ma's money. Let's remember he's been outta work for at least a week and a half, and before that, accordin' to my witness at the Winslow who told me her friend, the third victim Beatrix, had seen him dressed to the nines and livin' high around the Pierce Hotel once or twice before he killed the girl. That means money, boys, and I bet some of it came in a wire transfer from a bank in Dallas."

The other three men looked at each other, and then, one by one, they began nodding their heads and acknowledging Bass's supposition.

"Now listen, boys, this don't really qualify as much more 'n hunch. But I tell ya, the more I thought on it, the more I liked it."

McParland added, "I like it too, Frank. I doubt that C. C. Slaughter paid him much, and like you said, he didn't work for more than a week there after the shooting on the west side. He still had to pay the widow, Benoit, too. Where'd the money come from? Sweet ol' mom."

"I think it's about time to head back down to see Mr. E.A. Tolkar at his bank," Grooms said.

They all agreed, and hats and rain gear were snatched up as they walked to the cab stand out front.

9:35 a.m., May 30, 1888
First State Bank of Texas
500 Pecan Street
Austin, Texas

They arrived at the bank just as the rain began to fall and they all dashed from the Gurney cabs into the bank. The First State Bank had opened late due to the storm, but everyone was in now, and Mr. E.A. Tolkar was still eager to please.

"Oh certainly, gentlemen certainly. Money wires are easy to track down because there aren't that many of them to start with. Now do we want to use the same timeframe then?"

Bass looked at the others, who shrugged in agreement. "Yeah, please, the last ten days, maybe out to two weeks would be good."

Ed Tolkar left his office, and the three men saw him talking to a middle-aged lady with a pinched face and her light brown hair piled on top of her head in a bun. He returned to his office and explained it shouldn't take her long.

Bass took the opportunity to ask what kind of information they might expect to find on the wire transfer record. "Well, the name and address of the sender and the originating bank, of course, and then there'd also be the name and address of the receiver, you see, as a way of making identification. The address is important because we have to notify the recipient when the funds arrive."

Grooms Lee began smiling now which infected Cillian O'Dell and James McParland too. About fifteen minutes later, the office manager appeared with two pieces of paper in her hand, and she signaled through the glass door to E. A. Tolkar. He went outside for a moment to talk with her, and when he came back inside, his head was high, and his chest puffed out in an obvious statement of pride in his accomplishment.

"Gentlemen, I believe we have what you are seeking after. I have two wire fund transfer orders, both from Agatha Waters in Dallas.

The first one was addressed to Devin Smith on Second Street for fifty dollars, and the second one is made out to Harleigh Jones at an address on Bowie . . . also for fifty dollars."

They thanked E. A. profusely and headed back to the station.

Back at police headquarters, the four men acted swiftly. Bill Breitwish was summoned, and the current address of the killer was plotted on the street map of Austin. Grooms Lee talked quietly to himself as he searched for 350 Bowie Street and then inserted a bright red pin in the map when he found it.

"Looks like all residential dwellings around there though it's not too far to the Metro District by trolley. Cill? How do you see this arrest happening? You know the area best of all of us.

"Aye, Chief. I believe we keep our uniform coppers outta sight but use them to create a perimeter in case he tries to hoof it. Then, a few of us in street clothes'll approach the house quietly. Do we know then who and how many live there?"

Bass read from a slip of paper. "Yeah. The house belongs to Edward Landick. 'Says here he's a retired brakeman, so he's gonna be older. That's all, though. Nothing about any family."

"Right then, I'll go to the front door and knock, likely it'll be the owner who answers, and I'll whisk him outta harm's way quick as I can. Then we'll have Francis darlin' and the doughty Scotsman at the back, here at the corners, so they can see windows on the sides," O'Dell said, pointing to the rear corners of the house. "Now, we'll have to be careful in this, me dears, because the river is only a block or two away. And if the blighter makes it passed us and into the river? Be a mighty hard fish to catch."

McParland had been listening, and when he sensed that O'Dell was finished he asked, "When do you think we go on this, Cill?"

O'Dell took off his cap and scratched his head. "Well, me heart says, let's catch the bugger and be done. But reason, ah reason says, what if he's not there? It's the middle of the day, he could be out pickin' daisies for all we know. But . . . if we go in the early mornin' hours, say just before sunup tomorrow when there'll be a bit a light . . . we can be relatively certain he's home. That's how I learned it in Brooklyn."

"I doubt we could get our street officers organized and briefed before late this afternoon. Going at, say, 5:00 to 5:30 a.m. or so gives us more time to be ready," Chief Lee said.

Bass had been listening. "I like it too. The quiet morning hours make sense, but I'd feel more comfortable if we had a beat officer, maybe two, keeping an eye on the place overnight, out of sight, of course."

"Good idea, sure can't hurt. Besides, what if he decides to jump the gun and do the killing tonight? I'll assign a couple of our sturdier men to it," Grooms said.

"Let's all get some sleep tonight and plan to meet here at, what Cill, 4:00 a.m.?" Bass added.

"Aye, won't be any trouble getting there at that hour. 'Ats plenty a time."

The Chief closed it up by saying. "Well, good luck to us then. Our sides about due for some good luck."

5:15 p.m., May 30, 1888
Offices of Ballinger and Assoc.
Attorneys at Law
202 Congress Ave.
Austin, Texas

He had been waiting for her for twenty minutes at the trolley stop where he'd seen her just the day before. He'd calculated that the girl worked in the Ballinger Building as a secretary or clerk perhaps, and he should expect to see her emerging from the brick and limestone structure by 5:30 p.m. He was dressed in fine day wear. If he had learned nothing else from his mother, he knew that refined gentlemen catch more glances than the ill-mannered and poorly clothed. At 5:20 p.m., there she was, in a blue frock with a lace collar, an umbrella, and, though the rain had stopped some time before, of course, a shawl to signify her modesty. Her face was as lovely as he remembered: clear skin, not pale but radiant even in poor light. Her hair, deep brown with highlights of the subdued red color that gave auburn its name.

He stood in a small recess between buildings and watched as she prepared to board an oncoming trolley. He dashed forward as the vehicle stopped and boarded just after her, taking the seat next to her without even slightly acknowledging her presence. It was all part of the game, he knew, and he would play along until he had her. His only real concern was that she was early and by a full day. Also, there was no guarantee she'd agree to meet him tomorrow. *Ach . . . there were ways.*

The trolley was crowded with people going home after work, and this vehicle headed ultimately to the west side of town. It made many stops before returning to the metropolitan area, and the two of them rode silently together for some time. He knew it would be important for her to make the first contact, to take the initiative of opening a dialog. From then on, he knew, she would unconsciously believe that she controlled the relationship, that it was her doing that the two should become more than just strangers. This was something his mother had taught him growing up, and she said it was fundamental in manipulating relationships. It disturbed him slightly that she might be trying to goad him with her silence. After all, he knew exactly who and what she was, and she would recognize him as well for the power in his presence . . . unless she was a novice, a 'baby witch' new to the coven and the Black Lord. *She is young enough certainly, and if she is new in her training the Crone of the Coven might not have yet explained the nature of the Magi. Oh, this was going to be delicious.*

They'd been riding for nearly thirty minutes and had reached the state university stops when she finally spoke. "You're not getting off here?"

He smiled slightly and turned to face her. "I'm sorry?"

She seemed to be ready to engage . . . *a difficult time. 'Can't show too much interest but can't be too aloof either.*

She went on to explain. "You have the look of a professor, and I thought you might live near the school."

Again, he smiled at her weak attempts to draw him out. "Oh . . . no, I'm not a teacher."

She sat back and was quiet for a short while. Then she asked, "I certainly thought you might be; you have a look of intelligence."

Again, he smiled as he turned to her, "Why thank you, miss, aren't you kind. No, I can't afford to teach. That is to say, I'm already employed in the family business, and educators are historically underpaid."

She thought for a moment.

She's trying to determine how wealthy I am. Good God, she is a novice.

She said, "That's very true and shameful too. Our teachers should be paid much more than they are. They have such an important job."

He looked at her again with the same slight smile, "Yes, that's right."

And then it began.

"What is it you do, sir . . . for a living I mean?"

"I own a plantation to the north in Round Rock. It's a family concern, actually. We have several orchards, but the cash crop is cotton, of course."

Her eyes grew wider as he spoke, "Oh my, that must be quite a large operation. Do you employ . . . er . . . Coloreds?"

Again he smiled, "Oh yes, we have quite a few Negro laborers. But nothing like before the war, I'm told. In the Antebellum years, my father said the family owned near to three hundred slaves. Of course, we don't employ half that many now. And we're quite clear not to call them slaves. Today they are 'freedmen' and 'residential workers,' and we pay them a wage as well as providing them comfortable housing." He watched her face and could practically see the wheels turning. *This is becoming almost fun!* he thought.

They continued chatting like this for a brief time, and eventually, she revealed her name to be Annie Sumner and that she worked as a secretary for the Ballinger Law Firm. He shared his name as Harleigh Pace and that his grandfather, Hiram, had purchased land for their plantation from the Perez Rancho some forty years ago. Of course, it was all lies, but she was entertained and gradually warming to him.

As the trolley looped back around, he suggested "coffee or a cocktail" at the Capitol Club since it was close to a stop on the route and would be convenient when they chose to leave. She agreed. When they walked through the doors to be seated, it was 6:45 p.m., May thirtieth.

Chapter 23

4:15 a.m., May 31, 1888
  Police Headquarters
  Congress Avenue at Peach Street
  Austin, Texas

Bass arrived at Chief Lee's office a few minutes after 4:00 a.m. and took his usual chair at the Chief's desk. A few minutes later, James McParland and Cillian O'Dell arrived. After the usual polite *good mornings*, they sat in silence until Grooms Lee arrived. When he did, it was as though a whirlwind had arrived. With a clipboard in hand, he went straight to the Austin Street map that O'Dell had tacked to the wall. The Chief made a couple of quick notations on the map, and when he turned to the room, all eyes were on him.

"Mornin, boys . . . big day today. The two uniformed officers I set out at the suspect's house late last night have reported in. There has been no activity around the house since they arrived before midnight. I've already talked to our beat officers and given them assignments that I just made on the map.

"I've assigned men in pairs, and they know what they're there for. I also explained to them that for early risers, folks getting out to work, they're to politely request citizens to use an alternate route away from Bowie Street. I don't know what to expect from this guy, but we know he's no stranger to gunplay, and I don't want to chance any gunshot wounds to civilians.

"Now, we're gonna have two men at the corner of Bowie and Burnett, here. I've got another pair down at the intersection of Fannin and Burnett. These two will be most visible if this Harleigh character happens to look out the front window.

"Then I've got four men behind the house in the trees along the Shoal Creek Greenbelt to the river and two more at the Cotton Compress on West Avenue. These men will be out of sight of the house and are there to back you and McParland up, Frank. All these officers are already on their way to the scene. I've explained timing, and they're to listen for voice commands from any of us.

"And that brings us to the arrest. Here's what I want, and it ain't too complicated. It'll start to get light in about an hour, so Cillian and I will approach the front door when we're all in position. I'll knock . . ."

Cillian interrupted. "Chief, why don't you let me do the knockin' oy? And you can back me up on the stoop. You bein Chief and all, why put yourself in harm's way?"

"Cillian . . . I'll do the knockin', and I want you to watch the west side of the house when I do. Frank, you'll be at the south corner, and James, you're at the north. There is a back door that opens from the kitchen right here . . . and I'm thinkin' that's where he'll go, so you boys be ready. And watch your damn crossfire. If he bolts from the door, shoot him . . . don't ask him to surrender. If he comes out the back, he's already given up that option."

There was a brief pause, and Chief Lee said, "Any questions?"

There were none. Each man knew that arrests like these were fluid situations, dependent on what the suspect would do. The Chief had already done as much as could be done, so no one broke the silence.

"Good luck to us, then. Let's get on with it," Chief Lee said.

The eastern sky was lightening to a gray pallor as they rode west on Peach Street in a police coach. Weapons and loads were checked, there was very little talking. Each man was rehearsing his part repeatedly in his mind, determining his best course of action in each of the several eventualities that the suspect's actions would determine. The only thing each man had determined, separate from the others was if the suspect did not surrender immediately, he would not survive the day.

By 5:15 a.m., the gray light was usable, and the coach had crossed the Shoal Creek bridge. It stopped as instructed at the corner of Bowie and Pecan Streets. All four men climbed out and, without speaking, simply nodded or tipped their hats, wishing each other well. Bass and McParland walked down Bowie Street a hundred feet or so and then ducked back behind several houses on their way to 350 Bowie.

Chief Lee and Cillian O'Dell walked slowly up Bowie Street, and when they reached the house at 350 Bowie, they paused to make sure everyone had time to get to their position. Then Chief Lee adjusted his hat and climbed the steps of the small front stoop. He placed his right hand on his pistol, and he knocked on the door with his left. He knocked once and then again before he heard movement inside.

O'Dell stepped off the stoop so he saw the side of the house and heard the front door open. It was the old man in his long drawers, hair wildly mussed and a look of confusion on his face.

"What is all—?" Before he could speak further, Chief Lee grabbed his arm and pulled him from the stoop and down to the ground.

The Chief drew his pistol and stood at the ready as he called out, "This is the police! Come out now! Your hands empty, and where I can see 'em!"

A single shot sounded from inside, and the Chief went down, bleeding from a wound on his right side. Seeing the Chief go down, O'Dell gradually came back around to the front door and cautiously peered inside. He saw a shadowy movement in a hallway and fired three shots in rapid succession.

O'Dell began calling, "Come out ya Blackguard, you're completely surrounded . . . there's no hope for ya a' tall!"

Another shot whistled from inside and struck a neighbor's house with a *thwack*.

O'Dell then called to an officer to come help the Chief, who was lying in the yard, moaning and losing blood. A uniformed officer, Nathan Bates, dashed to the Chief's side as more shots from inside rang out. One struck him in the left arm, but he managed to drag the Chief and himself to the front wall of the house away from any view inside. Cillian O'Dell moved to their side of the house, firing inside as he moved. He stayed there, reloading his revolver and guarding against further harm to his wounded comrades.

Bass and McParland heard the gunfire and immediately rushed to the back door. McParland tried the latch, but it was locked, so Bass, inching closer, motioned for McParland to move away, and he shot through the wooden frame around the latch. The door swung slowly open.

McParland had the better angle, so he crouched low and peered quickly into the kitchen. He pulled back and sat on the small porch shaking his head as he looked at Bass. Next, Bass called inside, "You in the house! Buster, this just ain't your day. Don't matter what you do now, mister, 'cause I'm by God gonna shoot ya dead!"

Bass followed his statement with four loud blasts from his Colt, fired chest high into the house, and splintering woodwork as the heavy bullets crashed through walls. He dove through the door into the kitchen and, staying as low as he possibly could, scanned the area around him. A quick look told him no one was in the small room to the right. That only left the hallway and another room on his left. He stood slowly, hugging the kitchen wall, his back and sliding along the flowered wallpaper toward the hallway. Just as he got to the hall, a high-pitched shriek pierced the air, and then a wail as a figure dashed across the hallway and through the window, breaking the glass and falling to the ground.

Bass turned around and ran through the back door to the porch and jumped over a small railing to see a man in dark trousers and a white shirt duck into the brush of the Shoal Creek Greenbelt. He limped, favoring his right leg.

Bass squeezed off another round, but he was also mindful of the four officers stationed along the creek and held his fire as he gave chase. He saw the man's shirttails flapping as he ran, covering more ground than Bass thought would be possible for a man with a bad leg. He was making for the river using the thick cover along the creek, grabbing at low shrubs and limbs to help him along. Bass heard him still wailing and cursing aloud as he ran.

The Colorado River curls lazily around the south side of Austin, but today, with the recent heavy rain and runoff, it moved faster than usual. Bass heard it not too far away. He knew that if his man got to the river he could simply use its flow to carry him away from law enforcement and to eventual freedom. Certainly, that must be his plan.

Bass took the quicker route to the river along a pathway above the cover that his suspect was using. It meant he lost sight of him temporarily, but he'd get to the river first. When he came to the river outlook on the path, he looked back and saw movement in the low shrubs, blackberries, and ivy. He could also see that his man would have to leap about ten feet to the river from his position in the brush, and he'd be in the clear when he did. Bass had only one shot left in his Colt. He had no time to reload. So he waited, and he watched as the movement in the bushes got closer.

He heard other officers yelling as they approached, but he could not answer; he could not afford the distraction. He watched and waited . . . and then he was there, his white shirttail flagging behind him. He took two long strides toward the river, and in that moment, Bass fired. The momentum of his leap shuddered with the impact of the slug, and he clutched at his side, howling as he fell short of the water, landing on a broken log.

Bass let his shoulders sag, his pistol hanging in his hand alongside his right leg. So many thoughts rushed to him then that he couldn't decipher which one to focus on. He walked slowly to the edge of the pathway and looked down.

Just a few feet away lay the Annihilator, impaled through his middle by a pointed branch of the fallen log.

McParland reached him first. "Ja' get him, Frank? I saw you shoot."

Bass nodded his head toward the log along the shore.

McParland looked for a moment and just whistled. "*Whew* . . . that is Biblical justice, my friend." After a pause, he commented, "Well done, Frank."

Again, Bass nodded as McParland started walking back, and then he remembered Grooms being shot. "Hey, Heeltap, how's Grooms?"

"Not good, I'm afraid. Cill took him and the uniformed copper off to Doc Flotter. He lost a lot of blood, but he was awake and talkin so . . ."

When they got back to the house on Bowie, one of the officers ran up to them. "She's fine, gonna be just fine."

Bass looked at McParland and then back at the officer, "She who?"

The officer realized they hadn't been told. "Oh . . . we found a girl bound and gagged under his bed. Annie somethin'. She's alright though, bumps and bruises but nothing serious."

The officer walked back to the front yard and sat with several other coppers waiting for a ride back to Headquarters.

Bass looked at McParland, "Annie somethin' . . . that's right, huh. Today's the thirty-first. You talk about cutting it close."

Epilogue

In the three days that passed since the death of the Annihilator, one could sense the entire city of Austin breathe a collective sigh of relief. The local newspaper ran headlines each day regarding some new aspect of the Annihilator investigation and the incredible determination and courage of Chief Grooms Lee and his team. The story itself made national news at a time when the telegraph was not usually used for local news stories. One day, the papers focused on the actions of the madman's mother, a State Asylum Superintendent, and the promise made by the City Attorney in Dallas of a vigorous prosecution for the despicable crime of aiding and abetting the maniac.

Another day, *The Austin Statesman* led with stories of the modern techniques used in discovering the identification and lair of the murderer. These articles detailed the Pinkerton Agency's use of a method of "fingerprint identification" and the importance of the rapidly burgeoning sciences of photography and wire communications. Human interest articles abounded as sidebars highlighting the individual men responsible for the ultimate elimination of the killer.

Chief of Police Grooms Lee and Officer Nathan Bates—who were grievously injured by the killer—were both indisposed as they recuperated at City Hospital. Still, Detective Cillian O'Dell made himself available to the press. A Pinkerton Agency detective from Chicago was instrumental in the killer's downfall but declined to be interviewed and had requested anonymity.

US Deputy Marshal Frank Bass of El Paso (Buffalo Robe Bass, from the many dime novels) predominated, however, as the man directly responsible for the death of the villain. While Marshal Bass spoke only in limited sessions, he was generally adamant about the heroism of Chief Lee, Officer Bates, and Detective O'Dell. His one and only quoted reply to questioning was, "Justice was served, and Austin is safe from the Annihilator."

8:45 a.m., June 3, 1888
City Hospital
650 Lavacca Street
Austin, Texas

Grooms Lee had suffered a partial tear of his liver and had just undergone a hepatectomy performed by several surgeons from the teaching hospital at Baylor University. By all accounts, the procedure was successful, and though the Chief would have a long period of recovery, it was expected to be complete with no lasting effects. Officer Bates was not so fortunate. The bullet that struck him shattered his left elbow, and the arm—which was nearly detached by the impact—had to be amputated.

Bass had been waiting at the hospital for news of Grooms's operation, and when he was told of the success, he was immensely grateful. He wanted especially to express his admiration for the Chief in his fight against alcohol and the way hemanagedd the investigation in general.

Bass had gone through a similar time following the deaths of his first wife and baby several years ago of typhus. She had been working as a teacher at the Tigua Pueblo reservation when the illness decimated the village. Bass knew it would be sometime before Grooms saw visitors, and he intended to write to him as soon as he was home.

His train left for El Paso at 11:15 a.m., and with any luck, he should be home for supper the next day. It was a homecoming he truly needed. He'd missed his home when on manhunts in the past, but his need for its warmth and stability now was crucial. He had seen the grim side of city life and the sickness that close quarters fosters, and he'd had enough. He knew there was a measure of evil in all men, but the crowded, closeness of city life seemed to incubate the seed more quickly. He was ready to be done with it. He longed for the spaces of the prairie, the clean newness of his frontier.

Bass left the hospital after hearing the good news and went back to police headquarters to say goodbye to his friend James McParland. They had worked together the previous spring in Fort Stockton, Texas, when McParland was disguised as an eccentric prospector named Heeltap. In actuality, he was investigating a fraudulent oil scheme at the request of the Interstate Commerce Commission. Bass found him in the hallway to the Chief's office with Bill Breitwish and Cillian O'Dell.

The three were talking among themselves when Bass interrupted. "I just came from the hospital, boys, and talked to one of the doctors. Looks like Grooms is gonna be alright."

Everyone smiled at the news, and then Breitwish excused himself, shaking hands with Bass and McParland as he left. Next, it was time for McParland to make his farewells. Unlike previous conversations with Cillian O'Dell, this one was amicable and good-natured. As Cillian shook McParland's hand, he said, "So then ya kilt-wearin' Jocko, do ya tink you'll be back to see us again ever?"

"Cillian O'Dell, it's possible, I'd say even likely. I'll probably be asked to investigate a certain mick Sergeant who tends to lie to the press and drink too much Bushmills," McParland replied.

O'Dell smiled broadly at that. McParland went on, "Oh, and in case it comes up, the fingerprints we got from the house on Bowie match up to the ones from the Benoit house. Not a surprise, but it ties a loose end." McParland then looked at O'Dell and said, "Take care a yourself, *a chara*. You're too good a man to lose."

The two embraced, and McParland headed to the door.

Bass had separated from them slightly and was standing further down the hallway when McParland stopped and dropped his bag.

"Well, you did it again, didn't you, Marshal? Some men are just natural-born heroes. Now I s'pose you're gonna go back to El Paso and herd doggies, er whatever they're called, kiss your beautiful Sally, and bounce baby Lil on your knee. Don't you ever get tired of bein' perfect?"

Bass looked at him, remembering their prior working friendship. "Heeltap? It's always a struggle . . . but it's easier when you're around . . . and it's Deputy Marshal, actually."

They smiled at one another, and McParland shook Bass's hand, saying, "See ya around, cowboy." And he grabbed his bag and was gone.

"Cillian, my Irish whiskey-drinkin' partner, I'm gonna say goodbye here even though I still wanna pay a final call on the Mayor. Sergeant, it has been a true joy and a real learning experience fer me to watch you work. And if I ever need help detectin' a crime or drinkin' whiskey, you'll be the man I'll call for."

O'Dell smiled again. "Oh, thank ya, darlin'. You know you'll have a special place in me heart from now on. And I learned a ting or two from you, ya know, like how ta get a witness to remember, say."

They shook hands, and Bass walked back up the hall to find out where the Mayor's office might be.

The office of the Mayor was located in the courthouse which was on Congress Avenue just a block away. Bass had no appointment but simply asked the middle-aged secretary if the mayor was in.

"Oh my yes, Marshal, of course. I *ah* mean I'm awful certain he's in for you. Let me just announce . . ."

From inside, Bass heard the Mayor's voice call out, "Bass? Why, of course . . . of course, come directly in and sit. Can I offer you a whiskey?"

"Oh no thanks, sir. Tad early for me."

The Mayor nodded. "Why yes it is, I apologize. I'm just used to Grooms' habits with the bottle."

Bass's expression fell, and the Mayor saw it. "No, listen up to me, Mayor Nalle. Grooms Lee has been sober throughout this investigation and lies near death right now at City Hospital, put there on the city's behalf. If I were you, Mayor Nalle, I'd adjust my way a' thinkin' when it comes to Chief Grooms. Once he recovers, he'll be 'bout the biggest hero this town has seen. 'Wise man ought to appreciate that."

The Mayor was ashen white. The last thing he wanted to do was alienate the man who shot down the Annihilator and was a famous lawman on his own to boot. "Oh please, Marshal, don't misconstrue, I've always been one of Grooms's biggest supporters in City Government. *Ahem*, now. What is it I can do for you?"

Bass settled back in his chair. "Mayor, I want you to do something for me. Ordinarily, I'd just ask Grooms, but . . . well, do you remember the train robbers I arrested a couple weeks ago now?"

The Mayor nodded, "Yes, certainly, and may I say that was quite a piece of law enforcement if you know what I mean."

Bass was quiet for a moment, focused on the Mayor's eyes. "Yeah, well, there were five pretty nice-lookin' horses brought into town that day, and ordinarily, they'd belong to me. But here's what I want you to do. I want you, on behalf of the police department, to buy them horses. 'Like I said, they're pretty nice-lookin' nags. I want you to pay $40 a piece for 'em. That's what the Army pays, I'm told, and I want you to give the money to Steven Coe. He's a bartender over at the Winslow Hotel. You tell him it's from me, and I hope it helps him fetch his dream."

The Mayor looked confused, "But Marshal Bass, that's two hundred dollars . . . that's a lot a money."

Bass stood to leave and smiled, "I know it. He's a good bartender. 'Pours a healthy dram and don't skimp. You do that, Mayor; I'll find out if ya don't."

"Yes, yes, of course, Marshal. Anything you say . . ." the Mayor said, but Bass was already down the hall . . . and heading home.

7:00 p.m., June 3, 1888
Colorado River
South Bank
Near Austin, Texas

The Colorado River bends to the south at the Congress Avenue Bridge and curls back about a mile further on. Here at this bend the river had deposited over the millennia an aggregation of limestone and granite boulders. Monoliths that the river tumbled and rolled down from the hills in the west and then grounded, settled into the earth, and established as a natural sanctuary for the growth of Cottonwoods and Elms. From here, the river slowly receded and again wound to the north, shoring and preserving the natural retreat it had created.

The place was some distance from the city, not easily reached, and as such, it was not widely known. But those who did venture enjoyed its tranquility and unspoiled condition. Travelers in spring and summer relaxed in the quiet solitude and natural beauty it provided along the river. It was known as The Ravenwolf Garden, and by day, it was a delight.

But the forbidding blackness of night, so far from the glow of the city lights, offered different qualities. In the deep darkness of evening, certain women from the town met at their covenstead to form a sacred circle and worship their Wiccan deities. Here, they would practice the ancient rituals and repeat the chants and prayers to the Dark One. They would call on Him for his might and justice.

Air I Am

Fire I Am

Water, Earth And

Spirit I Am

The women were all known to each other. They led quiet lives of mundane existence, but at the new moon and the solstices, they would meet in their Ravenwolf Garden to create their circle, and by the light of a central fire, they would summon from their souls their Holy Pagan. They wore hooded cloaks of assorted colors to denote their position in the coven.

Their Crone was Amelia Brady, the judge's wife. She was the Priestess who divined their meetings and initiated the novices. She carried the knowledge of the ancient spells and approved or disapproved of their use. Her cloak was crimson for the blood of the pagans and the fire of the Dark Lord.

Air Moves Us, Fire Transforms Us
Water Shapes Us, Earth Heals Us
And The Balance Of The Wheel Goes Round

The others that attended were Bethany Wahlton, Mathilda Masters, and Megan Day, all dressed in the black cloaks signifying their doyen, masters of their craft and of their higher learning. They were the eyes and ears of the coven, providing information of the day to the Crone. She would then determine the actions necessary for the preservation of the coven and, when necessary, determine the best spells and curses to be used.

Finally, there were the novices in green cloaks there to learn the chants and rituals of the craft. To experience the heady excitement of casting spells. These were Fiona Fields and Annie Sumner. They carried communications to those of the Sacred Circle, and during meetings, they tended the fire and arranged the Circle.

And The — Wheel Turns
Never Ending
New And Old And New Again

The meeting held this evening was impromptu and weeks in advance of the solstice. The Crone had thought it advisable to bless the sisters lost to the Magus and reassure the coven of his death. The Magus had cut their numbers by three and terrorized their sisters near and far. She also knew it was necessary to obliterate his spirit as well as his flesh lest he rise again to cause chaos for the Wiccan.

She taught the chant:

I banish the Magus from my mind and my life.
I claim only freedom from strife.
I cast out the Magus on the knot of three.
Bring only harmony to me.

"We beg thee, Dark Lord, accept our sisters: Mollie Simms, Eileen Beretta, and Beatrix Lowe."

She then threw colored pitch into the fire, which caused it to flare and leap, its licks of red and yellow illuminating their faces. The members of the coven repeated the chant three times, and the Crone recited anew.

It's The Blood Of The Ancients
That Runs Through Our Veins
And The Forms Pass
But The Circle Remains.

Again, she threw the pitch, and the fire jumped and crackled as if to accentuate her authority. The coven again repeated her chant, and she finished the incantation with the Wheel Chant.

And The — Wheel Turns
Never Ending
New And Old And New Again

Finally, she ended her sermon with the prayer to Satan that all had memorized and spoke aloud.

Hail Satan
Ruler of the Netherworld
Master of the Ninth Circle of Hell
Beneath the Celestial Prison of Descent
Help me Overcome

The Pretending Forces of Light
Usher me in the Dark Void of Your Being
So I May Be Born Afresh
In Soul and Flesh of Your Design.

The End

The Annihilator

Slaughter is, first and foremost, a work of fiction. The fundamental premise of the story is, however, based in fact, and I've certainly taken liberties to make the story more compatible with our hero, Frank Bass.

In Austin, during the years 1884 and 1885, eight women were murdered in their beds as they slept, though five were dragged outside unconscious before being killed. The killer had inserted a sharp object in the ears of six of the victims, and three were terribly mutilated—an ax having been used on all.

Several men were arrested, but only one man was convicted for killing his wife, a conviction which was later overturned. An eyewitness to one of the murders gave conflicting accounts, and others who claimed to have seen the culprit varied widely in their descriptions.

William Sidney Porter, the author who wrote under the pen name of O. Henry, was in Austin during the period and dubbed the killings the "Servant Girl Murders" and the culprit as the "Servant Girl Annihilator."

The final two killings attributed to the Annihilator were committed on Christmas Eve of 1885, and there was no further activity in or around Austin after that. But in the early morning hours of August 31, 1888, the body of Mary Ann Nichols was discovered in the White Chapel District of London. Her throat was deeply cut, and her body mutilated. She is often considered Jack the Ripper's first victim.

There is a wealth of information readily available about the "Servant Girl Annihilator" case and the conjecture relating them to the Ripper killings as well. We are some one hundred and forty years removed from the murders, and no conclusive proof as to the perpetrator has yet been found.

H. Grooms Lee was the City Marshal of Austin and became the chief of police during the Annihilator killings. Reports of his drunkenness and ineffectual investigation caused him to be fired in December of 1885. Several Pinkerton Agents had been called in to assist but they too failed in isolating a suspect. Chief Lee was replaced by a former Texas Ranger, James Lucy, who expanded the police force, established curfews, and banned late-night liquor sales in the city. Still, late on the night of December 24, 1885, Susan Hancock and Eula Phillips were brutally murdered.

The information on fingerprint identification is historically accurate, as is the information on George Eastman's invention of the American Film roll, which allowed the storing of multiple photographic images inside a single camera.

The Greenwood Cemetery
Weatherford, Texas

The cemetery that Bass visited is still in place today in the little town of Weatherford, Texas, the County Seat of Parker County. And yes, the Witches' Tomb is still visited by para-psychologists and curiosity seekers today. Weatherford is about 30 miles west of Fort Worth, Texas, should you have the urge to visit. Locals still insist that the Cemetery casts an unholy pall over the city...and those who practice the Dark Arts can be heard chanting on the days of solstice at midnight. Of course, that's only hearsay, still....

Oh. And Mary Martin is buried there.

Acknowledgments

First, as always, I must thank my lovely wife, Sheryl, for being understanding while I lock myself away for hours at a time in my office. She is my first proofreader and most supportive critic.

Next, a special thank you to my friend and editor, Cass Costa. She is brilliant beyond words, a ridiculously hard worker, and tolerant of my eccentric writing habits. If you enjoyed the story much was due to her talent.

And finally to my writing group, the wonderful people who encourage me even after reading my rough copy. They take the punishment nobly and still allow me to participate in meetings.

And to you, my reader, a heartfelt thanks for choosing my story to read. Heaven knows there are many others you could select . . . but please keep choosing mine.

—*Will Astrike*

Slaughter

9 798822 762535 9